Human Gold

A Jenny Tallchief Novel

E. H. McEachern

authorHOUSE®

AuthorHouse™
1663 Liberty Drive
Bloomington, IN 47403
www.authorhouse.com
Phone: 1-800-839-8640

This is a work of fiction. Names, characters, places and incidents either
are the product of the author's imagination or are used fictitiously. Any
resemblance to actual persons, living or dead, business establishments
or events, is entirely incidental. Geographic place names have been used
to give the reader a better understanding of the setting, however, the
actions and incidents described did not actually occur in those locations.

Published by AuthorHouse 9/20/2013

ISBN: 978-1-4918-1724-7 (sc)
ISBN: 978-1-4918-1723-0 (e)

Acknowledgements –

*Thanks to the following for their patience
and professional assistance:*

Susie Cole and **Benadet Dittmar** –
Story Continuity and Editing

Lucy Mahaffey – *Human Trafficking Research*

Larry Martin and **Fred Dittmar** –
Genealogy and Historical Research

Michelle Cole, DVM – *Veterinarian Technical Advice*

Logan R. Wilson – *9 Oaks Artwork*

Joe Scavetti – *Research, Editing and Everything Else*

Dedication –

For my Billy

Preface –

1832

"… there is a young woman whom the trader kept in the capacity of his Mistress, until, either from weariness of her or in the hope of gain, most probably from both, he sent her along with the rest to be carried South and sold, probably in the New Orleans market, where a branch of this inhuman traffic is to sell pretty girls for Mistresses for white men: These command a very high price."

Mary Berkley Blackford "Notes Illustrative of the Wrongs of Slavery"

2013

"Studies show that 100,000 to 300,000 U.S. kids are moved into the commercial sex industry every year in America…creating the next generation of prostitutes that will meet the growing demand of men who pay for sex."

Oklahomans Against the Trafficking of Humans

Chapter One

Flashes from the patrol cars' light bars lit up the death scene in a visual staccato of pulsating light – blue/red/white – blue/red/white. They cut across the sleep-deprived faces of Undersheriff Caleb Tallchief and his boss, Pottawatomie County Sheriff Joe Holcomb, as the two leaned against the Sheriff's SUV. Occasionally one or the other would stamp his feet or flap his arms in a futile attempt to ward off the bone-chilling cold. Crime scene tape defined the perimeter and the small tent erected over the body protected their victim from the elements and the prying eyes. Neither man spoke - there was really nothing to say.

The young undersheriff wadded up his empty Styrofoam coffee cup, stuffed it into his jacket pocket. He'd had enough caffeine – more than enough. He was wired and his bladder was starting to complain. He glanced around searching for an impromptu bathroom.

His troubled blue eyes involuntarily slid back to the child's body in the ditch in front of him. It had been purposely thrown aside like yesterday's garbage. The horrendous damage inflicted on the small body was something neither Tallchief nor Holcomb had ever seen before. The child had been brutally stabbed – how many times Caleb couldn't even begin to guess. No telling what else had been done to her. She looked so small – so vulnerable lying there in the glare of the vehicle headlights – she couldn't have been older than ten or eleven, if that. Caleb's heart stuck in his throat as he fought back anger and tears. With a conscious effort, he looked away.

The same lightshow caught the stoic – almost expressionless – faces of the uniformed men scattered around. They stood in groups of two or three, some quietly talking – most just standing - the usual crime scene sarcasm and sick cop humor conspicuously absent.

Caleb's eyes came to rest on Travis Moore, the department's newest and youngest deputy, standing alone on the periphery. The young man's face was still white as a sheet – or maybe it was green. He'd puked up his guts when he first saw the body. "At least he had the good sense to run down the road a bit so the crime scene wouldn't be screwed up," thought Caleb dryly.

He yelled and waved. "Hey, Travis. Keep that traffic moving." Caleb gestured to the gawkers passing slowly along Highway 177– eager for a glimpse of tragedy – human nature at its sickest.

"Good idea," said Holcomb. "Give the rookie something to do."

The area had been secured, ready for the forensic team's arrival. There was nothing left for any of them to do as they waited for the county's medical examiner to take charge of the body. Nothing to do – yet, no one left the scene. None of them seemed willing to abandon her to the bitterly cold, black, night. It was up to them now to watch over this child – to give her some measure of care and protection in death that she had been denied in life.

So, together the men from the PotCo Sheriff's Office stood vigil and waited for the approaching dawn.

****

Some ten miles to the south, the rest of the Tallchief family slept. As the night gave way to morning, soft sobbing echoes, no more than whispers floating on the morning air, pulled at Jenny's dreamless subconscious, gently prodding her awake. As her eyes slowly opened to the grey light filtering through the lace curtains, the heart-broken sounds faded away.

"Did you hear that?" Jenny asked the critters that were her bed companions. At the foot of the bed Jesse, Jenny's German shepherd-collie mix, lifted her head and yawned prodigiously. The dog's bleary red eyes seemed to say, "Good grief, Jenny, it's still the middle of the night. Go back to sleep." The large dog plopped her head heavily back down on the bed and wiggled into a more comfortable position. Clue, now a fully-grown feline, and Curly Joe, a white male cockapoo, didn't budge. The only one missing from this early-morning conversation was Caleb, Jenny's husband. He'd been called out in the wee hours of the morning, but Jenny had been too sleepy to remember why. Oh well, he'd call home when he could.

"I know I heard something," Jenny assured herself, as she threw back the covers and padded across the hardwood floors. The bedroom door, as always, squeaked in protest as she pulled it fully open and stepped out into the gloom. Nothing – not even a bird's chirp or a creaking board broke the silence.

Jenny tiptoed across the cold hallway and peered oh-so-quietly into her son's room. Two-and-a-half year old Zachary Ryan was curled up in the crib he had outgrown, sleeping in his favorite position – arm draped across his Sippy cup and his behind straight up in the air. As always, his blanket had been wadded up and kicked aside. Jenny covered him, and backed silently into the hallway.

Reentering her bedroom, Jenny was drawn to the adjoining small sitting room that was being remodeled. The heavy oak door between the two rooms had been removed from its hinges and lay propped against the wall – the first of many changes to come. Jenny entered the space and felt an indescribable change in the air – not exactly a chill – but something…

The old rocking chair she'd just purchased from the antique shop in town sat in front of the large east-facing window. "What's that doing here?" she asked no one in particular. "If Caleb's been using it as a step stool, I'm going to kill him." She gently ran the tips of her fingers across the old scarred wood - somehow it made her feel warm and welcome – like home or belonging. An unfelt air current stirred the sheer curtains. Jenny looked around – nothing there.

"Oh well," Jenny yawned and shrugged her shoulders, "I guess as long as I'm up – I'll make some coffee." Pulling her favorite, but threadbare, robe from the closet, Jenny shot a guilty glance at the beautiful white robe beside it.

Caleb had given her that new robe last Christmas. It still hung in her closet – never worn. When he asked why she never wore the new robe, Jenny explained her old robe was like an old friend. She'd had it since college and they'd grown up together. She couldn't trade it in on a newer model just because it was getting a little frayed around the edges. Caleb just looked at her with an amused, but befuddled, expression. It was obvious Caleb had never had a true friendship with any of his clothing.

Jenny quietly made her way down the stairs into the darkness below. Soon, the aroma of coffee filled the kitchen and the gurgling sounds of the coffee maker erased all thoughts of her odd wake-up call.

Jenny's solitude was not long-lived. A couple of minutes later Jesse slowly lumbered down the back stairs and into the kitchen. "About time you got your lazy self up," Jenny commented as she poured her first cup of coffee. The shepherd ignored the sarcasm, stretched out her front paws and repeated the process with her hind quarters. Then she lumbered over to the large bowl beside the back door and lapped some water.

Within seconds the other two animals tumbled down the stairs and into the kitchen in one large ball of fur, paws and wet noses. Curly Joe scrambled upright and ran to the back door, loudly yapping. Jenny hurried to let them out before the loudmouth cockapoo woke the baby.

"Please God – just a little more peace and quiet," she thought as she pulled the door open and a blast of chillingly bitter wind hit her squarely in the face. She didn't bother to go back to the kitchen chair, but waited right by the door – one hand on the door handle – the other on the coffee mug. It would be only seconds before the trio was back and ready for breakfast. The colder it was outside – the quicker the return.

As expected, within a minute she heard familiar scratching at the door. She poured out dry dog food and, as the two canines dug into their respective bowls, Jenny quickly fed Clue. By now, she had the timing down pat. If Curly Joe finished too soon, he'd try to eat

Clue's food. Clue – never one to be outmaneuvered – would attack Curly Joe full-on. WWIII would ensue.

This morning, much to Jenny's delight, everyone finished at the same time and Armageddon was again avoided. She breathed a sigh of contentment and settled down to savor her coffee and the silence.

****

Jenny was on her third cup when Caleb dragged in. The big man had such a look of despair on his handsome, lean face that Jenny immediately came to her feet and wrapped her arms around him, "Caleb, what happened?"

She got him a steaming cup of coffee as he pulled out a chair, collapsed into it, and stared straight ahead. He didn't even bother to take off his jacket or stow his sidearm – first thing he always did when he came home. The tall blonde man remained deathly still for what seemed like a long, long time – lost in the memory of what he'd seen, but Jenny didn't prompt him. She knew he'd find the right words to tell her - he just needed to get his mind straight.

"You know, I've been a cop for a long time now and seen a lot of brutality, but nothing – *nothing* compares with this morning." He fell silent again.

He turned to his wife, "We found this young kid dead out by Highway 177– she was probably no more than 10 or 11 years old. She wasn't just dead - she was butchered. Not a shred of clothes on her, and you know it's colder than hell out there. She'd been beaten bloody - stabbed I don't know how many times and thrown in the barrow ditch like so much garbage."

He paused and absently took a sip of coffee, "What kind of monster does something like that?" The question was rhetorical, not really directed at Jenny, nor did Caleb expect an answer. He was speaking in general to the universe - to the uncaring cosmos - knowing there were no answers to the horrors of inhuman behavior.

"Caleb, I'm so sorry."

Jesse, sensing Caleb's need for normalcy, padded across the kitchen and laid her furry head in his lap. Caleb's hand absently reached out to scratch the big dog behind her ears as he sighed deeply.

The man, the dog, and the woman sat together silently for some time. Then, almost as if physical action would dispel his fugue, Caleb shook his head and fired off a wan smile towards his wife. The spell of despair was broken.

"I guess the Tecumseh Terror is still asleep?"

"Yes, thank God." Two-and-a-half years earlier Zachary Ryan, his parents' pride, joy, and source of greatest vexation, had been born to the Tallchiefs. Unfortunately, he came not only with all the standard equipment, but also with a severe case of colic.

For the first six months of his life, Zachary screamed, cried or fussed. Jenny and Caleb tried everything, breast-feeding, formula-feeding, designer-formulas, car rides – but the only thing that seemed to comfort the helpless infant was to hold him close – even when he was sleeping. Pediatricians assured the couple their baby was just fine and that, as he grew, the colic would abate.

And, eventually, the doctors were proven right – time was the cure. However, before time performed its magic, Caleb and Jenny spent many a bleary-eyed and caffeine-hyped night at this very table, holding their fitfully-sleeping son. Even now, any moments they shared here alone together in the silence were rare and precious indeed.

As if on cue, a loud shout blasted down the stairwell, indicating the apple of their eye was awake and ready to begin his day. Jenny, accompanied by Curly Joe, found Zachary jumping up and down in his crib, grinning from ear to ear, and looking nothing short of spectacularly adorable. Her heart jumped with happiness at the sight of her little rascal, and then, almost immediately, clutched with sorrow for the mother whose child lay dead in a ditch.

Chapter Two

Jenny took Zac to daycare and left Caleb at home to catch up on some much-needed sleep. As always, the toddler sobbed uncontrollably as his mother handed him off to his teacher, but Jenny knew as soon as she was out of sight, Zac would instantly revert to his normal happy and rambunctious self – just like somebody had flipped a switch.

When Jenny first began leaving Zac at school, she agonized over his reaction. She accused herself of being a horrible mother- of abandoning her son to strangers. Finally, logic trumped emotion. Jenny knew all the staff at the daycare very well – they weren't strangers; they were wonderful, caring people. They loved Zac and treated him like the little prince he was. And when she'd also observed the other toddlers performing the same "mind game," Jenny concluded the behavior signified at best a very short attention span or at worst an early form of parental manipulation. Either way, Jenny no longer worried about Zac developing permanent mental scars because he went to daycare.

As Jenny exited the building, the sun slipped behind dark glowering clouds and a cold March rain began to spit from the sky.

"Well," she noted to Jesse, seated beside her in the front of their old SUV, "I guess the weather matches the mood, doesn't it?"

In the fifteen minutes it had taken to reach the Tecumseh Veterinary Clinic from the Stay-N-Play Daycare Center, cold rain began to morph into a winter mix– snow and sleet bounced against the windshield. This was the kind of weather that sent icicles down one's spine.

"Great, I really hope this doesn't turn into ice," she thought as she turned into the gravel parking lot.

Snow was rare in Oklahoma and didn't really pose much of a health risk. Heavy snowfalls were generally welcomed, because nobody in his/her right mind tried to get out on the roads. For the most part Oklahomans were aware they didn't know how to drive in heavy snow and stayed home. A snow day was sort of a holiday declared by Mother Nature herself.

An ice storm, on the other hand, was the state's winter weather monster. It unleashed chaos- multi-car pile-ups, downed power lines, county-wide electrical outages, falls, and panic –havoc wherever and whenever it pleased. And, ice was sneaky – people couldn't always tell it had formed on the sidewalks and roadways. Accident victims didn't know until they were upside down in a ditch or sprawled flat on their backs on a sidewalk that they should have stayed home. Jenny crossed her fingers that the temperature would stay above freezing to keep any moisture that fell in a miserable, but manageable, liquid state.

Jenny pulled the Clinic's sparkling new glass door toward her as she juggled her purse and briefcase from one hand to the other. Jesse quickly slipped through the opening ahead of her and ran smack into Annie Hawthorne. Annie almost dropped the tray of hot coffee and sweet smelling croissants she was carrying.

As the clinic's receptionist righted herself and her precious cargo, Jenny heard her murmur under her breath, "For the life of me, I don't see why that dog has to go everywhere. That animal is always underfoot."

But Jenny knew why Jesse went everywhere with her and she knew that Annie knew, too. Jesse would always be at Jenny's side - for not only was the German shepherd Jenny's best friend and companion, she was also Jenny's savior. Four years ago when Jenny was a new doctor in the Tecumseh Veterinary Clinic, Jesse had saved Jenny's life. From that time forward, the two were inseparable.

Back on an even keel, Annie shot Jenny a smile and then blushed. "Uh, good morning, Dr. Tallchief. I was just taking Dr. Penn some coffee, would you like some?"

Jenny glanced at the tray and smiled inwardly. Annie must have brought those fine china cups and saucers from home to take the place of the worn, battered mugs generally found scattered around the ancient coffee-maker in the back. Jenny inhaled deeply as she thought, "Yep – the pastry is fresh and home-made, too." She looked at the woman more carefully - has Annie been dieting? She certainly was wearing more make-up and dressing more professionally these days. Jenny was pretty sure her middle-aged receptionist had a secret crush on their new doctor - although Annie would be appalled at the very thought.

"No, but thanks, Annie. I'll get some coffee in a little bit. Do we have a busy schedule today?"

"No, not too much – just routine stuff. We do have two surgeries scheduled – but those are for Monday morning. The Sutherlands called about one of their horses, but Dr. Penn can handle that if you need to do something."

"No, far as I know, I'll be here all day." Jenny smiled at the two ladies waiting in the reception area to see Dr. Penn. She walked briskly down the hallway, and turned left into "Doc's Office." Even though her name, *Dr. Jennifer Tallchief, DVM*, was right there on the door inscribed in brass for all to see, she thought to herself, "I guess for me, this will always be 'Doc's Office.'"

When Jenny first came to the Tecumseh Veterinary Clinic, she was an intern from the Oklahoma State University School of Veterinary Medicine. At that time her employer, "Doc" Martin was the lone veterinarian for the area and Annie Hawthorne was his receptionist. Even then Doc had an eye on retirement and finally, after three more years, that dream came true. He sold the clinic to the Tallchiefs and trotted off to his favorite fishing hole – grinning all the way. Doc promised Jenny he'd always be available for a consult if she needed him – that is, if Jenny could ever find him.

Back in the beginning, Jenny would comment to Caleb about the schizophrenic décor found in Doc's office. Old was mixed with new, the latest technical gadget leaned up against an antique telephone or Dictaphone. Doc had kept a loaded gun in his bottom right hand desk drawer – a gun that had saved her life. Yet, in the year since Doc had officially retired, Jenny had changed very little in the office. Her diplomas now hung on the wall instead of his and she'd gotten rid of the old couch – too many terrifying memories – but that was about the extent of her redecorating.

The clinic itself was a different story. The reception area had undergone a considerable cosmetic update, and there was a new surgery suite. She'd also carved out a small second office for her new associate, Dr. Logan Penn.

Logan Penn, too, graduated from OSU. He was a few years younger than Jenny, single, easy-going and drop-dead gorgeous – as attested by the increased traffic in the clinic. And, in addition to being a draw for local female population, Logan was a thoroughly competent vet and a very likeable character.

Jenny stowed her purse and briefcase in their proper places and donned her lab coat. She pushed through the door at the end of the central hallway into the kennels and waved a good morning to their technician, Mike Cady, and part-time helper Jake Sears. Jake had just come in from walking one of their boarders and was attaching a harness and leash to a big black lab. The dog was jumping and prancing and Jenny wasn't sure whether this reflected a real need to get outside or just that the lab was happy. With the natural gregarious nature of labs - it was hard to tell.

Jenny and Mike made the rounds, - Jenny checking on a couple of the more complex treatment regimens. Contrary to what one would generally find in most small rural veterinary hospitals, the Tecumseh Clinic treated animals from across the state – many with unusual or hard-to-diagnose ailments. Its reputation for being *the* treatment center of "last resort" was growing exponentially – primarily due to Jenny's extraordinary diagnostic skills. In just the last month, she had consulted on several cases in Texas and three in Arkansas. The race track in Oklahoma City had her number on speed-dial. Consulting fees now exceeded those generated by their standard practice.

Morning rounds complete, Jenny returned to her office. Annie hurried down the hallway to tell her that a Dr. Cooper from Austin had requested a call-back.

Jenny punched in his number and made an appointment for the following Monday to see a male Lhasa apso whose illness defied identification. Atypically for a vet, Dr. Cooper asked if he could accompany the patient rather than its "parent." Jenny, of course, said the doctor would be most welcome. Wondering what that was about, Jenny had Annie update the appointment book.

Early in the afternoon Jenny sat at her desk, eating lunch, when her cell phone rang. It was Caleb. "Hey. I thought you were going to get some sleep."

The voice on the other end sounded weary. "Well, I tried - but no luck. I feel the need to hit something. I think this might be a good time to knock down that wall between our room and the sitting room. Want to go over to Lowe's with me?"

"I think that can be arranged. I'll meet you at home in half an hour."

****

Everybody at Lowe's knew Jenny and Caleb on sight. They were such frequent customers the staff had begun to take a personal interest in each phase of their remodeling - offering unsolicited construction tips or decorating ideas. The Tallchief's old Victorian house had almost become a town-wide renovation effort. As Caleb and Victor Marshall discussed the pros and cons of various types of wallboard, Caleb's cell phone blared out the first notes of *Scotland the Brave*.

"Hey, Caleb. It's Mary Ellen. I know you're not due in 'til tomorrow, but with the Sheriff at that meeting in Oklahoma City, and Trucker off sick, I've got nobody to send. Since you're pretty close by, I just thought…." Mary Ellen Moore was the dispatcher and arguably the most important person at the Pottawatomie County Sheriff's Office in Shawnee.

"Sure, Mary Ellen, no problem. What do you need?"

"Well, the priest at St. Mary's in Tecumseh – you know – that little Catholic Church on the edge of town - called and said he's got a young girl there. He doesn't know whether she's a run-away or what. He doesn't know what to do with her. Can you go by and check it out?"

"Be glad to. I'll leave right now. I'll call you back when I know something."

St. Mary's was only a few minutes from Lowe's, but it looked like it was miles from anywhere. The small structure, built in the traditional shape of the cross, stood alone surrounded by an open field. Attached by a small breezeway was a tiny house which served as the rectory. The Catholic population in Tecumseh was very small.

Father Leland met Caleb, Jenny and Jesse as they pulled to a stop in the pounded dirt parking lot in front of the church.

The priest fluttered his hands. "Thank you so much for coming right away. I just didn't know what to do." Wasting no time, the elderly man turned toward the church. Jenny, Caleb and Jesse hurried to keep up. "About an hour ago, Mrs. Dell, our housekeeper, came rushing into the rectory to tell me there was this girl drinking from the font."

When Jenny and Caleb looked blank, he added, "You know, the bowl that holds the holy water just inside the church doors. Mrs. Dell was most aggravated at the child's lack of respect."

The small priest exhaled. By now he was so agitated he was almost dancing a jig. "Well, I went inside and found a girl sitting in the back pew staring at the crucifix – just staring – not moving – I couldn't even tell if she was breathing. She wouldn't say anything. I tried talking to her – even tried a little Spanish – but nothing. I touched her arm and she sort of screamed – made this high-pitched squeal. Her skin is ice cold and she's filthy. I didn't know what else to do. I put a blanket on the pew next to her – I sure didn't want to try to get too close to her again - then called the Sheriff's Office. I hope that was right…." His voice trailed off.

Caleb reassured the man. "You did exactly the right thing. Let's go see her, OK?"

The priest opened the heavy front door and, uncharacteristically, Jesse leaped ahead of the priest and disappeared into the gloom beyond. "Hey," Father Leland said, "Dogs aren't allowed in the sanctuary."

"Father, I'm so sorry - I don't know what got into her. She's usually so well behaved. I'll get her out right away." Jenny was puzzled, the only time she could remember that Jesse displayed this kind of aggressiveness was when she or somebody in the family was in trouble.

Jenny hurried into the darkened inner space. It took a few seconds for her eyes to adjust, but she soon spotted Jesse, sitting on the last pew next to a blonde, disheveled girl. It was difficult to see clearly, but it appeared the girl had her arms around Jesse's neck and her face buried in the dog's dark fur.

Instead of rebuking Jesse for her breech of etiquette, Jenny stood quietly at the end of the row. Now joined by Caleb and Father Leland, Jenny waited until Jesse caught her eye. Jenny raised her shoulders as if to ask, "What's going on?"

Jesse licked the top of the girl's head. After a minute or two, the girl, without releasing her grip on the dog, turned to face the three adults.

Caleb froze. "Sweet Jesus, it's not possible," he thought to himself. He backed up a step or two, grabbed the top of the pew across the aisle and sat down – heavily. The girl holding on to Jesse was the same girl he'd seen just that morning - the same cold, dead battered girl who'd been tossed aside in the ditch beside Highway 177.

Jenny saw all the color drain from Caleb's face and his forehead break out into a sweat. She honestly thought he might faint.

"What's going on?" Father Leland looked from the child to Caleb and back to the child. "What's wrong?"

"I don't know, Father." She turned to her husband, "Caleb? What? You look like you've just seen a ghost."

All he would say over and over was - "this is just not possible. This is just not possible."

****

When Caleb finally realized he was seeing not a ghost – but a twin - he strode outside to call Mary Ellen at the Sheriff's Office. Jenny and Father Leland followed on his heels, listening to the one-sided conversation and finally understanding. Jenny was speechless. Father Leland crossed himself.

Several calls later, it was determined the girl should be taken to the hospital in Shawnee to be examined and kept overnight for observation. Tomorrow, the Oklahoma Department of Human Services would assume responsibility. Caleb softly relayed the plan to Jenny and the Priest.

Jenny approached the twosome in the pew but the fear in the girl's eyes grew stronger the closer Jenny came. So, Jenny settled back and thought. She motioned to Jesse to come to her, hoping the child would follow. The instant Jesse leaned in Jenny's direction, the girl began shaking and moaning and gripped the big dog even more desperately. Jenny motioned to Jesse to remain where she was, and Jenny retreated to where Caleb and Father Leland anxiously waited in the vestibule.

"This isn't going to work," she explained. "That child has to have gone through something pretty horrible. She's holding on to Jesse for dear life. If we force her to go to the hospital – into the hands of more strangers without Jesse - I just don't know what that'll do to her emotionally."

"Can we give her some tranquilizers or something?"

"That'd be really risky. We don't know if she's already been drugged…and if she has - with what." Jenny continued, "Let me call Dr. Phillips, Zac's pediatrician. We need some professional help here."

Jenny made the call. Dr. Phillips listened to Jenny's description of the girl's condition and said he'd be over as soon as he could. In the meantime, Father Leland asked Mrs. Dell to fix something hot for the girl to eat. The housekeeper, obviously feeling guilty for her premature judgment, soon returned with a tray heaped high with a bowl of stew, some cornbread, butter and a big slice of cherry pie.

Jenny took the tray from the elderly woman and reentered the church. Jesse and the girl were still sitting side by side, but as the aroma of the food wafted its way into the sanctuary, both of them turned in Jenny's direction. Jenny set the food tray about halfway along the pew and retreated back into the foyer.

"Let's hope she's hungry enough to eat something," Father Leland remarked. Sure enough, Jenny saw Jesse leap down to the floor and then reappear on the center aisle side of the pew. Her head disappeared again and Jenny assumed the dog was using her nose to scoot the tray closer to the girl. In under a minute, Jesse's dark head reappeared and she turned to look directly at Jenny. The three adults could hear the spoon rattling as the youngster attacked the food.

Thirty minutes later, Dr. Phillips, accompanied by an attractive scholarly-looking middle-aged woman, pulled into the church parking lot. Jenny stuck her head outside and waved them in.

In hushed tones, Dr. Phillips said, "Sorry it took so long, but after I thought about your patient, I wasn't sure I could give you the best advice. So I called Melody to help us out. She's a child psychologist from Shawnee and consults with the Oklahoma Department of Human Services. She has much more experience with children in crisis than I do." Introductions were made all around.

Drs. Smith and Phillips accompanied Jenny into the sanctuary, but when the girl saw them, she jumped for Jesse, knocking the food tray to the floor. She wrapped her arms around the dog so forcefully Jesse yipped. Then she began to shake and make low moaning sounds. The trio stopped dead in their tracks and retreated to the foyer.

"Wow, that was some reaction! She's obviously terrified." Everybody looked at Dr. Smith.

"I don't think it would be wise to further traumatize her. It looks as though the dog has become her lifeline and separating her from the animal now would probably do more harm than good."

Dr. Phillips agreed and added, "I couldn't see any obvious physical trauma– it looked as though she moved quickly and easily. She's eating and cognizant. I didn't see anything that couldn't wait for a couple of days. I sure wouldn't want to force a more thorough exam that might throw her into a real tailspin."

"Okay," said Caleb. "What now?"

More phone calls. Dr. Smith conferred with her peers at the OKDHS, while Caleb called the Sheriff's Office. Luckily, Sheriff Holcomb had returned and the dispatcher put him on the line.

"Caleb, I just got back from OK City - about our Jane Doe. They believe she could've been kidnapped by human traffickers. I'm told these gangs are vicious -brutal – like we saw on the kid – if the kid in the church was kidnapped by them, too – she could be in a lot of trouble."

"So….what do you want to do?"

"Well, sounds like the kid has decided for us… she's not going to go anywhere without your dog, right? How about if you take her home? I can't see us trying to keep her at the Office, can you? I'll get you some additional protection at your house 'til we get this sorted out. Maybe by then the girl will be able to tell us what happened. Probably just be a couple of days, what do you think?"

Caleb agreed, knowing full well Jenny wouldn't abandon this helpless girl. "Who are you kidding?" he said to himself. "You can't leave her, either."

****

After everything had been coordinated with the OKDHS, the Shawnee Sheriff's Office and the Tallchiefs, Drs. Phillips and Smith left. Both asked to be kept in the loop as much as possible, and Dr. Phillips promised to stop by the Tallchiefs house to give the girl a more thorough exam just as soon as they thought she could tolerate it. Waving goodbye, the Tallchiefs promised to call and then watched as the pick-up's tail lights faded into the diminishing twilight.

"Well, I guess we should get back to the rectory," said Father Leland. Jenny could tell the diminutive priest was anxious to get back to his normal routine and away from the tragic figure in his church.

Caleb sensed their emotion. "Thank you for all your help, Father. And, you, too, Mrs. Dell," said Caleb, shaking the hand of each in turn and effectively alleviating the two from any further responsibility. Obviously relieved, they quick-stepped back to the small house beside the church.

****

Jenny and Caleb sat with Jesse and the young girl in the quiet of God's house. By and by, the girl's eyes became so heavy with exhaustion that she fell into a troubled sleep – her head resting against Jesse's chest - her arms wrapped firmly around the dog's neck.

While the child slept, Jenny and Caleb discussed the next steps, knowing that Jesse's help would be key in getting the girl home. After discarding several options, they finally devised a plan that might work. Jenny shared it with the shepherd while Caleb went out to the truck and returned with Jesse's leash.

Scarcely an hour later, the girl opened her eyes to see Jenny seated near her. She was startled but this time she didn't shake or moan. Jenny spoke softly and calmly to her.

"Hello, my name is Jenny," Jenny pointed to herself. "And, this is Jesse." She scratched her friend's ears. "What's your name?"

Silence.

"We want to help you. You're safe with us, OK?"

No response.

"We want you to come home with us. You'll be safe there. Jesse will come, too." Jenny stood up and clipped Jesse's leash to her collar. Then she left the pew, walked down the aisle and out the church door.

Jesse picked up the end of the leash in her mouth and put it in the girl's hand. Then the shepherd jumped to the floor and followed in Jenny's wake.

At first the young girl did not move. The leash grew taught and then pulled from her fingertips. Jesse turned and picked up the end of the leash - again placing it in the girl's grip. This time the youngster stood and followed, as Jesse led her down the length of the pew, into the aisle, and outside into the dark.

When the girl saw the SUV outside with the doors standing open, she stopped abruptly and would go no further. Jesse turned, reared up on her hind legs and placed her paws on the girl's chest. The shepherd stared directly into the twin's blue eyes. They remained in that position – eyes fixed on eyes - for a full minute. Whatever message was conveyed, some degree of understanding was reached; for when Jesse finally eased down, the big dog led the girl into the vehicle and they all headed home.

****

The next two days were interesting – to say the least. Jenny kept up a running commentary with their new houseguest even though the twin added nothing to the conversation. Although the girl seldom acknowledged Jenny's presence, at least she didn't repeat her trembling and moaning routine and even seemed to tolerate Caleb. She was calm as long as Jesse was at her side. Jesse didn't appear to mind – somehow sensing that the child needed her close.

Zachary, through some special intuition all very young children seem to have, did more to put their guest at ease than anyone. That boy was a showman, for sure. At times the toddler could get their guest to play, drawing her from her inner thoughts into his world of laughter and mischief. One activity they particularly enjoyed together was eating - especially bananas. She and Zachary split one each morning and afternoon.

On the evening of the second night of the twin's stay, Jenny was fixing dinner while Caleb was upstairs pounding on the wall that separated their bedroom from its adjacent small sitting room. Jenny heard a loud crash, accompanied by Caleb's swearing, and ran up the stairs to find Caleb flat on the seat of his pants and the antique rocking chair upended.

"Damn it, Jenny. Why'd you move that rocker in here? I tripped over it and nearly broke my friggin' neck!" Caleb slowly stood up and checked himself for injury, brushing white plaster from his jeans.

"I didn't move it, Caleb. As a matter of fact, just this morning I moved it from here to our room – over in the corner."

"Well, somebody did. What a goddamn mess!" Jenny looked around – caught Caleb's eye. Then they both started laughing – like that room could possibly be more messed up than it already was.

Jenny returned to the kitchen pondering the mystery of the mobile rocker only to find her beautiful baby boy had pulled one of the kitchen chairs over to the counter and was stretching to steal another banana.

"Hey, big guy, watch it. You're going to kill yourself." She picked him up and firmly set him on the floor. Zac's big blue eyes looked soulfully into hers – Jenny was a sucker for those eyes. "Okay, just one more." She handed him a banana, and the toddler gleefully escaped into the living room to share his booty before Jenny could change her mind.

"I wonder if we've got any prunes," she thought absently as she cut lettuce for their salad.

Zac was playing one of his favorite games, "What's this?". The game consisted of pointing to various objects, body parts, toys, pets, whatever came into his field of view and naming it. Generally, the toddler didn't wait for his game partner, but shouted out the answer himself. This evening, Zac was playing with Jesse.

Zac pointed to Jesse. "Zat?" he asked. When the shepherd didn't answer, Zac helped her out, "'Esse!"

He pointed to Jenny. "Zat?" Not waiting for a response, he yelled, "Mommy!"

Then he pointed to their newcomer, "Zat?" and immediately supplied the correct answer, "Nana!"

Jenny heard the monolog. Anyone within a three block radius of the Tallchief house would have heard it. "Is that Nana?" she asked, pointing to the twin.

"Yep." Suddenly, her son lost interest in the naming game and picked up his Speed McQueen car. "Rooom…. rooom!" and off he went.

"Well," Jenny said to the world-at-large, "I guess we have to call you something – 'hey, you' is just not working. Zac seems to think Nana is perfect. So, at least for now, Nana it is."

****

Running, running. Out of breath - can't breathe. Long, heavy skirts catching on the underbrush. I can hear the girls screaming in the distance. They're terrified and so am I. I've got to help them, but I just can't run fast enough. Oh, God, help ...help me save them. Screaming, screaming. I hit a tree full on. It knocks me to the ground. I try to stand, but my skirt is caught on a thorn bush. I've lost a slipper and my feet are covered in blood....

"Jenny, Jenny, wake up!" Jenny's eyes opened and for a moment she didn't know where she was. One minute she was running in terror, and, in the next - safe and warm in her own bed.

"You okay? Your legs were thrashing and you were whimpering. That must have been one hell of a nightmare…." Caleb's concerned voice trailed off as he tried to make out his wife's expression in the dark. "You want me to turn the light on? Can I get you something to drink?"

"No, no…. thanks, I'm okay. Boy, that was really weird – I was running through the woods someplace

– scared to death. I had to find somebody – some kids – I think. They were in danger and I couldn't find them. I could hear them screaming, but I kept catching my dress and falling down. ….." She was quiet for a moment. "Thanks for waking me up. That dream was not fun at all."

Caleb wrapped his comforting arms around her and they sat that way until Jenny quit shaking. Jenny said, "I wonder where that came from?"

Caleb shrugged his shoulders. "No wonder you're freaked – it's been a zoo around here lately…"

They both turned as Jesse poked her nose into the crack between their bedroom door and its frame and quietly slipped into the room. The shepherd leaped onto the bed and nuzzled Jenny's hand. Jenny absent-mindedly scratched Jesse's ears, assuring her, "I'm fine – I'm fine. It was just a bad dream."

As Jenny's eyes became more accustomed to the gloom, she could see the twin standing still as a statue just outside the bedroom door – eyes glued on the German shepherd.

"Hi, Nana. Want to come in?" As if hit by a bolt of lightning, the youngster turned and fled down the hallway. Jesse sighed in the way only dogs can do, jumped from the bed and followed, tail banging the door and frame as she scooted through.

"See what I mean?" Caleb turned over and closed his eyes.

Chapter Three

"What you mean, you don't have them?"

Julio Mendez swallowed nervously and averted his eyes from Sr. Ortiz. He shifted from one foot to the other and held his hands together in front of him.

"Well, those little bitches tried to get away when we stopped at the Oklahoma transfer house waiting for the crews from Kansas and California to pick up the other girls. The twins was really sneaky – one went right out that bathroom window and the other one almost did. Nobody ever got out that window before. I don't know how they done it…"

Mendez's hands let go of one another and began to move in ever-widening arcs as the volume of his speech increased, "That crazy bastard Wasp got one before she could get out. The kid bit him and he just went ape-shit. Started beating on her and took out his knife and stabbed her over and over. She was screaming and he was yelling – oh man – oh man - there was just blood everywhere."

The Hispanic man cleared his throat. "That guy is nuts, Sr. Ortiz. These gang freaks just want to hurt people and hurt 'em bad. I tried – but I couldn't stop him." He paused to let his explanation sink in - so that his patron would understand that the situation was in no way his fault.

"But we got rid of any evidence," he continued, "we cleaned up the house, stripped the dead kid and got rid of her body. Nobody'll find her. Nothing that can link her to us."

Mendez looked up. "The other one got away. It wasn't my fault, Senor. We looked for hours but we couldn't find her anyplace. Hell, it was so dark and cold out there, she's probably a frozen Popsicle by now."

The small man offered a slight smile at his own joke. When it was returned by only a cold hard stare, he continued - the cadence of his speech increased with each word. "We loaded up the other girls and headed here - quick as we could. We figured we better get out of there in case the cops got wind of it."

Mendez looked beseechingly at his employer, silently praying Sr. Ortiz would recognize that he, Mendez, was a loyal and competent member of the organization, and that he had done everything he could to fix an unavoidably catastrophic situation.

Inside Ortiz was boiling. He had a customer for those twins who was willing to pay big bucks – all that planning and effort - now he had nothing to sell.

"Let me understand - the other girls – you brought them here?" Ortiz kept his voice even.

"Si, Sr. Ortiz. But they are all fine – nobody else hurt or missing."

Ortiz cursed vehemently to himself. "How could any one person possibly be this stupid? This idiot Mendez brought these girls here – here for Christ's sake - where I have my legitimate operation's offices."

"Calm yourself," Ortiz instructed himself, "Don't lose your temper. No need to have a coronary. Nothing to do now, but minimize the damage." Not trusting himself to speak, Ortiz waved Mendez out into the reception area.

In the silence of his well-appointed office, the head of area operations for the Marta Cartel tried to figure out what he was going to do next. Like Mendez, Ortiz, too, had bosses – but his bosses were unaware of this latest international business enterprise with the twins and of the potential danger it posed for the entire network. He'd have to do some fancy "spin doctoring" himself to keep them in the dark and out of his business.

He cursed inwardly again and again. It had been hell trying to convince the 'big bosses' his human trafficking plan would be the perfect solution to their negative cash flow. All the Colombian cartels, and especially theirs in Marta, had been taking a financial beating from the Mexicans for more than two years, and you'd think those Colombian idiots would be leaping at his solution. That posturing bastard, Martin Gabriel, had been particularly insulting.

The memory of the Marta Board Meeting in Bogota eighteen months ago popped into his head. Oh yes, he remembered that meeting very well - every word – every gesture - every insult. His stomach muscles clenched.

Ortiz had been called in to 'make his pitch' before that self-righteous collection of old bastards – like he was a child currying favor. There they were - sitting in judgment as if they were respectable businessmen – respectable – ha, that's a laugh – and Ortiz was shit. That fat, bloated dinosaur Gabriel – so sanctimonious – so belittling - vehemently opposed the idea, for – believe it or not – moral reasons. He said stealing children for prostitution was an insult to God. Insult to God –could you believe it? Like any of them cared about anything but money. It took Ortiz many hours and one surreptitious bribe for the cartel to provisionally accept his proposal.

Shit – everything had been going so well – great in fact – until this fuck-up. Profits were through the roof – well in excess of his estimates. In less than one year more than $500 million had come in from cross-country money alone.

But none of that would matter if he couldn't hide the damage done in this debacle. If Gabriel found out what Ortiz was up to – it truly would be a disaster. He'd sworn never to resort to kidnapping. Gabriel made a point to remind the other board members that kidnapping was what had destroyed the Cali cartel many years ago. So what? Who cares what those shitheads did a hundred years ago?"

Ortiz tried to calm down and think clearly. He had had the twins kidnapped and they had been younger – much younger - than anyone involved in the trafficking so far. Ortiz had promised the Cartel he'd keep away from the really young kids. The fact he was going to sell them to a client in Eastern Europe wouldn't make a bit of difference to them, either.

"Shit, shit! Shit!" he shouted aloud. He pounded his desk until his fist bled.

"Well, that was helpful."

Ortiz turned and glared at the figure standing in the dark corner. The man, nonplussed by the Director's angry glare, pulled an old-fashioned white cloth handkerchief from his back pocket and handed it to the overwrought Ortiz.

Ortiz wrapped it tightly around his bleeding knuckles. He pointed a shaking finger at the door Mendez had used and said, "Kill them both – Mendez and that crazy piece of shit from the gang. Make sure Mendez' body is never found, and as for that moron Wasp, kill him ugly and make sure the rest of his gang sees it. Maybe then they'll understand what happens when you fuck with the Cartel."

Ortiz paused, "Then I want you to go to where they dumped that kid and see what the real damage is, OK?"

MacIntosh nodded and left the room. Ortiz settled back into his comfortable cordovan leather chair. He rubbed the palm of his uninjured hand across the soft masculine-scented hide – it always seemed to calm him – made him feel in control.

"At least I don't have to worry about MacIntosh screwing up," he thought. He and MacIntosh went back for years – one of the very few friends Ortiz had allowed himself. They'd met when they were just kids in the seedy back streets of St. Louis.

One late night Ortiz had been trying to get home without running into any of the A5's – the gang who ruled his neighborhood. Always on the prowl looking for trouble, for new recruits, for whatever – the gang was one of the most vicious in St. Louis's underbelly. Until that night Ortiz had been lucky enough to stay under their radar.

That night, the slender eleven year-old stealthily slipped down the alley - in and out of the shadows – taking care to be silent and invisible. Taking this route had always been safe before, but this night he'd run out of luck. He stepped from between two trash bins and directly into four A5's. It couldn't have been worse – one of them was Fat Boy – an honest-to-God sixteen-year old psychopath. Ortiz had heard stories of kids caught by Fat Boy – boys or girls – didn't matter – he raped them and slit their throats. Ortiz was terrified – he was certain he was going to die just for Fat Boy's perverse entertainment.

"Hey there, Ortiz, been lookin' for you … you wasn't trying to run away from us, was you? I mean I been startin' to think you didn't wanna' be my friend…" Fat Boy looked at his gang, grinned, and the three others snickered. "Show me I'm wrong…why don't ya?"

One of the four flipped him around and slammed his face against the bricks – he could hear Fat Boy come up behind him and unzip. All four started laughing and joking – egging the pervert on. Ortiz still had nightmares about that sound – could still smell the stink of the garbage and feel the ragged brick scraping his face like sandpaper.

That's when MacIntosh- meaner-than-a-snake, MacIntosh stepped in. The thirteen-year old Irish kid lived right around the corner from Ortiz and he was as notorious as Fat Boy – but for different reasons. The other kids said MacIntosh was vicious in a fight and totally fearless. That night Ortiz found out something else – the recalcitrant dark-haired teen loathed the A5's.

In the blink of an eye, MacIntosh had taken out two of them with his baseball bat, and Ortiz, with a well-placed kick, put Fat Boy out of business. The fourth kid ran off into the night.

Ortiz and MacIntosh, unscathed except for a small crescent-shaped cut to MacIntosh's chin, forged a friendship that night – a friendship that was as strong today as it had been that night twenty-five years ago.

When Ortiz started working for the Marta Cartel, he brought MacIntosh with him and he'd never been sorry. MacIntosh still had his back. They made an extraordinarily solid team - each had his own skills, a shared love of money, and a total disregard for morality.

Reverie broken, Ortiz popped back to the here and now. He sighed - first things first – he had to break the bad news to his soon-to-be disappointed customer. He reached for his cell, and realized he'd have to punch the numbers in with his left hand. It was extremely awkward and it took three attempts to get the number right. The failed effort reignited his anger and Ortiz pounded the desk again, "Those damn idiots – this is their fault, too."

The Director took a couple of deep breaths to calm down before he pressed 'call.' After two rings a familiar voice answered. Ortiz began, "Mr. Ulmani, I'm afraid I have some rather unfortunate news for you…a temporary set-back."

****

The Tallchief house slept. Upstairs in the little sitting room adjacent to the master bedroom and amidst the construction chaos, the antique rocking chair squared itself in front of the large window overlooking the front lawn. Imperceptibly at first, the chair stirred on its rockers– back and forth – back and forth - until it reached a slow rhythmic cadence. Clue, perched on the top of Caleb's chest of drawers, watched with unblinking eyes. After a bit, he jumped down and padded silently across the bedroom floor and into the sitting room. The cat stared for a moment or two at the rocker's empty seat. Then he settled down on the floor beside it and began to purr.

The cat and the chair kept a quiet vigil over the night until the first rays of dawn kissed the morning awake.

****

Caleb was up and away early Monday morning. He barely had time to get a cup of coffee before Holcomb's SUV pulled into the drive. Holcomb and Caleb had a meeting in Oklahoma City with the Oklahoma Bureau of Narcotics and Dangerous Drugs Control. The OBNDC had recently been granted more wide-reaching authority to investigate human trafficking, and Caleb and the Sheriff were meeting with the director of the seven-member anti-trafficking unit, R.T. Huff.

The two Pottawatomie County lawmen discussed the case from any number of angles on the 45-minute ride into the City. Given the limited resources at the Sheriff's disposal, they knew they'd have to call on several of the state's law enforcement agencies for help – maybe even the Oklahoma State Bureau of Investigation, the OSBI. Caleb tried to talk Holcomb out of contacting the OSBI – he and one of their field agents had locked horns some years ago and Tallchief was still pissed.

"Caleb," said Holcomb, "You know better 'n anyone this is bigger than we can handle alone." Caleb didn't respond. "OK- let's see what the OBNDC can do. I'm not ruling out the OSBI though."

The rest of the trip passed quietly, but companionably. Then Caleb said, "Now I know why you wanted to get such an early start."

"What?"

"I didn't know you wanted to take a scenic tour of the City – we should have brought brochures."

"What're you talking about?" Caleb pointed straight ahead.

Holcomb looked out the windshield. "Well, shit!" Straight ahead was the archway to the Oklahoma City Memorial with the time of 9:01 etched boldly at its apex. Caleb was only a kid when Timothy McVeigh blew up the Alfred P. Murrah Building. 168 people, including many kids, died, but he still remembered it. The drama – the horror – maybe that was one of the reasons he decided to go into law enforcement.

Tallchief's attention snapped back. This was the third time Holcomb had driven by the Memorial – obviously, the guy was lost.

"Want me to drive?" Caleb asked, chuckling.

"No, damnit. I got this." Holcomb turned left– retracing the route he'd taken twice before. Caleb thought he could hear his boss mumbling something about construction and dumbass one-way streets, but this time they managed to find the multi-level parking garage directly across from the Federal Courthouse. Once parked and out on the street, Holcomb and Tallchief walked a couple of blocks east and easily found the address for the offices of the OBNDDC. They arrived on the 12th floor exactly on time.

The two were led into a small, but nicely appointed office. One entire wall was floor-to-ceiling windows. Caleb and Holcomb walked over to view a large swath of the City's panorama. Fast-moving scull racers dotted the surface of the Oklahoma River, several people were zip lining across the river above the scullers. They could see the Chickasaw Bricktown Baseball Stadium, where the OKC Triple AAA Class *Redhawks* played and, if he leaned forward and put his nose to the glass, Caleb could see the Chesapeake Arena, where the pro basketball team – Thunder – played. The Devon Tower dominated the skyline – it was almost twice as tall as any other building in the city. Many locals still weren't sure whether they liked that building or not – it had already garnered several odious – but descriptive - nicknames.

"Downtown OKC has really changed," thought Caleb. "I need to bring Jenny over for a weekend real soon. Maybe we can go to a game or see the Crystal Bridge. We could even bring Zac – ride on a canal taxi."

Caleb's reverie broke when Director R.T. Huff hustled into the room. The director was a small fiftyish woman, slim of body but large-chested, with short salt and pepper hair, minimal make-up and a friendly, but reserved air. Holcomb and Tallchief exchanged wary glances –Huff'd be a force to be reckoned with – good force or bad – that seemed to be the question. Caleb guessed they'd find out soon enough.

The lady walked briskly forward to shake hands.

"Hello, gentlemen, nice to meet you both."

"Sheriff Joe Holcomb and this is Undersheriff Caleb Tallchief. Please call me Joe."

"Caleb."

"Most folks here call me Bobbi. The "R" is for Roberta. Please - let's sit." She led her guests to the small round table in the corner of the office.

"We appreciate you seeing us so quickly. We've got a friggin' mess on our hands," began the Sheriff.

Director Huff smiled and answered. "Hey, we appreciate being asked. Not every county sheriff wants us around."

She continued, "I think you both probably already know that since the Sawyer case last summer, the OBNDC has ramped up its efforts to get a handle on the human trafficking situation in the state. We've learned from confidential informants that some of the same criminal elements trafficking drugs and guns in Oklahoma are now dealing in people. They don't care – the fact they're selling human beings means nothing to them. Only profit matters – and unfortunately, there's a lot of profit in buying and selling kids and young adults."

Caleb said, "You know, I couldn't figure out why of all the state agencies, we were meeting with you -what narcotics and drugs had to do human trafficking. Now it makes sense."

"Just like with the drug and gun smuggling, Oklahoma is prime territory for human traffickers. We're on the crossroads of main east-west and north-south interstates – not to mention I-44 up through Missouri and Illinois. Oklahoma has a high rate of poverty, domestic abuse, teen pregnancy and homelessness. Vulnerable people are prime targets for traffickers. Needless to say, we've got an uphill battle on our hands. We're just starting to get our minds around it."

"Are you familiar with our Jane Doe?" Holcomb asked.

"A little….but I'd appreciate hearing it from you."

"Early Friday morning, we got the call that a child's nude body had been found in a ditch near Highway 177 – just south of I-40. We went to the scene and found a girl, I estimate her age at about 10 or 11. She'd been beaten, stabbed and probably raped. Her wrists showed she'd been bound. From what we gathered at the scene, we believe she was killed elsewhere - 177 is just where they dumped her. We've sent the body along to the Oklahoma State Medical Examiner's Office for autopsy, but it's still too early for their report - probably be some time yet. We've also asked for some help with the forensic evidence from the OSBI."

Caleb raised his eyebrows and looked at Holcomb.

Bobbi asked, "Who called it in?"

"A ranch hand - name of Jack Millard – just a kid himself really - works for Bill Taylor –- owner of one of the larger ranches in Pott County. He'd been out at the Stone Pony - casino just outside Shawnee. Apparently, on his way home he stopped on a dark stretch of 177 to take a whiz and glanced around. He saw the poor kid lying in the ditch and called us."

"Any chance he's involved? Had he been drinking?"

"No, I'd be real surprised if he had anything to do with it. He was real shaken up. If he'd been drinking, he was sure cold sober when we got there…he'd thrown up all over the place. But that's not the strangest part of the whole thing. Caleb, why don't you tell Bobbi the rest?

Caleb continued, "Later that afternoon, we got a call from Father Leland, the priest at our local Catholic Church. He had a trespasser – a young girl. I was off-duty, but close by; so my wife who was with me and I went to the church. At first I thought I'd seen a ghost."

Noting Bobbi's surprise, Caleb went on, "No kidding. The same girl as we'd seen dead earlier that day. I tell you, that was a shock."

Bobbi nodded, following his narration without comment.

"Of course, she's gotta' be the twin sister of our Jane Doe. The poor kid hasn't said a word yet, obviously something really bad happened to her – but, she's attached herself to our dog. When we tried to separate the two – hell, the poor kid almost had a heart attack. After we talked the whole situation over with the powers that be, we decided she should come home with us – my wife and me. Not only were we concerned with her emotional state, we're afraid for her safety – those bastards who killed her sister may be looking for her."

Huff sat back in her chair and folded her arms across her chest. Caleb could almost see her brain calculating behind her intelligent eyes.

Caleb continued, "She's staying at our house until we can figure out who she is or where she belongs. Our son, who's two, has nicknamed her Nana, but we don't know her real name or where she's from."

"So what do you think? Do you think she'll be able to talk – tell us what happened?"

"No idea. She doesn't seem to be as terrified as she was and she seems to be comfortable in our home, but..."

Holcomb broke in, "We've sent her clothes to the OSBI as well. We're hoping something will give us a clue as to where she's from or at least where she's been."

Director Huff thought a minute. "Twins, huh. That's a new twist – but why not? I agree with you, Sheriff. This has all the earmarks of a human trafficking deal gone south. What can we do to help?"

"Well, we need access to any information you might have about trafficking rings operating around here and we'd really appreciate some help with missing person reports – that kind of thing – to help us locate this child's family. We're kind of limited on our resources, especially since I've assigned some extra security to watch over Caleb's house and family."

"Done and done. How about if I assign Mark Hamilton, one of the members of our task force, to work directly with you? He can handle the research and anything else you might need from our end."

****

Jenny, Nana and Zac, too, were up and around early. Jenny had two surgeries scheduled and then there was the consult with the Austin vet. That whole thing was strange – the man seemed pretty reluctant to talk about the dog's problem. Oh well, she'd find out soon enough.

Jenny dropped the baby at day care and she, Nana and Jesse made it to the Clinic in less than fifteen minutes. Nana and Jesse settled into the reception area with Annie hovering over them, plying Nana with her home-made apple strudel.

Later that morning with rounds and surgeries complete, Dr. Penn stuck his head into Jenny's office and asked, "Hey, OK if I sit in on your consult with the vet from Austin? I want to see you work your magic."

"Fine by me," Jenny replied, knowing full well her special skill as a diagnostician could never be learned. It had come to her as a special gift – but at a tremendous cost.

Dr. Cooper arrived about fifteen minutes early and Jenny welcomed him and his patient, "Charley." They talked 'vet' for a few minutes and then Cooper got to the heart of his problem.

"You see, Charley's my mother's dog – he's more like her baby." The two vets understood that feeling perfectly. "She loves him more than any human – probably even me. For sure, I'd never want to make her choose." Jenny chuckled.

He continued, "Charley's a rescue I got for her - oh – about ten years ago now, and I've taken care of his health needs ever since. That dog has had every shot, every treatment – everything. I don't know what's wrong."

Jenny asked, "So what're his symptoms?"

"Charley's hair is falling out. He won't eat. He sleeps or lays around all the time – no energy. No interest in anything. I've run every test I can think of and they all come back negative. I'm stumped – really stumped."

He leaned over and patted the small dog. "Charley seems to be slipping away a little more every day. If he dies, and there was something I could've done, Mother would never forgive me. Hell, *I* wouldn't forgive me." He smiled, but Jenny could sense his underlying anxiety.

"Well," Jenny responded, "I'm sure you've thought of everything I might, but since you drove all this way, how about if I look him over?"

"I can't tell you how much I appreciate this," Dr. Cooper continued. "A couple of my colleagues in Austin examined Charley and they can't figure out what's wrong either. Mike Sheehan recommended I bring him to you. I think you've consulted with him before, and he swears you are in a league of your own when it comes to diagnoses."

Jenny smiled at the compliment, but said nothing. "If you only knew," she thought to herself, "I don't do the diagnosis – my patients do it for me."

Jenny gently set the little dog on the examining table, just as Dr. Penn slipped into the room. Jenny stroked the animal's thinning coat, quietly talking to Charley as if he were human – Logan later swore they were actually conversing. She looked into Charley's big brown soulful eyes, then his mouth, and began to gently probe his underside. Although Charley didn't jump or offer any outward signs of distress, Jenny could sense this was the pain center. Then she got a flash of insight from Charley. Male dogs seemed to be overly interested in him – sniffing him aggressively – like he was a female in heat. She could sense the poor animal's despair – he hurt – he was abused by other dogs and he was just too tired to fight back – it was too much. Jenny thought, "Hmm….abdominal pain, exhaustion, hair loss and hormone imbalance – hormones are about the only reason for the other males to be *that* interested. What – what could it be?" A glimmer of an idea seeped into her consciousness. "Could that be it? Wow – that would be really unusual, but – hey – unusual is what I do."

Logan and Dr. Cooper watched Jenny closely. "So, what do you think?"

"I'm not sure. Let's take Charley outside for a walk around the building." The three doctors and Charley circled the Clinic as Jenny closely watched the small male dog slowly make the circuit.

Jake, walking a large male bulldog in the opposite direction, nodded and smiled. Suddenly the bulldog wheeled around and started enthusiastically after Charley. Taken by surprise, Jake was barely able to rein in the animal before it reached the smaller dog. It took all Jake's strength to pull the bulldog away. Embarrassed, Jake hauled the big dog around the corner of the Clinic, and Jenny could hear him say "Sorry, Doc," as they passed from sight.

"No problem, Jake."

"Happen much?" Jenny asked of Dr. Cooper.

"I don't really know. I can ask Mother." He picked up his cell phone and learned that it was only within the last two weeks or so that his mother noticed other dogs taking an unusual interest in Charley.

The little Lhasa decided to mark a place the bulldog had just sprayed – probably in retribution for the bulldog's bad behavior. His stance was just a little bit off-kilter – sort of a half-hiked leg and a half-squat.

When they got back to the examination room, Cooper pressed Jenny for her thoughts. She took a breath. This was really a long shot – but she was pretty certain she was right.

"OK – I think Charley has a sertoli cell tumor."

Logan and Cooper looked at her with disbelief.

Logan said, "But that can't be – the dog was neutered, right?" He looked at Cooper, who nodded.

Jenny asked Cooper, "Charley was a rescue dog, right? Was he neutered before your mother got him – you didn't perform the surgery did you?"

"Right, he was neutered at the shelter. Why?"

"I think Charley is a cryptochid – only one of his testicles ever descended into the scrotum – and the other one wasn't removed. Now it's cancerous."

Cryptochids were rare – in fact, Dr. Cooper had never seen one in all his years of practice.

Jenny said, "Let's do an ultrasound and also look at his hormone levels to see what we can learn."

The ultrasound revealed that Charley did, indeed, have an abdominal mass that could've been – and probably was - a retained testicle. Hormone testing found elevated amounts of estrogen. The good news was that if it was a sertoli cell tumor - and there didn't seem to be any doubt about that now - there was no indication the cancer had spread to other parts of the Lhasa's body.

Dr. Cooper left with Charlie in tow, having determined he would operate in his Austin Clinic, so his Mother could be near. He happily shook his head from side to side in amazement – looking at Jenny in awe and at Logan with gratitude. He enthusiastically shook hands with each one in turn and then gave Jenny a big hug. "I can't tell you how grateful Mother will be," he said, then added guiltily, "Hell, how grateful I am."

Charley's expressive brown eyes connected with Jenny's - an unspoken "thank you" conveyed, acknowledged, and accepted.

After he left, Logan crossed his arms over his chest and leaned against the doorframe of Jenny's office. "Okay, Houdini, what made you think of a sertoli cell tumor? Never in a million years would I ever have considered that – after all, the dog had been neutered as a puppy."

Jenny smiled, "It just came to me...and the fact that Charley had to be emitting some kind of odor that attracted that bulldog – it made me think of the large amounts of estrogen emitted by testicular tumors. I thought maybe – just maybe – if Charley was a cryptochid, the vets who neutered him may have removed just the one descended testicle and left the other one where it was. So he wouldn't have been totally neutered, and as he grew older, the embedded testicle became cancerous. After all, it wasn't Dr. Cooper who performed the original surgery, so he'd have no reason to think the dog still retained one testicle. I know it's rare that this happens, but obviously it did happen to Charley."

Logan Penn gave Jenny a long puzzled look, shrugged, and left her doorway.

Jenny smiled to herself knowing she'd never be able to tell Logan what really happened – that it was Charley who told her what was wrong.

****

On the way home from the Clinic, Nana, Jesse and Zachary shared the big backseat. Zac was loud and boisterous as usual, but Nana seemed even more distant. At one point, Nana's eyes locked with Jenny's in the rear view mirror.

"My sister is dead, isn't she?" Nana said softly, tears welling in her big blue eyes.

Jenny was so shocked she couldn't respond for a moment. Nana was actually speaking for the first time since she came to the Tallchiefs, and she seemed so coherent. Jenny pulled to the side of the road and turned to face the girl who had been through so much. Taking in a deep breath, Jenny slowly replied. "Yes, I am so sorry, sweetheart, but she is. Do you remember what happened?"

"No," replied Nana. "I just feel very sad and empty in here," as she touched her heart. Jenny didn't know whether she should try to comfort the girl, hug her, or let her alone, but Jesse resolved the dilemma by laying her head in Nana's lap. Nana turned to stare out the window, tears tracking slowly down her cheeks.

****

Jenny couldn't wait to tell Caleb her news - Nana spoke to her. Jenny hadn't been sure they'd ever be able to communicate. Just as importantly, Nana was starting to remember.

During dinner Jenny and Caleb made several attempts to get Nana to talk, but she wouldn't. After dinner, she sat at the table and colored with Zac's crayons and coloring books.

Jenny and Caleb went upstairs to call Dr. Smith. The psychologist was excited, too. She said she'd stop by and assess Nana's emotional state as soon as she could, but this was a real break-through. Caleb, anxious to find out anything Nana might be able to tell him, suggested Dr. Smith get the child to open up about what had happened. Agreeing to stop by the next day, the doctor cautioned them against pushing too hard, too soon.

No sooner had Jenny and Caleb disconnected when the phone rang again. Emma's bright voice spilled out over the speaker just as soon as Jenny picked up.

"Hey, you got room for an itinerant traveler?"

"Emma. I'm so happy it's you. Are you okay? I thought you weren't coming home to visit 'til summer. Is everything alright?"

"I'm not coming home to visit – I'm coming home for good." Her voice cracked, "Oh, Jen, I've tried and tried to make this work for me and, well, it's just not happening. I think I've been rejected by every single shitty script writing group in this whole crappy state and I'm getting fed up with the "Don't call us – we'll call you" routine. They may not think my scripts are worth a damn, but I do, and they're just too stupid to know good work when they see it!"

Jenny knew her sister was on the verge of tears. She seldom swore and had to be really upset to even say "shit." Rejection was something Emma rarely experienced and obviously she'd had a lot of it in California. She had gone to the west coast with rather limited funds, so she probably was out of money as well as hope.

Caleb jumped in, "Hey, Emma. Come ahead. We really need you here, we're in the middle of a big mystery and I, for one, would love your help. Can you come in the next couple of days? I'll get you a plane ticket right now."

Emma had been in California for the past two months, trying to make contacts, sell her screenplays, and maybe even land a job as a writer. Jenny had read the scripts she took; they were good – no they were more than good – they were excellent. Emma shouldn't have had a problem in selling any of them – especially when compared to some the trash coming out of Hollywood these days. But politics and prejudices being as they are – Emma's acceptance as a professional writer was a long shot. The professionals in California probably didn't even bother to read anything she'd submitted. She was an unknown – and even worse, an unknown from redneck Oklahoma.

Caleb went on to explain about their new houseguest and the mystery surrounding her origins. Instantly, Emma was beyond thinking of her California woes and empathizing with the trauma of their little girl lost. She agreed they needed her and that she'd be on the next plane – or at least the flight that Caleb would arrange.

Then Emma fell silent for a minute and the atmosphere became strained. Caleb's intuition told him it was time for him to go. Emma needed to talk to Jenny – alone.

He said, "Okay Em, here's Jenny. I'm going to go in the other room and find a plane ticket for you – don't go away until I give you the flight numbers, OK?"

Jenny took the phone off speaker and said, "OK, Em. It's just you and me now. What's up?"

Emma was silent for a minute. "Jenny, how do you think Matt will feel about my coming back with my tail between my legs?" So that was part of Emma's emotional melt-down, too.

"Emma, you know Matt is crazy about you. He was from the moment he set eyes on you and will be until the day he dies. He's been moping around here since you left, acting like nothing at all is the matter, but desperate for any word about you – especially if you're okay and worried sick that you might meet somebody new."

Emma Cochran, Jenny's little sister, and Matt Tallchief, Caleb's younger brother, had been engaged before Emma went to California. Although she dearly loved Matt, Emma's professional heart was set on becoming a screen writer. Following college graduation, Em worked as an office assistant for an Oklahoma City oil company, honing her writing skills at night, and even writing a screen play about her kidnapping by a serial killer some four years earlier. She dutifully sent her scripts to various firms. When she was lucky enough to receive a response – it was always a rejection.

At her wits' end, Emma sought advice from her former college advisor and mentor. Dr. Sloan recommended she personally take several of her scripts to Hollywood and promised to 'pave the way' by providing introductions to many of the industry's elite. Although Dr. Sloan assured Emma that the process wasn't easy and that nothing was guaranteed, Emma, ever the optimist, knew in her heart it would be only a matter of a few weeks before her dream became a reality.

Matt, ever the pragmatist, was less enthused. Emma begged him to go with her, but he wouldn't, citing family responsibility for running his grandfather's feed store. He said spending all their savings going to Hollywood was just plain stupid. Matt, in what he considered to be his most kind and tactful manner, tried to tell Emma that if all the scripts she'd submitted so far hadn't received even one positive response, why in the world did she think going to Hollywood would make any difference? Maybe her scripts weren't what studios were looking for. Apparently Matt needed to work on his tact, for Emma was completely insulted that Matt considered her selfish and uncaring and even more insulted that he considered her writing insufficient to impress Hollywood. Finally, in the heat of the moment, they broke their engagement – and she headed off to California alone - leaving both of them mad and miserable.

Caleb and Jenny wisely stayed out of the fray.

****

Emma's arrival, as always, was like a tornado ripping through a tranquil country landscape. Jenny picked up her sister at Will Rogers International Airport in Oklahoma City late the following evening and Emma talked non-stop during the entire hour ride to the Tallchief house. Jenny heard all about the Hollywood fiasco and provided 'uh huhs' and 'uh uhs' at all the right times. The only subject Emma did not discuss was Matt.

Although it was almost midnight when the sisters arrived home and Caleb had long ago put Zac to bed, Nana was still awake. Emma went to her and took both of the girl's hands in hers. Much to the astonishment of everyone, Nana smiled. Emma had that effect. She could charm the birds right out of the trees, and apparently, looking at Nana, she could bring sunshine out of the darkest of places.

The four of them sat for another half-hour at the kitchen table with Emma providing humorous, if sarcastic, tales of Hollywood. Suddenly the back door flew open and Matt strode across the kitchen floor directly to Emma.

As if she weighed nothing, he lifted her from her chair and held her tightly. "I am so sorry, Emma, I should have supported you, gone with you, believed in you. I was just afraid if you went to Hollywood, you'd never come home again. Please forgive me. I love you and I never – never want us to be apart again."

Emma began laughing, crying and tightly holding on to Matt. She said, "I was planning to go to the Feed Store early in the morning and make an absolute fool of myself until you forgave me. Now I've been upstaged again!" Then they kissed as if no one else was within twenty miles. Probably for them – no one else was.

When he finally came up for air, Matt said, "I just knew that Hollywood bullshit was not for you."

"Oh – shit," Caleb frantically made the 'stop' gesture with his fingertips drawn across his neck. He knew Matt was headed for disaster. Matt was a wonderful guy, and generally knew just the right things to say – that is – he knew in every situation that didn't include Emma.

Either Matt didn't see Caleb's frantic signal or he didn't understand, because he blundered right on. "Tecumseh is the best place for you and me. Settled down – married and kids – that's what matters – not this writing stuff. If you really want to write, why don't you try some children's books or something like that...?"

The temperature in the Tallchief kitchen plummeted about fifty degrees. Emma pulled back from Matt – holding him at arms length and looking directly into his happy eyes. Matt's euphoric expression drained away.

"What do you mean – my writing is unimportant?" She began to thump his chest with her index finger. "I'll have you know that I'm an excellent – maybe even exceptional - writer – and my work is just as important as yours - babysitting your grandfather's feed store – what I do is probably even more important!"

"Uh oh," thought Jenny. "This is going downhill fast."

Emma was on a roll. She'd had enough of stupid people taking shots at her writing – and now even Matt. She thought for sure he now understood how important it was to her – but apparently he was just as big a self-centered jerk as those shitheads in California.

Matt recoiled from Emma's spate – then joined in. "Oh yeah – just how much money have you earned lately? At least I help support my family – keep it together. You don't see me running off to the ends of the earth in search of a fantasy. Family is everything – if you don't get that – maybe we *don't* belong together!"

Matt stormed out, slamming the door so hard it shook the house. Emma burst into tears, ran to her room and slammed her door.

Upstairs, Zachary started to wail.

****

That night the dream came again. As before, Jenny was running, terrified, hearing the distant screaming of children and being unable to help. Only this time as Jenny emerged from a thicket of trees and brush, she came face-to-face with an incredibly dirty teen, barely bigger than she and dressed in threadbare Civil War era rags. The boy jerked in surprise and the pistol he held in his right hand discharged. Jenny looked at her chest where blood was slowly spreading across her blouse.

"Oh my God, oh my God, ma'am, I am so sorry," the words poured from the ragged boy's mouth. His expression was one of surprise and horror. "I didn't mean it, oh my God." Then she slowly sank to the ground and woke up shaking in her own bed.

****

Although Dr. Smith wasn't able to coax any words from Nana, she was very pleased that the child seemed so well physically and relatively secure at the Tallchief home. "No promises," she told Jenny as she picked up her purse and folders, "but I'd be real surprised if she didn't start talking more real soon."

"How about her memory?"

"That's another story altogether. We won't know whether she'll be able to recapture that until she does – or doesn't. Just keep doing what you're doing – it seems to be working."

With Zachary safely ensconced at day care, the three girls had the rest of the day free. Emma could always be relied on to provide timely entertainment and she didn't fail them now.

"How about a trip to the Shawnee Mall? Nana, you really need some new clothes, and there's no better way for a woman to spend a day. What do you say, Jenny?"

Shopping wasn't Jenny's choice of fun activities, but Emma was right. Nana was in desperate need of some new clothes. Sheriff Holcomb had taken the shirt and jeans she was wearing at the church for analysis, and the poor kid had been switching between two sets of hand-me downs ever since.

"Sounds good to me, Em. But if we go to the Mall, Jesse can't go. They have these stupid rules about no dogs in the Mall. Can you do that, Nana?" she asked.

Jenny could see Nana waging war within herself over the issue. Jesse was her security – and to be without the dog was scary. But – a chance to go to the Mall and buy new clothes was just too good to pass up. Vanity won out. Nana nodded in agreement.

Travis Moore, the deputy assigned to protect Nana, sighed and rolled his eyes – "a shopping trip for God's sake. I'm a deputy sheriff and I'm going to take three women shopping. I hope the other guys don't find out." Then he reconsidered, "Oh well, maybe it'll be less boring than sitting around here - besides, I really need a new pair of Levis – and maybe a new shirt?" He checked his money stash – "Oh well, there's ATM everyplace now, right?"

When Moore and his contingent arrived at the complex, the deputy checked in with Mall Security - not that he thought there'd be any danger. And if there was – he could take care of it -he touched his sidearm. But protocol was protocol and Deputy Moore was one who followed the rules.

The three and their escort spent several hours wandering the Shawnee Mall, making jokes – pointing out all the latest absurd fashions and buying Nana several new and very cute outfits. Although the youngster didn't say anything, she seemed more animated and positive than Jenny had ever seen her. "Maybe shopping *is* a cure-all," she thought.

Just as they exited Dillards, they heard a loud commotion directly across the atrium from where they stood. Deputy Moore pulled his firearm and hurried his charges toward the nearest exit – just as he'd been trained. As they neared the south doors, an overweight, grey-haired Mall Security guard, breathing heavily, caught up with them. He bent over double, wheezing loudly, trying to catch his breath. Obviously, physical fitness was not a prerequisite for a Mall Security employee.

"Hey, deputy." The man heaved out a breath or two. "You know a guy – big guy – name of – uh." He looked at a note he held in his hand. "Tallchief – Matt Tallchief?"

Jenny stepped up. "Yes, we know Matt. He's my brother-in-law."

"OK. Well, he's been following after you guys for quite a while. He was actin' all sneaky – obviously didn't want you to see him. We've been watchin' him watchin' you. Anyways, the whole thing looks pretty suspicious to me. Maybe he's your terrorist."

The group retraced their steps and found Matt – handcuffed - sitting in the center of a circle of mall cops. Two had guns drawn and pointed at the big man. A large crowd had gathered watching the excitement, and another security man was trying – ineffectively – to get them to move on.

"Matt, what's going on?" Jenny looked at the security man – her voice becoming icy. "This is my brother-in-law. He's okay – he's a member of my family. Will you please put those guns away and take off those ridiculous handcuffs?"

"You sure, lady?" Jenny shot the security guard a look guaranteed to turn the fires of hell to ice. The man signaled to his officers to holster their weapons and release the prisoner.

The grey-haired security chief reached over and extended his hand to Matt. "Hey, man. No hard feelings, I hope."

Matt stood up – embarrassed, angry and oh-so-busted. He gave the gawkers a look that immediately disbursed the crowd.

Matt took in a big breath. "No, no hard feelings." He shook the guard's hand. "In fact, thanks for watching out for them - you did the right thing. I should've told you what I was doing."

Matt, the girls and Deputy Moore walked down the Mall in silence. Emma waited until they were outside before spinning around to confront her former fiancé. "What the hell was that all about, Matt?"

Matt knew he couldn't claim coincidence – he hated to shop and never went to the Mall voluntarily. So, he decided he might as well come clean.

"Damn it, Emma. I was worried about you. Caleb told me about the traffickers – they're violent – hardcore - don't care who gets hurt or who they kill… I was just watching out – covering your back, you know?"

Truth be told, Matt was more qualified to guard them than Deputy Moore – except for the whole getting-caught-by-the-security-cop thing. Matt was former army with combat experience in Afghanistan. Tough and brave, knowledgeable about weapons, Matt had the best of all reasons for keeping them safe. He was still head-over-heels in love with Emma.

Emma said, "Look, Matt. I'm a big girl – I can take care of myself. I don't need you to cover my back – alright?"

"Yeah, just like four years ago," Matt snapped. "You did a great job that time, didn't you?" Emma had been kidnapped by a serial killer when she was still in college. Her family and a huge dose of luck had saved her.

Deputy Moore didn't know what to do. He just looked from Matt to Emma and back again with big round eyes and an expression of helplessness.

Jenny stepped in. "Matt, go home. Emma, shut up and get in the truck."

****

The foursome returned to Tecumseh late in the afternoon and decided to stop at Ellie's for lunch. Ellie's Deli and Café was, in many respects, the social center of town. At noon it was impossible to find a table and in the evening many of the locals congregated to drink coffee, gossip or both. But in the late afternoon, the place was almost deserted. The four hung their coats on the back of their chairs and seated themselves.

"Well, almost empty," Jenny thought as she glanced around and spotted Paul White Horse. Jenny inwardly groaned - she had conflicting emotions about the Seminole medicine man – she knew he was good and honest – but truth was – he was weird. "To be fair," Jenny thought to herself, "maybe he just knows too much about me…"

Jenny nodded and he did the same. The elderly man lit his pipe – never taking his eyes from Jenny. She was the first to look away.

Amy Greenburg, Ellie's granddaughter, slowly sauntered over to their table - pad in hand. She exhibited about as much professional enthusiasm as a duchess collecting trash. The patrons at the Café had stopped complaining about Amy's supercilious attitude and abominable service long ago. They knew the girl was a fixture at the Café for as long as she chose to stay. After all, Ellie often said, "Family is family and that is that."

Jenny, Travis and Emma ordered then Amy turned to Nana. "What about you, kid?" Nana lowered her eyes to the tabletop and seemed to shrink. When she didn't answer, Emma explained, "She's really shy, Amy, and doesn't talk much. Bring her a cheeseburger, fries and a Dr. Pepper."

Amy turned around and languidly strolled toward the kitchen. "Shy, my foot…I bet she doesn't talk at all. Ha- she must be a lot of fun to have around. What a moron." Amy congratulated herself on her own superior communication and social skills – something this kid obviously didn't have.

****

They picked up Zac on their way home, still basking in the glow of their successful shopping adventure and totally avoiding the whole Matt episode. As soon as they got home, Nana and Jesse ran upstairs so the twin could try on her new clothes. Jenny called Caleb and found out he probably wouldn't be home until late – the Sheriff's Office and the OBNDC had several teams in the woods searching for the murder site. The hounds they'd used in tracking Nana's movements backwards from the church had lost the scent a couple of days ago - now the teams were scouring the woods for clues. At dusk, they were to meet up at the Sheriff's Office to debrief. He had no idea when he'd make it home.

No sooner had Jenny disconnected than Nana appeared coming from the direction of the front staircase. Emma started to compliment her on her new clothes when she noticed the girl was trembling. All the color had left her face. Jenny rushed over and held Nana until the girl stopped shaking.

"Nana, what's wrong?"

Nana opened her mouth, but no sounds came out. When she tried again, her voice squeaked, but at least they could make out some words, "The chair – the rocking chair – it moved .... all by itself ..."

The three rushed upstairs through the master bedroom and into the little sitting room. There, in front of the window overlooking the drive, sat the antique rocker with Clue, purring rhythmically, curled up in its seat.

"I moved that chair into the bedroom just this morning - *again*," Jenny told Emma, "I know I did.

Caleb's been complaining that it's always underfoot – so I made sure to get it out of the way. Now it's back. How could that happen?"

Emma slowly approached the chair and touched its back. Then she poked it with her index finger - rocking the chair back and forth a couple of times. Clue opened one eye, sighed, and settled back into the seat.

Suddenly there was a loud banging at the kitchen door. All three of them jumped at least a foot. Nana squealed. Jenny hurried down the stairs, threw open the door, and looked directly into the rheumy brown eyes of Paul White Horse.

****

The elderly man slowly shuffled around the outer perimeter of the upstairs sitting room, pausing every now and then to wait and listen. As he moved, his low, gravelly voice chanted softly in sounds that were both indecipherable and ancient. His arms were in constant motion – high – low - out to his side – straight ahead. His right hand firmly grasped a small well-worn leather talisman; his eyes shut tight.

"I wonder how he keeps from tripping," thought Jenny, "Caleb seems to wind up on his butt at least once or twice every time he's in this room - and *he* keeps his eyes open."

Jenny's relationship with Paul White Horse wasn't exactly adversarial, but it was complicated. He'd come into her life four years earlier when Emma's disappearance had driven Jenny to the point of desperation. There wasn't any doubt the man possessed some unusual psychic gifts – that's probably what made Jenny so uncomfortable. She, too, had similar gifts and she wasn't entirely happy about it. She felt the strangeness of her abilities – her 'differentness.' She didn't want to be 'different' – but she was - and Paul White Horse knew it.

Gradually the cadence of the medicine man's chanting, the rhythm of his hands and shuffling foot movements seemed to alter the atmosphere in the room. Jenny caught a faint whiff of roses – of something or someone quite old – stillness - even the quality of light was not as it was – maybe softer – Jenny couldn't quite define it. She had the feeling – she'd had it before – that time had slowed.

Nana and Emma were spell bound - they weren't even breathing – eyes locked on the old man as he slowly, slowly circled in toward the antique rocker. He touched the chair lightly – ran his hand back and forth across its back, the arms and seat. The chanting stopped and White Horse stood rock-still.

Finally he turned, locking eyes with Jenny.

"There is a spirit here," intoned Paul White Horse in his ancient rumbling voice. "An old spirit. She is very sad and seeks or waits for someone or something."

The three females looked at each other. A ghost in their house – a ghost attached to the rocking chair? Is that even possible?

"That's all I know," Paul said, still looking directly at Jenny. "But your cat knows more. Use your gifts, Jenny, help this spirit." Then the old man turned, descended the stairway and disappeared out the back door. The atmosphere in the room snapped back into the here and now.

"Whoa - that is one weird dude," observed Emma. "What did he mean, Jenny, use your gifts? Are you talking to dead people now?"

"Very funny, Em."

She knew exactly what Paul White Horse meant. He wanted her to communicate with Clue to see if she could pick up anything about the spirit. Jenny scooped up the grey and white tomcat, but didn't get any images or feelings at all.

Jenny scowled, turned and tromped down the front staircase. Maybe White Horse was just full of it, but in her heart, Jenny didn't think so. She remembered the recurring dreams – dreams in which she is running, afraid, and then very, very dead.

Chapter Four

Emma was on a mission and woe be unto anyone who got in her way. The petite blonde may have had the appearance of a winsome spirit, but in fact, she could be extremely focused and determined when she felt strongly about something. And, apparently solving the mystery of the haunted rocking chair was just such a something. Nana, too, now that the initial shock of seeing the rocking chair self-propel had worn off, didn't seem afraid at all.

"Do you think we can find out who the ghost is? Do you think we can help her?" she asked.

"I don't know how," said Jenny. "What do you think, Em?"

"Well, let's see if the chair has any clues. No pun intended," she looked at the cat. Sure enough, on the underside of the seat, there were some initials carefully carved into the wood, but so faint they couldn't make them out.

"I know, I know," said Nana and took off down the stairs. She quickly returned with Zac's crayons and a sheet of plain white paper. She placed the paper over the carvings and ran the crayon back and forth, back and forth, over the design. In a minute the women were able to decipher several of the letters and a year.

"WSC, AMC' or could be ANC and E or FRC and the year 1858 or maybe 1859," said a pleased and proud Nana.

"Well, that's a great start," Em said, as she hugged her young co-conspirator.

"Yes," thought Jenny, looking at the smile on her young friend's face, "just the perfect start to bring Nana back."

****

"Eric, hey, it's Caleb Tallchief from Shawnee."

"Hi Caleb. It's been awhile. How's Jenny and Emma?

"Fine – Emma's just back from California and Jenny's the owner of Tecumseh Veterinary Clinic now. Zac's almost three."

"Tempus fugit, my friend. Tempus fugit. What's up?"

Although in general Caleb had a low opinion of the OSBI, he had met one agent he liked, respected and trusted – Eric McBride. Caleb told him about the discovery of the Jane Doe body, Nana, and the lack of progress in finding the murder site. He briefed Eric about the involvement of the OBNDC Task Force and the thinking that the twins' kidnapping had something to do with human trafficking.

"The OBNDC has promised to keep us in the loop – but you and I both know how that goes. I know the OSBI has been called in to assist and I need somebody inside that I can trust. Most of these statewide bureaucracies think we country boys just got off the turnip truck, you know what I mean?"

McBride laughed. "They'd sure be wrong on that count, but, yeah, I know what you mean."

"I trust you, Eric. Jenny and I have the surviving twin living with us and I really need to keep on top of what's going on, both for the kid's sake and for my family. This has all the earmarks of something really nasty – there are some vicious bastards out there connected with human trafficking."

McBride had heard a little about the case, but it wasn't something he'd been asked to work on, so he said, "OK, Caleb. Let me see what I can find out. I'll call you back when I know something."

Caleb disconnected, somewhat relieved that he and Holcomb would not be totally left out of the picture, but deeply concerned over the potential danger this case had brought into his home.

****

A phone call to Tecumseh Antiques revealed that the Tallchief rocking chair had come from a store in Van Buren, Arkansas. Van Buren was a mid-size city near Fort Smith – just across the border from Oklahoma.

The next phone call to the Van Buren antique shop owner hadn't been nearly as satisfactory – not satisfactory at all. The elderly lady confirmed she had, indeed, sold the chair to Tecumseh Antiques but didn't have any idea of its origin or previous owners. It had just come to her along with a consignment of many items from an old storage building that had passed through many, many hands over the years. There was no way one particular item could be traced to its owner. Besides, she was a very busy woman and couldn't be bothered to do the research on all these pieces, for heaven's sake. "If you have to know who owned it – do the research yourself," she squawked at Emma and hung up rudely.

Emma disconnected, frustrated and a little angry. Just the initials and a year sure wouldn't be enough to research their resident spirit. Emma needed more – much more - to go on.

When she discussed the situation with Caleb, he suggested, "Maybe you should go to Van Buren, sometimes you can find out more in person than over the phone."

"Good idea," Emma responded, "we'll go tomorrow."

Caleb called later that afternoon. "Hey, looks like you'll have to postpone your trip to Van Buren for a while."

"How come?" Emma and Nana were both deeply disappointed – they really wanted to get on the trail of the mysterious ghost.

"The Sheriff needs Moore tomorrow and the next day. Don't have anybody to spare for the next couple of days. In fact, we'll have to make arrangements for both of you to come to the office…"

"Oh, Caleb. Isn't there somebody – anybody you can draft to go with us?"

Silence. "How bad do you want to go?"

"Really – really bad. This is the great detective adventure of all time, don't you know?"

Emma winked at Nana – who smiled.

"OK – the only one I can think of who might be able to go is --- Matt."

"What…."

"Well, he's had training, combat experience, can take care of himself and watch out for you, too. That's your choice. Sheriff's Office or Matt. You can't be unprotected until this murder is solved."

Emma looked into Nana's pleading eyes. She breathed in heavily and said, "Ok – if he's just going to be our protection – we'll go."

Nana jumped up and down and clapped her hands together - a big smile covering her face. Emma had a sneaking suspicion she'd just been had.

****

Matt arrived at the Tallchief house in the wee hours of Saturday morning. He wanted to get an early start - be sure they'd be in Van Buren when the antique shop opened. Bowing low and graciously pulling open the passenger and back seat doors, Matt said, "You don't think I'd let you two beautiful girls – oh, excuse me Jesse – you three beautiful girls go alone, do you?" Matt looked at Nana and wiggled his eyebrows up and down.

She giggled.

Emma glared.

Just as Matt started to close the truck doors, Clue jumped in and settled down for the trip. "You want to go, too….well, why not?" said Emma.

"Why not indeed," affirmed Matt. He got in, started the engine, and the fivesome headed east on the great ghost adventure.

Nana, Clue and Jesse snoozed for the entire two and a half hour trip. Emma reluctantly discussed strategy with Matt.

"You've already pissed off the shop owner," Matt said, "so how about if I go in and appeal to her better nature?"

"You mean flirt, don't you?" Like his brother, Matt had a way about him. People immediately liked and trusted him – often telling him secrets they would never have told another soul. "One of these days, Matthew Tallchief, some little old lady is going to sue you for alienating her affections."

Matt shot Emma a sarcastic glance and replied, "Well, some of those little old ladies *are* pretty cute."

Emma punched Matt in the arm – hard.

Descending towards Van Buren along Logtown Road, Emma could see the Arkansas River at the bottom of Mt. Vista winding its way past the city and Fort Smith. Barges made their unhurried way up and down the wide expanse of water while vehicle and train traffic sped across bridges spanning the boundary between Van Buren and Ft. Smith. You could smell springtime in the air, and see traces of its vibrant colors shimmering in the sunlight. It was a truly beautiful sight.

Just below the crest of the hill on the right stood several old Victorian homes – all but one had been restored. On the left, a large, beautifully landscaped cemetery quietly watched over the valley. It wasn't hard to imagine what the area might have looked like during the Civil War.

At the bottom of the hill just past the restored turn-of-the-century railway station, Matt made a hard right onto Main Street. Emma no longer had to imagine what Van Buren might have looked like in the Civil War, because they had just stepped back in time. She and Matt gazed down a street that could have, and probably was, built decades before 1850. Old shops, a theater, a brick bank and county buildings - all of them looked at least 150 years old. If not for the twenty-first century vehicles rumbling down the street, Emma would have sworn she would soon see women in hoop skirts and bonnets accompanied by gentlemen dressed in Confederate gray. It was incredible.

The SUV slowly cruised the street. The address they needed was on the left. Matt drove to the end of the street, passed a theater and an ice cream shop, and turned around in the Crawford County Courthouse parking lot. Reversing his route, he found a parking place directly in front of the antique shop.

It was a corner store in need of a little repair. The mortar between the red bricks looked a little spare in places, and there was a crack extending from the foundation halfway up the side wall. But the newly-painted front door and trim glistened pristine white in the early morning sunshine and the two outsized wooden planters overflowed with yellow and purple pansies. The large front picture window sparkled. Old-fashioned script in gold and black letters proclaimed the store as Alma's Antiques, Established 1902.

"Looks like we're the only customers this early – good," thought Matt, as he stepped out of the SUV, and stretched out some of the road-mile kinks from his arms, legs and back. Matt glanced around – there weren't even any parking meters to feed. He smiled broadly and swaggered into the store, full of confidence. Everything was going according to plan.

And the plan was for Matt to sweet-talk the proprietor into giving him a little more information about the chair – where it had come from – maybe some of the history of the town – that sort of thing - and then they would spend the rest of the day tracking down any leads he'd uncovered. Emma and Nana rolled down their windows preparing for a long wait while Matt worked his magic.

It was a big surprise then to see Matt pull open the store's door after just a few minutes inside. Emma chuckled to herself – apparently the old Matt charmthing wasn't as foolproof as he thought it was.

But then an odd thing happened.

While Matt stood in the open door – back turned speaking to someone inside, Clue jumped from the back seat into Emma's lap, out the window, through the shop's open door and disappeared from view. He was immediately followed by Jesse. Nana threw open the back door, yelling, "Jesse, come here, Jesse" and followed the big dog. Emma had no choice but to join the parade, calling after all three.

The shop's proprietor, Mrs. Alma, a small grizzled woman with large glasses circa the 1970's was beside herself, throwing her arms around in a frenzy and shouting indignantly. "We don't allow animals in here....get them out. All of you – out!"

An elderly gentleman, cleaning some of the antiques on display, dropped his feather duster and began to laugh. Funniest thing he'd seen all week.

Clue ran directly through the shop and an open doorway at its back into what looked like a storage room.

Matt, trying his best to calm the old lady, said, "Mrs. Alma, we're so sorry. We'll get them out of here right away." Then he joined the hunt, close on Emma's heels. The four adults, for by now Mr. Alma had joined in, searched for Clue, Jesse and Nana. Up and down the tightly packed aisles, they caught occasional glances of their quarry, but when they ran to intercept, there was no one in sight. They could hear Jesse bark from time to time and Nana's voice, but none of the adults could find them. "Boy, what a Chinese fire drill," thought Matt laughing, "I hope the old gal doesn't call out the militia."

Finally, at the far end of the storage area, perched on a high shelf, Emma spied the grey and white cat. Jesse and Nana stood below, looking up.

"Good grief, Clue," giggled Emma. "That lady is going to shoot us all. Come down."

Matt caught up with Emma, with Mr. Alma close behind. Both were laughing so hard they couldn't breathe.

"Mrs. Alma went back up front to tend the store. She told me to get you all out of here right now or she was going to call the police." Nana's eyes grew large.

"But don't worry - she won't. I swear - this is the most fun I've had in years." The man wiped the tears from his eyes. "Besides, it's my store." He took a few more deep breaths, "So, okay, how do we get that cat down – call the Fire Department?"

"No, I think I can take care of it," said Matt, finally bringing himself under control. "Is there a ladder handy?"

Mr. Alma brought up a twelve foot ladder, settled it securely against the metal rack, and Matt ascended to Clue's perch. The cat had his claws sunk deep into the lid of an old large wicker trunk about three feet wide, two feet across and maybe two feet deep. Two wide leather straps held the trunk tightly closed.

"I can't get him to let go," Matt complained, as he wrestled the animal.

"Bring the trunk down with you," shouted Emma and Mr. Alma simultaneously.

Matt juggled the trunk with its feline attachment down the ladder and set it at Emma's feet. The cat delicately extricated his claws from the wicker and gently leaped down, as if this sort of thing happened every day. He began licking his back leg.

Emma was intrigued. "Let's see what's in the trunk, OK?"

Matt looked at her suspiciously.

"Well, why not? We've come this far."

The four of them gently lifted the lid. Inside were bundles of letters, a lot of photos – some even dating back to the Civil War, business records, some old clothes, a locket with somebody's hair inside and, lo and behold, inside a worn and faded velvet draw-string bag, a family Bible. Emma gently lifted the book out of its wrapper and blew away the dust of decades. Nana hovered over her. With shaking hands she opened it and flipped slowly through the fragile pages until she came to a family tree. Matt and Nana held their breath. After what seemed to be an interminable wait, Emma looked up, her voice a little strange.

"Look, Matt. Look Nana. Look at the kid's names – William Samuelson Chapman, Anna Marie Chapman and Evelyn Rose Chapman."

Nana's eyes grew wide. "It's the initials from the rocking chair – WSC, AMC and ERC – and look at the years. They would have been kids in 1859."

Matt got it. He stared with unbelieving eyes at Clue who was still busily cleaning himself.

"Mr. Alma, how much for this wicker trunk?"

The elderly gentleman didn't even look at the contents. He smiled widely at all three. "How about twenty bucks?" He chuckled again. "Maybe I should be paying you for all the fun; this sure has been a morning to remember. Let's just take it out through the back, OK? Pull your car around here and I'll help you load it up. I think Mrs. Alma has had enough excitement for one morning, don't you?"

Chapter Five

Sierpe Gang Headquarters
Houston, Texas

The jacked-up Chevy barely slowed as it disgorged its bloody cargo against the fence surrounding the Sierpe Gang Headquarters in South Houston. Most of the gang members were sleeping off the after effects of the previous evening's party and the sentries were not quick enough to see who was in the departing vehicle.

Inside the warehouse, the newest leader of the Sierpes, Viper, lounged against his latest woman, Lottie or Lettie, or something like that. Who cares what this stupid bitch's name is, he thought, she'd be around as long as he wanted her to be around and then it'd be somebody new. Women got boring real fast, and Viper never liked to be bored. He rubbed his aching head. The party last night had been rockin' – best in a couple weeks. He especially got off when his 'wifey' Carmen, slapped around that new girl. That bitch was good – she'd have that white chick towing the line in no time at all. He sighed and looked over his domain. "Some these old guys gonna have to go," he thought to himself – "can't keep up."

Parties were an every night occurrence with the Sierpes – they lived the high life – every day and in every way. When there was no action, they created it.

Viper's name suited him well – like a poisonous snake, he exuded evil. Just looking at him made the hair on the back of your arms stand up. His ascent in the Sierpe chain of command was legendary – swift, and vicious. Early on his rivals thought him skinny and weak, but they didn't think so for long. New recruits spoke his name only in whispers.

Viper lost count of the number of people he'd taken out. Nowadays just to look at him made people turn and run – not because he was ugly – but because he was truly and completely bad.

The door at the far end of the warehouse slammed open, and several of the brothers screamed at the sentries to shut it quick – the sunlight streaming in was hurtful and way too bright.

But the outside sentries, Kevie and Snark, paid no attention to the colorful language, successfully threading their way to the back of the warehouse through the barrage of garbage and empty bottles hurled their way. They came straight for Viper, bearing what appeared to be a ball of some sort – "No, holy shit…. It's a head."

Kevie said, "Man, this old Chevy truck come by and someone throwed this out – right at us!" Kevie was shaken and scared – that was obvious.

"Chill, man. Ain't no …." then Viper took a closer look at the head. "My God, that be Wasp."

Kevie began shaking. "Man, who do that to Wasp? That man's a dead man walking – dead man walking…"

Viper slapped him across the mouth. "Shut up, you fuckhead."

At that moment, Viper's phone shimmied. A text from an unknown sender. Viper tapped the box. The text lit up - "A man who can't keep his head during a delivery doesn't need a head." There was no signature, but Viper knew full well who it was and who had decapitated his crew. It was Viper's new partner - Ortiz. Something must have gone wrong with the twins – shit….

****

Amy was on duty when the handsome stranger came into Ellie's. "Ooo…tall, dark and handsome. And look at that cute little scar – must be pretty tough, too." she thought. "Well, maybe not so tall, but definitely dark and handsome."

Instead of her usual laborious shuffle to her customer's table, she hustled right over and asked politely how she could help him.

He ordered coffee and pie. When she turned away from his table, he glanced casually around the café. "Probably not going to hear much at this place," he thought looking at several elderly Native American customers sitting separately. "Looks like they don't even talk to each other."

Amy brought a large slice of hot apple pie and set the plate in front of him. "Here you go, sir. Best apple pie in Pottawatomie County. Homemade this morning." With the steaming pot held in her other hand, she poured a cup of hot coffee adding, "You're not from around here, are you?"

"No," MacIntosh answered, "I'm from L.A. Free lance reporter."

Amy wasn't sure what a free-lance reporter was, but it must be important. And he was from L.A. "Wow, an L. A. reporter. You know, I'm going there someday – not going to be stuck in this dump forever." She paused, unwilling to end the conversation. "I bet you see a lot of movie stars…"

"Some, but not as many as you'd think."

"I bet there's cool stuff happening out there all the time. Nothing ever happens here," she whined.

MacIntosh took a chance that this kid might just know something about the twins. After all, this was a small town. His business had taken him in and out of several of them over the years. Everyone knew everything about everybody. He assumed a conspiratorial whisper. "Well, that's not what I hear."

Amy was astonished. "I thought nobody knew about that …."

MacIntosh raised his eyebrows, inviting Amy to continue.

She didn't hesitate, "That kid killed over on 177? Wow, you reporters really have got the inside track."

MacIntosh wisely nodded.

"I just know because the guy who found her is best friend with my ex-boyfriend's sister and she told me. But he's such a liar, you never know if what he says is true or what. My ex-boyfriend, that is – not his friend, you know." It would have taken a psychic to follow Amy's circuitous thinking pattern, but MacIntosh understood that this teenager probably did know something.

"Well, tell me what you know and I'll let you know if it's right."

Amy lowered her voice, "Well, I heard the Sheriff over in Shawnee ordered everybody to keep their mouths shut, because they don't know nothin' and he wants to find out something before it all gets out – so they won't look so stupid, you know?"

MacIntosh nodded sagely.

"The dead kid was dumped in a ditch, naked, if you can believe it. But that's not where she was murdered. The cops haven't been able to find that place. And, the

Sheriff didn't want anybody to find out about that kid's sister – they're twins, you know?"

"Yes, my sources told me the twin sister had been found," his tone inviting further conversation.

"Well," Amy said, sitting down, and leaning in even more closely. "I saw her right here just a couple of days ago. She was with Jenny Tallchief, and Emma Cochran – that's Jenny's sister, you know. Dr. Tallchief is our town vet and she's married to Caleb Tallchief – the Sheriff's right hand man. They're keeping her in protective custody," Amy said the words with great emphasis to impress the stranger with her inside knowledge, "but for the life of me I don't know why."

"Why do you say that?"

"Because that kid is an absolute retard. No sane person would ever be worried she'd tell the cops anything, much less testify in court. She can't even talk and won't even look at you - just stares at the table cloth. Poor kid - she'll probably spend the rest of her life in a nut house."

Although the teen's information was third-hand at best and no doubt wildly exaggerated, MacIntosh was sure it contained a substantial amount of fact. Anyway, it was probably the best he was going to get without arousing attention. If he asked around too much, people would notice.

Back in his car, MacIntosh delivered his assessment to his friend and employer. "Enrique, I've found the surviving twin. From all accounts, she's not an immediate threat – apparently she's experienced some kind of mental breakdown. She's currently living in protective custody at the home of a deputy sheriff. The rumor is that the local sheriff doesn't have any evidence about the dead girl except for the body and the murder scene hasn't been located. What would you like me to do?"

Ortiz thought for a moment. "Just leave it alone, MacIntosh. Killing the second kid will bring on too much attention. Let the hick cops flounder 'til the case goes cold. They won't find anything. Come home."

Little did Amy Greenburg know, but her penchant for gossip and exaggeration had just saved Nana's life.

****

Emma pulled into the Clinic's parking lot and shut off the engine. She sat there for a minute or two, collecting her thoughts. The trip back from Van Buren had been less than satisfactory. Emma had given Matt several chances to atone for his stupid chauvinistic attitude towards her career – but he didn't say a word. He just talked as if they were mere acquaintances – polite, but reserved. "What an ass," she thought to herself. "How could I possibly have thought I loved him?"

Emma would never admit that her heart ached for him, but she couldn't be the one to make the first step. Uh uh – no way – not in this lifetime. After all he'd been the one to dismiss her dreams as stupid. She ignored the part about sniping at his plans – ego being as it is.

She gathered her purse and some random papers and pulled open the Clinic's front door. Logan Penn was just coming out of one of the examination rooms carrying a miniature black poodle. At his elbow a dark-haired fat woman – Emma sort of recognized her but wasn't sure of her name – kept step with the doctor. The doctor was explaining something, and the woman hung intently on his every word.

"Mrs. Sanders, you have to quit feeding Solomon so much – and cut out the table scraps, OK? He's got to start getting a little bit of exercise. He's extremely overweight and sedentary. It's not healthy." Mrs. Sanders nodded vigorously. "I'm recommending we put him back on that special low calorie diet – at least 'til we get this weight thing under control. Are you okay with that?" She nodded again. "Other than that, I can't find anything wrong with him." He handed the dog to its owner. "Annie, would you please get some of that weight loss dog food for Solomon?"

"Certainly doctor. Right away." Annie hustled off to the stockroom.

"Oh, thank you, Dr. Penn. I really will keep Solomon on his diet this time. I promise."

"I know you will, Mrs. Sanders," Penn said. He knew darn well she wouldn't. He patted the woman's shoulder and turned her toward the counter.

Annie carried in a tray of canned dog food, added up Solomon's bill and checked them out. As Mrs. Sanders pushed open the door, Solomon in hand, she wiggled her fingers at the young vet in goodbye.

"I swear," Annie harrumphed, "I think Bessie Sanders overfeeds that poor animal just so she can bring him in to see you, Dr. Penn."

"Oh, I doubt that, Annie." But he was grinning as he turned away. His eyes lit up when he saw Emma. She stuck out her hand. "Hi – you must be Logan Penn, Jenny's partner. I'm her sister, Emma."

"Hi – guilty – that's me. Nice to meet you - I've heard a lot of good things." His eyes sparkled when he took her hand, and Emma caught the full impact head-on. "Whoa," she thought, "no wonder the ladies of Tecumseh overfeed their pets." Aloud, "I just came by to see if Jenny's ready to go. I've got her car."

Penn leaned in closer – still holding Emma's hand. "You know, I'm really not Jenny's partner – more like her trainee– like a sorcerer's apprentice." They laughed and he dropped her hand. "Hope to see you again soon."

Penn turned back to his office. Annie's adoring gaze followed him.

Jenny was ready to head home and the two picked up Zac on the way. "That Logan Penn is really something," said Emma. "He's got to be good for business."

"Yeah, I've noticed a definite uptick in traffic since he started - especially among the ladies," Jenny said laughing.

****

Jenny, Jessie and Nana sat side-by-side on the beat-up overstuffed couch in the Tallchief living room. Nana and Jenny occupied the two ends, while the large shepherd stretched out between them; Nana's hand resting on Jesse's haunches. The dog's head was snuggled up against Jenny's thigh.

The late afternoon sun napped behind thick grey clouds while the wind hummed a monotonous tune loud enough to mask the rhythmic cadence of the grandfather clock in the hallway, but not loud enough to be bothersome. Zac was asleep upstairs – Curly Joe was snoozing belly-up in his favorite chair. Clue, as usual, was nowhere to be seen. Jenny began reading through a stack of letters and clinic correspondence, inventory lists and all the necessary, but boring, paperwork she needed to address. Some of the letters were from other vets – either requesting her assistance with a particularly troublesome diagnosis or in one case, a request to speak at an upcoming professional conference in Washington, D.C.

By and by, words on the pages began to swim and Jenny yawned widely. She glanced at Nana and Jesse -

both had succumbed to the quiet and peace. Jenny shut her eyes, welcoming the few minutes of release a nap would bring. She sighed deeply and wiggled down into the depths of the cushions.

Just as Jenny began to drift away, Jesse pushed her snout under her hand. Jenny absently patted her, but Jesse pushed against her more urgently. "What is it, girl?"

Jesse looked over at Nana, who was deep into a troubled dream. Her face was flush with fear and she was making small, barely discernable mewing sounds. Nana's hands were firmly embedded in Jesse's fur.

Again, Jesse's nose urgently burrowed under Jenny's hands, the shepherd's expressive brown eyes seeking Jenny's. At first, Jenny thought the dog wanted her to wake Nana. But that wasn't it at all. The canine wanted Jenny to see what Nana's subconscious was telling her and somehow make Jenny understand.

Jenny leaned back into the couch, closed her eyes and gently held the dog. After several breaths, Jenny could see an old dilapidated two-story farm house almost completely hidden among trees and wild vegetation. A sagging front porch with two broken treads peeked out from behind an ancient willow tree. The entry door lay a little crooked on its hinges and a wide boarded-up front window ran almost the whole length of the first floor. At some point in its distant past, the house may have been painted white or yellow – but now it was a nondescript no-color gray. Next to the house an overgrown field surrounded a derelict barn tilting at an impossibly obtuse angle. Jenny wondered how it could still be standing. Across a small country gravel road, cattle grazed peacefully. A cell phone tower dominated a far hill to the right of the farmhouse. Then, as quickly as it came, the image dissolved. Jenny opened her eyes and saw that Nana was still sleeping, but more peacefully.

Jenny eased herself off the couch and went to call Caleb. She knew the vision of the house was important, but how it was important or how it fit into the overall picture, Jenny wasn't sure. She had no qualms telling Caleb about the unusual way the information had come to her – Caleb had seen that miracle at work more than once.

****

Undersheriff Tallchief gathered the Pottawatomie County detectives around a large, detailed map of the county.

"I know we've been chasing our tails trying to locate the murder site of our Jane Doe without much to show." Some of the men nodded and Mary Ellen Moore, holding a red magic marker, crossed her arms in front of her.

"But we've received a reliable tip that we may be looking for an old run-down two-story farmhouse close to a cell tower and across a country gravel road from a cattle ranch. It's got an old barn leaning way over on its side."

He waved the men in more closely to see the map, "Mary Ellen has plotted all the cell towers in our county and we'll concentrate our search in these areas." Caleb noted the circles drawn in red. He divided the men into groups and gave each a smaller version of the map.

Maps and assignments in hand, the deputies hurried out to catch the few remaining hours of daylight.

Chapter Six

Caleb pulled his SUV into the barely discernable turn-around in front of the ramshackle house, stepped down, and held the door open for Jesse to follow. Immediately he sneezed three times in rapid succession. "Damn that red cedar to hell," he complained as he approached the young deputy coming to meet him. "Hey, Travis, I thought you were assigned to watch over my family."

"Yes, sir. I was, sir. But your brother Matt was there today doing something for Jenny so Sheriff Holcomb said it was okay for me to let him take over the bodyguardin' for this afternoon. I hope that's alright," he asked, obviously seeking Caleb's approval.

"Yeah, that's fine." Caleb smiled inwardly. Even though he and Jenny had solemnly promised not to interfere in the Emma-Matt drama – both of them had. Caleb had told Matt about the shopping trip and obviously Jenny was trying her hand at getting them back together, too. This was so – so stupid. It was obvious the two of them loved each other – pride was screwing everything up.

He turned back to Travis. Travis Moore was PottCo's newest deputy and Mary Ellen Moore's youngest nephew. He was a great kid, smart with good instincts and anxious to prove himself. He had the natural enthusiasm of the young – and an overwhelmingly if irrational fear that if he screwed up; he'd best move to another state – maybe clear out of the country. After all, the people in the Sheriff's office were Mary Ellen's second family and nobody – but nobody - messed with Mary Ellen's family. That lady could be one relentless force of nature.

"Maybe Travis's fear isn't so irrational after all," Caleb thought. Aloud he said, "So what've we got?"

"Undersheriff Tallchief, we think this is our Jane Doe's murder site. They're signs of recent occupation, fast-food wrappers and like that. There're some sleeping bags inside, the kitchen and bathroom work – even though they're pretty gross. We've got blood evidence, too."

While the two men talked, Jesse began investigating on her own. She traversed the open area in front of the house, nose to the ground, tail down, and when she finished with the front yard, she disappeared around back.

For the next thirty minutes, the deputies went about their work, forgetting about the German shepherd. Then Caleb heard her strident bark. The two took off at a run to find her. About thirty yards into the deep brush Jesse sat on her haunches, looked straight at them and barked continuously.

"What'd you find, girl?" Caleb scooted the big dog aside. On the ground, almost buried beneath a thicket of dead vines, was a cell phone. And if the cell phone belonged to one of the perps – well, if it did, it would be pure gold. Travis and Caleb grinned widely – finally, a break.

Tallchief wasted no time in getting the cell phone to their OBNDC liaison, Mark Hamilton. He was almost as excited as the deputies had been. All kinds of valuable information could be gleaned from cell phones. Though normally gang members used burn phones, they were notoriously lax about deleting messages. There had to be phone numbers they used – text messages – who knew what? Hamilton rubbed his hands together in anticipation of the treasure at his fingertips.

****

Jenny met Matt at the door. "Thanks, Matt, for bringing this stuff." Matt hauled in the folding tables he brought from the feed store and set them up in the Tallchief living room. Jenny continued, "Do you think you could stay for a while and help us get organized?"

"Well, I don't know… I don't think Emma really wants me around…"

"Who cares what Emma thinks…we need you." And, in truth, Matt did have exceptional organizational and business sense – although Matt knew full well that wasn't the reason Jenny asked. Matt shrugged his shoulders - "OK, I guess I can stay for a couple of hours. Let's try to inventory this mess and see what we've got."

Emma stopped short when she saw Matt helping Jenny, but the look her sister shot in her direction told her not to complain.

Letters, receipts, official documents, and other potential treasures were pulled from the old trunk. There were ledger books from a firm called Chapman & Samuelson Shipping and Drayage and the Chapman family Bible. There was a locket and several photos from what looked like the Civil War era or maybe just before. There were files of correspondence from the mid-1800's until the 1920's. It was overwhelming. From the information recorded in the Chapman family Bible, Emma drew a large version of the family tree on poster board. They set the poster on a table easel to help them figure out who was who and what was what.

Matt wrote down a description of each item and Emma and Nana placed it on the table. Emma and Nana stacked like things together. They ordered and reordered the contents several times. Since the ghost in Jenny's dream seemed to be dressed in Civil War era fashion as did her killer, they put aside all correspondence dated after 1890. Finally satisfied with what they'd done, they called it a night.

****

In the quiet of the early morning, Emma gently untied the faded ribbon holding together a thick bundle of letters addressed to Mrs. Benjamin B. Chapman – the mother of the children who had carved their initials into the underside of the old rocker so many years ago. She, Nana and Matt planned to read them together later that day, but Emma couldn't wait. She carefully unfolded the fragile letter on top and began to read.

October 28, 1862
Dearest Mother,

I am writing this by the light of our meager camp fire. I am well and adjusting to this new experience. Although Father and I disagreed on almost every point about this war, I am sure he would be pleased to know I am now serving his beloved Confederacy. I keep my opinion about the issue of slavery to myself and pray you do the same as you know it is treason in the eyes of many to hold the sentiments we do about that subject.

It was nothing short of miraculous that Cousin Lawrence was able to successfully bargain for my position as his medical assistant. Over the past two weeks Cousin Lawrence Chapman has become my great friend and mentor. He is a true gentleman and a fine and compassionate doctor. We have been most busy for the last week, vaccinating all the troops against small pox, and Lawrence takes care to explain each procedure to me carefully so that I might at some point assume more responsibilities.

Although I will, of course, be required to fight should the situation arise, my primary duty will be to support Cousin Lawrence in his surgeries. I will not be assigned to the front lines, as many of our neighbors have been. You may remember

Jefferson Spence, from two farms south of us. He was also conscripted, but, unlike me, he was assigned to the infantry. He asks that you send word to his mother that he is well.

Thank you for your foresight in sending Old Thomas with Cousin Lawrence and me. Although Thomas remains taciturn, he is ever in good humor and helps to keep my loneliness in check. In camp and on the march, he has been constantly at my side. Last night I told him once again that as I am now the head of our household, I hereby freed him – formally executing a written act of manumission, witnessed by Cousin Lawrence and one other soldier, Private Phillip Odell, and as a free man Thomas was not obligated to remain. He opined that since he was a free man, it was his choice to serve me and Cousin Lawrence. He also said that "Miz Mary Elizabeth would skin me alive if anythin' ever happened to you or Master Lawrence—free man or not." He obviously holds you in high regard, Mother.

After Cousin Lawrence and I left Nine Oaks, we bivouacked with several hundred other Confederate soldiers on Mazzard Prairie, south of Ft. Smith. There we were issued new uniforms and a new Enfield Rifle. Our food and ammunition are primarily on our own or by the good graces of the community. Lawrence and I are among the best mounted, both of our horses being from good old Virginia stock, excluding, of course, the old hack Thomas rides.

As soon as possible, I will send this letter by way of Old Thomas, so that your mind might be put at rest as to my well-being. I must trouble you to send me as soon as you can the following articles: one small oven, two heavy blankets, dark if possible, a bottle of ink, two camp stools and a camp bed – so made that they will fold up and occupy very little room. The ten pounds of *coffee-sugar and other foodstuffs you packed are holding up well and are much appreciated as is the laudanum and other medicines you included.*

I will write as often as I can. I worry that you have no one to protect you in these most difficult times save Uncle Dwight and he is much occupied with the family business in Ft. Smith and not as close as I would wish.

Your loving son,
Billy

****

November 10, 1862
Dearest Mother,

Old Thomas arrived this morning with the supplies you sent and I thank you from the bottom of my heart for your loving thoughtfulness. Lawrence and I much enjoy the camp stools and the thick blankets do much to stem the chill of the night.

We have been bivouacked here near Mazzard Prairie now for about two weeks and it has been both a time for learning and military training. I have officially been given the rank of "Hospital Steward" which I understand is equal to the rank of an Orderly Sergeant in the medical department. Cousin Lawrence has loaned me two books to learn, specifically the "Sanitary Commission Report of 1861" and "The Practice of Surgery: Amputation" which are apparently the two preeminent texts of the medical profession. I study these for hours each day, and learn as much as possible so as not to dishonor the agreement Cousin Lawrence made for my position.

In addition to the routine hospital rounds we make each day, we drill in all manner of soldiering, excepting on Sunday, when the chaplains give services. Although many, like me, are within a day's ride of home and could attend services with our families, none are given leave to visit even for one day. Perhaps Hindman is in fear that some of us may not return – and that is probably a valid concern. We also engage in hunting and I can call it by no other word than "scavenging" as there are not enough food supplies or ammunition to satisfy the needs of our growing hordes. Troops, some conscripted and other volunteers, arrive hourly from across Arkansas and a few, I believe, even from Missouri and the Indian territories. We are an odd crew.

My skill in shooting and horsemanship has apparently been the subject of some discussion by several of our officers. I must give Father and Old Thomas their due in training me in these two useful arenas. Major Gen. John S. Marmaduke himself stopped by our camp and discussed my joining his group of cavalry and sharp-shooters. He offered me the rank of 2nd Lt. in a field unit – (Perhaps because Father was a Col in the regular Confederate Army and he therefore assumed I, too, have the requisite skills to be an officer. Or perhaps it is because I have my own horse.) I declined, saying I had already committed to serving in the medical corps with Lawrence Chapman and I would not absolve myself of this responsibility. I did commit; however, to serve with Marmaduke's men should they need my skills and I could be freed from my medical duties for a short time. May the Lord forgive my vanity, but I must admit, it was quite a heady experience for me to be sought out and asked to serve by such a prominent figure as Maj. Gen. Marmaduke.

*A rumor is afloat that we will be soon moving
north toward engagement with the Union, but it is
only a rumor and I know nothing of it. I will write
as soon as I can.*

Your loving son,
Billy

****

December 3, 1862
Dearest Mother,

*I may yet come to regret my vanity and
agreement to serve with Marmaduke's troops, as
on the morning of November 25th, I, along with
three other young men – were called to join with
all possible speed his band of cavalry near Cane
Hill, some twenty miles southwest of Fayetteville.
Our mission was to scout out any Federals and
gather food and other supplies as best we could.*

*My scouting party was traversing north
and east early on the morning of the 28th when
we heard the boom of artillery fire behind us.
We rushed back to camp only to find the battle
fully engaged and Marmaduke's pickets rapidly
giving ground. From what I understand, Blunt's
army had force-marched from Fayetteville and
surprised our troops. Because I had the fastest
horse, Capt. Scott quickly wrote out a message
to Gen. Hindman urgently requesting assistance
and, most importantly, additional ammunition as
his troops were running dangerously low.*

*Mother, you of all will appreciate what
transpired during the ride. As I was making my
way with all possible speed, suddenly a horseman
in federal attire appeared beside me and ordered*

me to halt. He brandished a large pistol and I had no choice but to accede. I was certain it was the end of the war for me and that I would soon be escorted to a federal prisoner of war camp. Although doctors and their assistants are generally returned to the field, I was at this time not engaged in my medical role, but in that of a courier. My heart was sick. The cavalryman led me to a copse of trees and there emerged a dozen other men similarly attired. I am sure my expression bespoke my inner terror, although I was doing my best to appear fearless and resolute. Suddenly, my captor broke out in laughter and was joined by the rest of his men. He then introduced me to William C. Quantrill's Company of Missouri guerrillas, dressed in captured Federal uniforms. Their mission was to create havoc and confusion among the enemy troops. They certainly had succeeded with me. They wished me Godspeed and sent me on my way. I can still hear the echoes of their laughter in my mind.

En route I encountered no true Federals, but soon met up with scouts for Col James Monroe, 1st Arkansas. The order was given to move with all possible speed in relief of Marmaduke's forces. I continued my wild ride until I met up with Hindman's forces. After passing the message, I rejoined Cousin Lawrence to prepare for marching orders and they soon came.

As I send this letter to you, we are headed north toward Cane Hill and Fayetteville.

Your loving son,
Billy

****

December 13, 1862
Dearest Mother,

I am but 16 this day, yet I feel the weight of 100 years of living. We have been heartily engaged in battle for the last several days and our comrades have suffered so very much. I feel blessed to be wound and illness free, yet, in some ways, cursed by the visions of all the misery I have seen. I know these horrible images of death and dying, men blown apart by uncaring cannon and rifle shot will remain with me all the rest of my days. How can any sane man wish to go to War with his fellow man? Perhaps we are all insane.

On December 3rd, we crossed the Arkansas River and quick-marched for two straight days – with little or no sleep and even less food. In the early hours of December 6th, we arrived at Cove Creek and almost immediately engaged Federal forces. Union troops held the high ground on Reed's Mountain for most of the day, but were finally pushed back to Cane Hill with Monroe's forces securing the high ground on Reed's Hill. Under the cover of darkness, the main body of Hindman's forces, including the hospital, moved north toward Prairie Grove. Monroe's troops remained on Reed's Hill as a diversion – lighting fires and making much noise to lull Blunt into thinking Hindman's full army was in residence. I saw little of this action myself, as I was in the surgery tent most of the day, but learned of it from one of Monroe's lieutenants who was brought into the surgery with a wound to his arm.

At Prairie Grove, Hindman's army secured the ridge above the open field below. Hindman set up headquarters in Prairie Grove Church. He placed infantry behind the crest of the south ridge to protect them from artillery fire. The battle at Prairie Grove commenced against Union forces brought up to reinforce those at Cane Hill.

E. H. McEachern

Our field hospital was hurriedly set up south and east of the field of battle and we were besieged with the wounded from the moment our wagon stopped and even before the tents were erected far back into the woods. It is the practice to set the surgery as far away from the battle as possible to protect our wounded and surgeons as they try to render assistance.

Our comrades, some walking, some on stretchers, some in ambulances, all sought the field hospital and all giving proof by their injuries as well as their tongues of the terrible carnage of the battle. Their sheer numbers gave lie to the news that Hindman's troops were winning the day.

The actual loss of men I do not know but the dead and dying extended around the hospital as far as the eyes could see and the wounded filled every tent or outside shelter. They suffered so much. I dealt primarily with those less injured, tying off arteries and setting broken limbs. We could do nothing for those with chest wounds but pray. Cousin Lawrence had the more grisly duty, amputating arms and legs with chloroform as his only aid. When our supply of that drug was exhausted, men bore the operation with a mouth or two of whiskey or nothing at all to alleviate the pain never complaining and even expressing gratitude. Old Thomas ran hither and yon, bringing water, medicines, and encouragement to all he encountered. Never have I been more proud to be associated with both these fine men. Although we rendered all aid in our power, there were many deaths.

At one point during that horrible day, Old Thomas came to me and bade me come outdoors. There under a small scrub oak tree lay Jefferson Spence, of Van Buren. I knelt beside him and asked if I could render any assistance, but he

110

*declined saying he was mortally wounded and
would soon die. He said it without regret – almost
cheerfully – but asked if I would let his mother
know that he had died bravely. I promised him I
would. He passed over into our Lord's hands just
minutes later, and two of his comrades removed
his body. Although I have seen many men die this
day, Jefferson Spence's death was a great shock
for me, as I had known him from boyhood, and
though he was older than I, we had met during
many trips into Van Buren.*

*Your loving son,
Billy*

****

*December 21, 1862
Dearest Mother,*
*We bivouacked in the field after travelling
all the night following the Prairie Grove battle
without tent or any shelter but oilcloths we found
abandoned by the side of the road. They were of
the very best material and we gladly abandoned
ours or kept them to throw over our wounded
carried in wagon or caisson. An open field is not
a fit sanitarium for the sick or the cold ground a
good bed for a feverish and chilly man.*
*Although we hold ready for marching orders,
most of the men are too exhausted and battle-
weary to do much more than rest.*
*Cousin Lawrence and I still do not know
whether the Confederate or Union forces were
victorious at Prairie Grove, even though the term
victory in this context seems so farcical to me, for
any conflict in which so many good men on both*

sides were killed or badly mutilated can have no winner.

Your loving son,
Billy

****

January 10, 1863
Dearest Mother,

The most violent storm of wind and rain within my memory burst upon our camp last night. My tent was thrown about and the rain streamed right in between the flaps so relentlessly that everything became thoroughly soaked. But I slept very well despite it. This morning Sean O'Reilly (he is Major McAndrew's servant and the most perfect Irishman I have ever seen – and who hates Col Broadworth, because of the latter's arrogance and disagreeable temperament) came over to our camp. I heard him telling, in the most perfect brogue, that last night in the worst of the storm he cut the Colonel's tent ropes and let the tent fall on the Colonel creating a great stir in camp. I laughed until the tears ran down my cheeks. It felt wonderful.

I hope your Christmas was filled with happiness and that my sisters received the letters and small gifts I was able to send. I think of you all and home so often. Every day will be Christmas once this War has ended and I can rejoin you.

Your loving son,
Billy

****

January 12, 1863
Dearest Mother,

Well, here I am at another encampment we call Camp Mud. We are still moving somewhat south and west, but I do not know our destination. After the last wagon was packed this morning I went down to headquarters to see if the spring-wagon had come, and sure enough there was the mess kit I had requested from you. I am more comfortably supplied with everything than anyone I know in the army, principally owing to your thoughtful love.

I have just unpacked the chest and at every turn I find new examples of your ever thoughtful love. Be assured you never sent sugar to a sourer group of men. We have been without it for some time and with careful rationing this supply will see us through the next month. Please take care not to send us any of your household allotments, and by so doing deplete the foodstuffs and medicines you must have to remain well and healthy.

Your two long, sweet letters reached me as well along with the sweet picture of Nine Oaks drawn by Evelyn Rose. It is a precious memento and I will carry it close to my heart. Kiss my sisters for me and tell them I think of them constantly.

Your loving son,
Billy

****

February 15, 1863
Dearest Mother,

Nothing of interest transpired this day or by my way of thinking within the last few weeks. For this I am exceedingly grateful. After Prairie Hill, I have had my fill of this War and its inhumanities. I can only pray it will soon end.

In the past several days, I have even begun to recapture some pleasant daydreams and shed the morose and melancholy attitude that so pervaded my soul earlier this year. I hope you, Anna Marie and Evelyn Rose are well this winter and able to keep warm and cozy at Nine Oaks. I have not received any letters from you in several weeks, but I know that you write daily. None of the men in our company has had any news from home for quite some time. I can think of no greater pleasure than to receive a dozen or more of your sweet letters all at once and spend many happy hours in a written conversation with you and my sweet sisters.

Our hospital is relatively uninhabited, save for those with dysentery and other maladies. We have been singularly free of any person with small pox – most likely due to the inoculations we executed last year. We spend much of the time these days hunting and fishing and doing our continuous "scavenging." It has been our fortune to travel though the Nations where the game and water are plentiful. It is not unusual for our scouting party to bring back as many as two deer from one days' hunt. The meat is certainly welcomed, and I am proud to say I do my part in feeding the men.

You will be happy to know I have been promoted to "Assistant Surgeon," equivalent to the rank of Capt.

Your loving son,
Billy

****

March 1, 1863
Dear Mother,

Sometime in the predawn we awoke to the distinctive sound of the cannon and well knew that a great battle was being fought somewhere in the distance. We quickly assembled our gear and made ready for orders when Major Johnson rode up and ordered me to join the sharp-shooters party he was sending out in the event of a Union attack. I could not disagree, nor could Cousin Lawrence, as the men in hospital were few and recovering quite well, and at any rate I was anxious to see for myself. I quickly gathered up my rifle and rations for one day. After a short ride, Major Johnson threw us into a line on the brow of a hill which overlooked a river, with quite a wide valley expanding below us. On the other side of the river, the bluff rose quite steeply, but on the top of it there was an open field. Major Johnson rode on to meet with another officer and left us to observe.

We anxiously awaited orders to go somewhere else and do something; but none came. After a time the cannon fire ceased, leaving us to wonder what had transpired on the far side of the steep bluff just out of our view.

Later that evening I was assigned to scout ahead. I came into an area where many Yankees lay dead, I thought by the cannon fire we had heard earlier. As I traversed the field I happened upon an old doll-baby with no limbs, save one arm. It lay just beyond the outstretched fingertips of a dead Federal soldier as if he had drawn it from his person and clasped it with his last breaths. It was so obviously something a little loved one had given him – perhaps a memento which he always carried even into battle to remind him of love and home. It was strange to see that symbol of childhood - that sign of a father's love - lying there among the carnage. I could not help but think of the sweet picture Evelyn Rose drew for me and that I, too, keep folded inside my uniform and next to my heart. I dismounted, picked it up, and stuffed it back into the slain man's tunic so that it might accompany him into his silent grave so very far from his home – a resting place which would likely never be known to the child who presented her cherished doll-baby so lovingly to her father or brother.

I encountered nothing beyond that field of bodies and returned to camp before dark. We went into bivouac a little after sunset, for it had become cloudy and rain was thick upon the air. We supped on a piece of stale bread and a piece of fat (mostly fat) meat, and a tin cup of coffee. There has been no sugar for at least ten days. Food supplies are almost nonexistent as the commissariat is far from our position and cannot provision us.

I cannot keep from thinking of that dead soldier and wondering who will mourn him.

Your loving son,
Billy

****

Emma slowly folded the last letter and placed it into its envelope. Then she cried for the boy who was forced into a War that stole his father's life, his youth, and his hope. Maybe she cried a little for all the soldiers on both sides. She wondered what had become of this eloquent Southerner, and whether he was the one for whom their spirit searched. Maybe, like the nameless soldier he had written of, Billy never came home either.

Chapter Seven

"Hey, Caleb. It's Eric McBride. I just got the autopsy results on your Jane Doe. Have you gotten a copy yet?"

"No, we haven't. No surprise there," replied Caleb sardonically.

"Well, she didn't go down without a fight. She had skin under her fingernails and some more stuck in her teeth. She probably bit the hell out of the bastard who killed her."

"Good for her. Any luck at matching it?"

"Yeah, actually we did - belongs to one Trevon Adams, 24. Nasty dude. He's got a long sheet; assault, domestic abuse, burglary – suspected of murder, but never charged with murder... anyway, some pretty hardcore stuff and mostly gang-related. But what's interesting is that everything's in Houston...looks like he belongs to, uh" Caleb could hear papers rattling... "the Sierpes. Sierpes dabble in some human trafficking for their prostitution ring – but it's all local - definitely nothing out of their city. No idea what he was doing up here."

"That is weird," Caleb agreed. "You don't think the gang is moving north, do you?"

"The OSBI doesn't have anything on that and the feds don't seem to think so," McBride continued, "but I've got a buddy in a Houston gang unit. Let me give him a call and see what he can find out."

"Thanks, Eric. I appreciate the call." Caleb disconnected. This was not good – not good at all. Gangs were notorious for their violence and disregard for human life. He felt more than ever that Nana and, by association, Jenny, Zac and Emma were seriously at risk.

****

Holcomb pounded on Clement McRae's front door. A check of the county's land records showed the murder site had belonged to Malcomb McRae. When the old man died, the property had come to Clement.

"Come on, Red, I know you're in there. Your piece of shit truck's right here." Louder, "Come on out or I'm going to kick this damn door off its hinges." The Sheriff hammered on the door again.

"You go around back – just in case Red suddenly decides he's gotta' go fishin' or something." Caleb quietly eased off the front porch – if the sagging, termite-ravaged planks could still be called a porch - and disappeared from view. Sure enough, two minutes later, Holcomb heard a loud crash, some male voices swearing and finally Caleb's voice. "Hey, Joe, come see what I found trying to sneak out the back door."

Red McRae was splayed face down in what appeared to be a sticker patch – little nettles covered the his filthy once-white T-shirt and hung randomly off his unshaven face and hair.

As Caleb cuffed the subdued man, Holcomb squatted down near his head and said, "Damn, man. All we wanted to do was to ask you a couple of questions about your grandpa's old house. You gonna talk to us?"

Red burped loudly – his breath was so foul, Holcomb fell back on his butt to get out of its reach.

"Drunker' than shit," observed Caleb.

"Ok, Red. I guess we'll have to do this the hard way. Clement McRae, you're under arrest as an accessory in the murder of Jane Doe..." Caleb pulled out his card with the Miranda warning printed on it and began to read, "You have the right to remain silent....

Red raised his head and looked at the Sheriff through red-rimmed, uncomprehending eyes. "Huh? Whadidyasay?" Then he flopped face down into the nettles and began to snore.

****

"Shut up, Red! Just shut the fuck up!" Exasperated and more than a little bit angry, Sims Towson looked at the filthy, bloated figure sitting on the bottom bunk of a cell in the county jail.

Red McRae sobbed uncontrollably holding his head between his hands, stopping every once in a while to pick a particularly bothersome nettle from his beard, hair, ears, or nose. Occasionally, Red added a groan or two to his repertoire. His head pounded – he felt sick at his stomach. But worst of all - he was sober. Red hated being sober.

"Oh man, oh man, I am so fucked." Then he started sobbing again.

Towson had known Red since they were kids. They'd gone to the same elementary, middle and high schools together. Sometime during the first grade, Towson had taken on the role of Red's friend - he was probably the only friend Red had.

Red had been a joke and a target for as long as Towson could remember – hell, even his nickname was an insult.

When McRea was a kid, his grandfather called him Clem Kadiddlehopper, after one of Red Skelton's comedy personalities, maybe because the kid's first name was Clement – but more likely because Red was so stupid. Clem's father somehow put a stop to the name-calling (Towson wasn't sure how, because that old man had a mean streak in him a mile wide), but Grandpa finally dropped the Kadiddlehopper and started calling him "Red." "Red" stuck – it was, after all, better than Clem or anything else the other kids had called him.

Knowing the connection between the two, the Sheriff had called Sims an hour ago. He hoped Towson would be able to talk some sense into the drunk. All they wanted was some information about his deceased grandpa's house and farm – they didn't really think Red had murdered the little girl - but the man wouldn't say anything. If they couldn't get him to talk to them – they'd have to formally charge his stupid ass and get him a public defender.

So, Sims pulled a chair up to Red's bunk – not too close – nobody could be that good a friend - Red stunk something awful – sat down and tried to find out what happened. At least maybe he could get him to stop that God-awful caterwauling.

"So – tell me. What'd they get you for…public drunk again?"

"No – worse. Way worse."

"So, either tell me or shut up."

Red looked at his friend. Towson's expression told him he wasn't kidding and right now, Red needed a friend.

****

"Caleb – Joe," Sims Towson shook hands with both men as he took a seat in the Sheriff's Office. "To tell you the truth, I think Red had better keep quiet 'til he has a chance to get himself a lawyer. I'm afraid he might be into something pretty bad."

The two lawmen looked at each other – surprised. Neither thought Red had the brains to get himself into that much trouble. "You got to be shitting me, Sims," said Holcomb.

"Nope, I guess it don't take much to dig a hole you can't get out of and, believe me, I think Red's hole is deep."

Caleb jumped in. "Sims, we've got to find out what Red knows and we need to know fast– you heard about the girl who was murdered out by 177?

Sims nodded.

"My family's got the other twin staying with us – she's just a little kid – and she could be in a lot of trouble…" Caleb was getting a little hot.

"I know – I know, Caleb. But Red is my friend and I can't just abandon him. I gotta look out for him, too, he's got nobody else. Look, my son's wife is a defense lawyer over in Norman…"

Caleb and Holcomb groaned.

"No, no, look. She's really pretty straight – smart and she's reasonable. I can get her to come over – probably this afternoon and let's see what we can work out. Maybe something that wouldn't put Red away for the rest of his life. What do you think?"

The two men agreed. What choice did they have?

****

Andrea Towson was not at all what the Sheriff expected. Young, dark and petite, she shook hands with the lawmen. Neither Caleb nor Holcomb detected the aggressiveness or belligerence they usually got from defense attorneys. Ms. Towson sat beside her father-in-law and tugged at the hem of her skirt.

"So, Ms. Towson," Holcomb began, "Where are we?"

"It's Andrea...I think we're going to have to work together on this one..."

Caleb felt slightly relieved – maybe even a little hopeful.

"I believe my client can provide you some important information about the case involving the young girl murdered here," she started. Holcomb's eyes lit up. "That is, if we can work something out regarding his charges."

"So, what kind of deal are you talking about?"

"Truly, I don't feel Mr. McRae is a bad man. I don't believe he would have become involved in anything that would result in harm to another person – especially a child – if he'd understood what he was getting into at the time. You know," she looked at Sims, "I guess everyone knows Mr. McRae is not ... um..." she searched for a polite way to say it.

Sims broke in. "We know Red is stupid and he's also a drunk. He's been drinking for so long, he's probably fried what few brain cells he had."

Andrea continued, "Well, – I'd ask for immunity and a possible relocation in exchange for a full and complete disclosure of what Mr. McRea knows."

Holcomb was confused. "Relocation?"

"Yes, that'll be made pretty clear if you can see through it and accept the deal."

After Sims Towson and his daughter-in-law had left, Holcomb reached for his phone to call Bobbi Huff in Oklahoma City. As he punched in the number, he thought, "What the hell does that old drunk know?"

****

"I'm feeling really sad about my sister." Nana, sighed deeply, tears welling in her eyes. She sat down on the edge of Emma's big bed. "And I miss my mom."

"I know you do, sweetheart," said Emma, sensing not only a chance to console her young friend, but maybe get some more clues about Nana's home. "What do you miss most?"

"I don't know." Nana sighed again and thought for a moment.

"My mom was sick a lot. Me and my sister would take care of her. We'd fix her soup sometimes or go down to the corner to get her medicine. Mom really didn't want us to go there– she said those dudes were mean as snakes – but sometimes she really needed her medicine bad. Me and my sister always went together

– we had each other's backs, you know? I was scared to go there - that black dude - he was super scary and had tats all over his arms and face and talking smart. But my sister was always so brave. She didn't take any of his shit."

"I guess that would be really scary."

Nana averted her eyes. "I know it wasn't really medicine – it was drugs. Drugs are bad stuff – we learned all about it from school. But my mom couldn't help it. She really tried, but she couldn't." Nana was silent for a while and Emma willed herself to be patient, fearing that more questions might cause Nana to lose touch with her tenuous memories.

Nana finally continued, "But when Mom felt good, we had a lot of fun. She told funny jokes and we played games or sometimes we all danced together. We were a good team. That's what she'd say – we're a good team."

The girl began to cry and Emma hugged her tight.

****

Two days later, Director Bobbi Huff, Eric McBride from the OSBI, OBNDD's attorney, Andrea Towson, and Red McRea joined Caleb and Joe Holcomb in the Sheriff's small conference room. Deals had been proposed, counter-offers made, and agreements reached. Everyone was ready and anxious to hear what McRea had to say.

"Go ahead, Red," Andrea prompted. "Tell them what you told me. Don't hold anything back – that was part of the deal, OK?"

Red had taken a shower and was wearing clean clothes. And, much to his chagrin – he was still sober. He took a couple of breaths and started talking – slow and hesitant at first - he was soon into the flow.

McRea told them that sometime last fall – he couldn't remember exactly – but he thought sometime between Labor Day and Halloween, a well-groomed man in his forties, driving a "really slicked out new black Escalade – Man oh Man – that truck had everythin' – just everythin' – this big old handpainted St. Louis Cardinals logo on the tailgate… anyway, he come by and wanted to rent Grandpa's place."

"What'd this guy look like?"

"Well, let's see – had on new jeans and a black leather jacket…I'm gonna get me one just like it…"

Holcomb nodded.

"Um, he had kinda dark brown hair – about as tall as me – wasn't skinny, but not fat… he was friendly alright, but he looked like you wouldn't want to cross him – kind of a mean look in his eyes."

"What color eyes?"

"Uh, blue, I think – not brown anyway…"

"Damn," thought Holcomb, medium build – dark hair – don't even know what color eyes – except not brown. How's this gonna' help?"

"Any distinguishing features, Mr. McRea?" This from Bobbi Huff.

"Huh?"

Caleb translated, "Did he have any scars...tattoos. Did he walk with a limp – like that?"

"No, he moved just fine." Red thought a minute – they could see the strain on his face.

"But come to think of it – he did have a funny-looking scar – right here on his chin – kind of like a quarter-moon."

Sensing this was the best description they were going to get, Holcomb asked him why the man wanted to rent the old McRea place.

"He said he needed a place to stay from time to time – someplace his wife couldn't find him." McRea chuckled at some inside joke, "He said she'd been screwing around with his best friend and now she was gonna divorce him... can you believe that?"

Towson patted Red's arm and urged him to continue.

"Anyway, he said he had to hide some of his stuff every once in a while 'cause he was afraid that if his wife's bitch lawyer knew what he had – especially his new Escalade – she'd go after it in the divorce."

Huff shot a look at Towson, who just smiled.

"And he was going to hide his stuff in your grandfather's house?"

"Yeah - he give me $10,000 – *cash* – and another $1,000 each and every month for supplies. All I had to do was keep a special phone on me all the time – couldn't be used for nothin' else - and when I got a message on that phone, I was to run out to the house, get rid of any trash, make sure all the windows and doors locked good, make sure there were some groceries, toilet paper – like that – oh yeah-and that the propane tanks were filled 'cause sometimes he'd stay over. That's all.

"What was the message – the message on the cell?" Caleb asked.

"Uh – just a date – you know, like Tuesday, April 10 – or Monday, June 1 - sometimes it was the next day – sometimes the day after."

"Red, come on - didn't you think his story was just bullshit?"

"Yeah," Red lowered his eyes to the table, "But then I thought - who the hell cares – I was getting' $10,000 cash, clear and clean, and I didn't even have to tell the damn tax man."

Andrea Towson winced.

****

Hamilton, OBNDC's tech-man, was sifting through McRea's cell phone's text message history. The phone itself was a throw-away – no surprise there - purchased at a Best Buy in Tulsa – so that was no help. He began transferring the numbers into a spread sheet program, when the phone chimed and a message popped up. Hamilton fumbled the phone – almost dropped it. He retrieved the text, and it was just as McRea had said - Saturday, March 31st – the next day.

Hamilton called Bobbi Huff, who, in turn called McBride at the OSBI and the PotCo Sheriff. By late that evening, they had the sting in place.

****

2:00 am. Pitch black-no moon- and, thank God, no rain or ice - only a cold wind.

"Damn, I'm freezing my ass off." Caleb shivered and hunkered down in his camouflaged high-hide in the branches of a tall oak tree. But he wouldn't have wanted to be anywhere else. Maybe they'd be able to catch these sons-of-bitches. He'd like to get his hands on the monster that killed Nana's twin. That would be something worth freezing for.

The radio beside Caleb vibrated. Eric McBride, stationed a quarter mile up the road, whispered, "Incoming."

From his vantage point Caleb could see headlights on high beam as they cut through the leafless trees. The lights jumped up and down in sync with the road's potholes and rocks. He heard a loud metallic screech and smiled – the vehicle had scraped high center.

Then a battered old utility van pulled up in front of Grandpa McRea's house. Caleb put on his night vision goggles. Two men, one small and wiry and the second, taller – with quite a bit more heft - got out of the van and stretched. Caleb watched, "Huh, looks like fat-boy's got a gun."

"We got a sawed-off or maybe even a machine pistol," Caleb whispered into his radio. "Take 'em before we get anybody killed."

A half-second later, ten men charged out of the brush. Their protective gear displayed various acronyms, OBNDC, OSBI and PotCo Sheriff – but their actions were perfectly coordinated. After two minutes of orchestrated chaos, the hapless driver and his sidekick found themselves disarmed, lying face down on the ground, and cuffed. Holcomb signaled Caleb to come down - his voice sputtered out of the radio, "No muss – no fuss."

When the back doors of the van were unlocked, three girls – all in their late teens - were helped down. Shaking from the cold and terrified, two started crying hysterically and the third just stared wide-eyed at the men splayed on the ground. One of the cuffed men tried to say something to her, but just at that moment a PottCo deputy 'tripped' and placed a well-positioned kick hard into the man's right side. The deputy had, in fact, been the Shawnee high school's star field goal kicker just a few years before he joined the department.

"Oops, sorry. I tripped. Sure is dark out here." Nobody disagreed.

Two hours later, the men were in a cell being held on charges of suspected kidnapping and interstate human trafficking.

The euphoria from the bust was not long-lived. When Holcomb got into his office the next morning, Bobbi Huff was waiting for him.

"Looks like we're not going to be able to charge these bastards with much more than interstate trafficking of illegal weapons."

"What're you talking about? They had those girls…"

"Yeah, but those girls aren't talking. They're scared out of their minds – retaliation against anyone who talks is a strong possibility – not just themselves, but their families as well -. Hell, it's more than a possibility – it's a certainty – and these girls know it."

She continued, "The good news is that the guy riding shotgun had an illegal automatic machine pistol – you know the kind that starts out as a legal semi-automatic – but by some miracle of nature gets transformed and the guy can't figure out how it happened?"

Holcomb smiled. He'd heard that story before.

"So we can keep the guys locked up – at least for a while anyway. Also gives us access to their cell phones and anything else we can find. We've got their prints and DNA and we're running backgrounds now."

Both were quiet for a minute. Huff continued, "Looks like the van came from Denver. The girls weren't sure where they were headed, and I believe them. They probably weren't told much of anything. They say they were just going with these guys voluntarily on a site-seeing trip…one big happy party. Can you believe they'll hang together with a story like that?"

"When I asked them why they were locked in the back of a windowless van, and why the guy in the front had a machine gun - they stumbled around a little, and then said they guessed he was just trying to keep them safe… sometimes I just despair of the human condition."

"Shit…."

"Shit, indeed. The men aren't saying anything. They lawyered up just as soon as we got them in custody and haven't said anything since – except to call a guy in Denver – told him to get them a lawyer down here quick, so I expect we'll have somebody knocking on our door pretty soon."

****

The guy in Denver swore "on a stack of Bibles" that he'd told his subordinates to avoid the Shawnee way station, but apparently one of them didn't get the word. The Denver man had sent one of his attorneys to handle the legal defense for the driver and the guard, but the law in Oklahoma had them dead-to-rights on the gun charge. He thought the men might serve a little time, but they'd never say anything. Ortiz and the network were safe – absolutely and completely safe. As he and Ortiz concluded their discussion, the man in Denver promised to keep his boss informed.

As the Denver operative clicked off, sweat trickled off his brow. He could smell the fear on himself, as he swiped at his forehead and eyes. "God help me if Ortiz finds out the automatic pistol the guard was carrying had been slipped out of guns stolen from Buckley. Ortiz would shit a brick if he heard that. He'd have to make damn sure none of those other bastards still had one... fuck a duck!" Maybe this'd be a good time for him to get out – get lost...as far away as he could go.

Several hundred miles to the east, Enrique Ortiz ended the conversation with a four-letter expletive and spun around. MacIntosh was lounging in a chair across the room.

"Jesus Christ – this whole thing's turning to shit!" Ortiz fumed. "That was Fredericks in Denver. One of the vans got waylaid by those hicks in Shawnee. They got the whole load *and* the driver *and* the guard. Goddamn it to hell!"

After a minute, he continued, "We've got to make sure everybody knows to stay away from Shawnee – maybe we ought to stay the hell out of Oklahoma altogether..."

In his reasoned and quiet voice MacIntosh responded, "Don't see how we can stay out of Oklahoma - all the interstate roads we need pass through there – and we can't shut down – the big boys in Colombia would want to know why ..."

"I know...I know. But we can't afford any more fuck-ups....first the twins and now this..."

Ortiz sat back in his chair, his hands unconsciously stroking the leather. How could these gangs be so incredibly stupid? It was beyond belief.

Ortiz thought a minute. "OK, here's what we'll do. For the next couple of weeks, tell the drivers to go straight through – no stops - except for gas. If somebody has to piss – give 'em a bottle. In the meantime, let's set up another way station – maybe someplace further east – or north - someplace way out in the damn sticks. And nobody – and I mean *nobody* better get busted – make sure everybody gets the message!"

MacIntosh nodded and left his friend to fume in solitude. MacIntosh was by far the calmer and more practical of the two. If something was messed up; fix it – don't rant and rave about it. Ortiz was a ranter and a raver – but he was also brilliant at organizing and bullshitting – two skills MacIntosh lacked. Ortiz thought it up; MacIntosh got it done. It worked – as long as Ortiz didn't have a heart attack.

In his office Ortiz shrugged...well, this problem wasn't insurmountable. Those Denver shitheads may have been caught – but they didn't really know very much – nothing about the overall operation – certainly nothing that would trace back to him. He didn't need to get upset or worry – sure didn't want to spoil the mood for tonight.

He was escorting Donna Sebastian to that benefit for … what-the-hell was it? – the homeless shelter? What a laugh...her dress probably cost more than the shelter's annual budget …. Oh well, didn't matter…. she was gorgeous and rich. He wasn't sure which attribute was more appealing. He'd talk her into leaving early and later talk her out of her evening wear. He smiled at the thought – Donna in diamonds and nothing else.

Ortiz pushed himself out of his chair and wandered over to the window – the floor-to-ceiling window that looked east over the arch, Busch stadium and beyond to the Mississippi. He wondered if any of the barges were his – the ones running guns south to New Orleans… probably….

St. Louis was a fine city – not too big – but big enough. From here he could supervise all the Cartel's Midwestern operations – the guns, the drugs, and now - the women. He smiled – who'd have thought he'd come this far – this fast. He was one of the many movers and shakers in the city. He had enough money to do whatever he wanted – well, almost enough - he laughed to himself, "I guess I'll never have enough."

It was, all things considered, a beautiful day.

****

Emma, Nana and Matt spent the next few days sorting through the piles of papers regarding Chapman & Samuelson. Matt was especially astute at weeding out those pieces of correspondence that probably had nothing to do with their search – routine shipping manifests, request for payment from dead-beat customers. Nana soon lost interest. "I bet she can't understand this mid-nineteenth century English very well," Emma thought to herself. "I wonder just how much schooling she's had."

Emma looked over at Nana, who was coloring a picture of Cinderella and the mice. "Nice job, Nana. Did you do many art projects in school?"

Nana replied, "Well, we didn't go to school every day like some of the kids, but when we did Sister Mary Agnes would let us color sometimes. I really liked going to school, especially reading and computers, but Katie hated it – everything except basketball. She was really good at basketball."

Emma went on high alert.

"Nana, was your sister's name Katie?"

Nana looked surprised. Her eyes grew wide and she smiled. "Yes, I just remembered that, didn't I? Her name was Katie and mine was…. Mine was…." Nana looked crestfallen. "I don't remember my name."

Emma was thrilled. Now they had two new pieces of information- names they didn't have before; Katie and Sister Mary Agnes.

Emma sought to reassure the girl. "That's okay – you probably won't remember everything all at once. But you remembered something really important. You'll remember more if you just don't try so hard. Like tonight – stuff will just pop out."

The girl looked somewhat mollified, but said, "I really want to help Caleb."

Emma hugged Nana, "and you will, Sweetheart, you will."

****

Matt broke the silence. "Em, I think I've found something important here. It's a letter from William (Billy) S. Chapman to Dwight Samuelson." Matt consulted the family tree board. "It has to be the son of Mary Elizabeth Chapman writing to his uncle. The same Billy that wrote those letters home. This says, no… I'll let you read it for yourself." Matt handed Emma the letter.

> *April 30, 1863*
> *Mr. Dwight Samuelson*
> *Chapman & Samuelson Shipping and Express*
> *Van, Buren, Arkansas*
> *Dear Uncle Dwight,*
>
> *Please accept my sincere apologies for failing to respond to yours of March 25th until now, but your letter was much delayed in its journey. I am currently stationed at Perryville in Indian Territory and it takes quite some time for news to reach our post and for our letters to reach the States. I also must admit I have had to take several days to compose myself in good enough order to write a coherent response.*
>
> *My mind and heart will not accept - cannot accept - that my dearest Mother and my two sweet*

sisters have been brutally murdered by a raiding band of heartless bushwackers. I cannot fathom what kind of monster would purposefully take the life of such sweet innocents. They, who have never harmed another person in this life, could certainly have posed no threat to them or their nefarious activities.

I am inconsolable. Where is God? Why did He not, in His infinite understanding, save them from this horrible fate?

Uncle Dwight, lest I be borne away by grief before I express this, please accept my heartfelt gratitude for the many very difficult tasks you have had to perform for Mother and my sisters. I know Mother, Anna Marie and Evelyn Rose were as dear to you as they were to me. I wish with all my heart I could have been at your side to take this burden from your shoulders, but apparently fate deemed it otherwise.

It is good that Ma'am Sissy survived. She was ever devoted to Mother and my sisters. I know Mother would wish Ma'am Sissy to have her freedom and I ask, for Mother's sake, that you take care to see that she receives her letter of manumission. If you should be able to find a place for her in your service, I would be most grateful.

The loss of Nine Oaks is of no consequence to me. Had it not been burned to the ground, I would burn it myself, knowing it is the scene of such indescribable horror against those I loved best. I know it was with much personal danger that Ma'am Sissy saved the few things she could from the fire – Mother's chair, the family Bible and some photographs, but I do not wish even these dear mementos. They would be to me unbearable reminders of a life now lost to me forever.

Do what you will with all that remains. I do not believe I can ever return.

Your nephew,
Wm. (Billy) S. Chapman
Assistant Surgeon

"My God, Matt – Billy's mother and sisters were murdered by bushwackers. That has to be what Jenny sees in her dreams. What a horrible heartbreaking ending for this family – I wonder if Billy is the only one left? Have you found anything else?

Matt shook his head in the negative and they both began in to search for next chapter in Billy Chapman's tragic war-time saga. Soon, they came across another letter dated October 5, 1863.

October 5, 1863
Mr. Dwight Samuelson
Chapman & Samuelson Shipping and Drayage
Van, Buren, Arkansas
Dear Mr. Samuelson,

I enclose herein a letter written to me by the right Rev. Peter Thompson of Russellville, Arkansas. As you can see, in the letter he refers to a crime committed against a Van Buren family that I cannot help but believe must be that of your dear sister, Mary Elizabeth, and her sweet daughters.

Although I know this information can in no way ease the pain of their loss, I thought perhaps it might bring you some small measure of comfort to know the villainous perpetrators of your sister's and her children's deaths have been made to atone for their heinous acts. I only wish her son, William, had survived long enough to see justice done.

> *We know that our good Lord works in mysterious ways - ways that we mortal men can never comprehend. We can though rejoice and take comfort in knowing that the entire Chapman family is once again reunited in Heaven.*

> *Your most humble servant in God,*
> *Rev. Ernest Baylor*
> *First Episcopal Church of Van Buren*

Folded inside the Baylor letter was a second note from a minister in Russellville, Arkansas. It concerned the capture and execution of a gang of bushwackers in the fall of 1863.

> *September 30, 1863*
> *Rev. Ernest Baylor*
> *First Episcopal Church of Van Buren*
> *Van Buren, Arkansas*
> *My dear Reverend Baylor,*
> *I write this letter in the hope you might assist me in the fulfillment of a promise I made to a young man who was about to meet his fate with the hangman.*
> *In late August a Confederate patrol assigned to protect our good citizens from the terrors wrought by roving bands of bushwackers and jayhawkers caught four men robbing and burning a farm just outside the city of Russellville (also known as Shinnville), Arkansas.*
> *Mr. Pauley Campbell, a boy of about 16 years, was captured in the act of burning the house to*

the ground. Along with his fellow blackguards, he was sentenced to hang by the neck until dead at noon the next day. Mr. Campbell did not ask for any special consideration because of his youth; yea, he was in fact quite stoic about his fate and ready to pay the price for his black deeds. He did ask to speak to a minister in preparation for his Heavenly judgment and to atone for his many sins, and I was asked to bring what comfort I could.

Upon meeting Mr. Campbell, I saw he was of such slight stature that he scarcely looked more than a boy, and in such a state of raggedness and ill-nourishment, I could scarcely help but feel sorry for his fate even though his quick intellect was sufficient to have guided him away from the criminal enterprises in which he was so obviously a participant.

We talked for at least one hour of salvation and forgiveness and prayed together. It was then he asked that I make his deepest apologies to the family of the woman and two daughters who were murdered by his gang near Van Buren last March. He did not know the names of the persons, but he was, I believe, sincerely sorry for their deaths. He said that he, himself, shot the mother totally by accident, when she stumbled upon him outside the home in the woods. I consoled the young man with the promise of God's infinite forgiveness and that his contrite heart was sure to be taken into consideration by our Heavenly Father. The other men, being uninterested in making a confession, did not wish to make their peace with God and I am certain now find themselves damned and burning in the pit of Hell for all Eternity.

I hope you are aware of the family so despoiled by these criminals and will forward the *sentiments of the lost soul I counseled before he met his ugly but well-deserved fate.*

With greatest regards,
The Rev. Peter Thompson
Episcopal Church
Russellville, Arkansas

Matt and Emma just looked at one another, unable to comprehend the loss this family had suffered more than 150 years ago. First, the father at Pea Ridge in 1862, then the mother and daughters, sometime in March 1863 and then sometime before October 5, 1863, Billy died, too. All of them gone in the span of 18 months. It didn't seem possible, but it was.

The sorrow Matt and Emma felt was just as real as though the Chapman family's heartrending story had happened yesterday. Matt didn't know what to say. He just put his arms around Emma and they held each other close.

****

When Jenny returned home that evening, she, Emma and Matt read, reread, and talked at length about the letters. The tragedy of the Chapman family was one, they knew, that had repeated itself many times over during the horrible and bloody conflict of the Civil War. But to them, this family's story was much more personal and poignant - perhaps because of the letters from Billy to his mother, maybe because of Jenny's dreams, but for whatever reason, the three of them vowed they would do everything they could to bring peace to the spirit attached to the old rocking chair.

They were still talking when the phone rang. Emma jumped up to answer and apparently the call was for her, as she spoke for a minute or two and then went out on the front porch to finish the conversation.

Jenny gathered up a sleepy Zac and headed upstairs. Instead of his usual 'tubby' before bed, she turned into the sitting room and stared at the old rocking chair. Clue lay on the floor at its side, purring softly. She straightened the chair in front of the wide window overlooking the front lawn. It was quiet outside - the strong winds of spring temporarily in abeyance. Moonlight reflected off the far woods, giving an almost ethereal quality to the scene.

Jenny eased down into the chair, holding her sleepy baby close to her. The chair was much more comfortable than it looked; its seat and arms seemed to wrap her and her child in a loving embrace.

She began to rock back and forth, gently humming and thinking of the spirit who lived in her home. In the peacefulness of the twilight and the rhythm of the rocking, Jenny and Zac slipped into a light slumber. Jenny began to dream,

Grief endures. It slips undetected into the conscious mind and saps the joy from one's soul. It is also cunning. It leaves just enough to allow hope to grow to the point it can return to feed again.

There is no pain for me – only emptiness. Sounds barely register and those I can hear come to me as if from under the water or through a thick impenetrable mist. It is neither hot nor cold, wet nor dry. Things happen around me but none of it touches me or seems to matter. There are no others here; I am so alone. Perhaps I am an unborn child still in the womb, waiting to come into the world. But that cannot be. For if I were an unborn babe, I would be full of hope and joy. But there is no joy – no hope here; only a heavy sadness lying across my shoulders like a shawl I cannot throw aside.

I see Nine Oaks. I know it is burned, but I see it as it was. I wait for my dear son to come home – to see him once again and know he is safely returned from this terrible War – this hell into which we have been unwillingly thrown. I wait, but he does not come. I cannot rest until he is home with me again. I pray it will be soon.

Jenny's eyes slowly opened...and knew for certain what she had only suspected - the ghost of her chair was Mary Elizabeth Chapman, the Arkansas mother whose world had been shattered and her life ended by the senseless brutality of war. After 150 years, she was still waiting for Billy to come home.

Chapter Eight

Caleb's phone blared and he snatched it up before it had a chance to wake Jenny.

"Caleb," came Joe Holcomb's voice, "sorry to call so early, but we may have something on the twins' kidnapping. One of the undercover men working Houston Vice has some information to pass on, and we might have a break on the burn phone you recovered from the crime scene. There's going to be a joint operational meeting in Oklahoma City at 8:00 am and we've got to hustle to make it. I knew you'd want to be there. Pick you up in 30 minutes, OK?"

Caleb grunted his assent, and kissed Jenny on the ear. "Jen, I've got to go to OKC right now. May have something on Nana's kidnapping. Don't know for sure when I'll be home."

"OK, sweetheart. Why don't you grab a quick shower and I'll make some coffee. Joe will probably appreciate some to keep him awake on the road, too."

On the forty-five minute ride, the two men speculated on what had been found. Maybe they'd lucked out and had a name and address for the twins.

When the men entered the room just a couple of minutes late, they recognized several faces around the table – Agent Eric McBride from the OSBI, OBNDC technical liaison, Mark Hamilton, and Bobbi Huff, OBNDC.She scooted aside as the face of a 30ish scraggly-bearded man came into view on the wall monitor.

"Everybody, this is Chris Dover, or "Padre" as he's known by Houston's gangs. He's with the Houston Multi-Agency Gang Task Force. Chris, let me introduce these people." She named the men and women sitting around the table, each acknowledging his or her introduction by a nod or hand wave.

"Chris has been undercover vice for the last 12 years, and he's heard some interesting rumors over the last few days. One of them regards our suspect in the Shawnee Jane Doe murder.

Dover's voice boomed into the room. Hamilton jumped to turn down the volume.

"One of our newest local gangs, the Sierpes – that means "Snakes" - has a new leader, name of Viper. This is one scary dude. We have no idea how many of his "brothers" he's taken out on his climb to the top, but it's been quite a few – some of them very, very bad. I haven't met Viper yet, hopefully, I never will, but here's his photo."

The picture of a skinny, but well-muscled black man appeared on screen. Dirty dreadlocks topped his head. His chest, arms, and face were almost totally covered in gang tattoos. And there was something different about him – maybe not different – but definitely more evil - than other gang members Caleb had seen. Just looking at this guy's photo sent chills down his spine. Something told Caleb that others at the table had the same reaction.

"The BOLO sent out for Trevan Adams, aka, Wasp, is why I called you. Rumor is that he is - or at least he was – one of the top members in Viper's crew. Couple days ago, Wasp's head – minus the rest of him – was tossed into the front yard of the Sierpe Headquarters."

That little piece of information got everyone's attention.

"What's interesting is that Sierpe hasn't retaliated against another gang. That's just not done in gang culture. If somebody hits you – you hit back harder."

"So what does that mean?" asked Huff.

"That says to us Wasp was taken out by someone outside the gang world – someone powerful enough to keep Viper from going after them."

Dover paused a moment to let this sink in. Then he continued, "So just maybe somebody from outside is trying to take over or, worse still, partner up with these psychos – and Wasp pissed 'em off. That somebody would have to have a lot of clout or some really big 'cojones.' Maybe both."

Eric McBride jumped in, "Could Viper have killed him?"

"He could have, but if that was the case, why all the secrecy? Viper's taken out plenty of his own and shot the finger at any of the members to do something about it. Why would Wasp's killing be different? Besides, beheading isn't Viper's style. He goes more for dismemberment, skinning his victim alive or beating them to death."

"Our guys thought maybe one of the Mexican cartels is making a move – partnering up with 'em. But no cartel in its right mind would deal with the Sierpe Gang – they're way too out of control."

Dover continued, "The Sierpes' claim to fame is prostitution by way of human trafficking and they make a hell of a lot of money at it. They recruit women in their teens or early '20s and keep them in line through terror, beatings, threats to kill family members, all kinds of nasty stuff. When coercion doesn't work, they've been known to resort to kidnapping those they really want, get them hooked on heroin, cocaine or crack – anything to keep them in line. Then they use them for as many as 10 johns a day and keep all the profits – anywhere from $500 to $4,000 a day per girl, if you can believe it. If one tries to get away, she either disappears or we find her body beaten to death."

"What about somebody you've got in custody…can you turn them to give something on Wasp's death?" Holcomb asked.

"What custody? We almost never make a case against a gang member for human trafficking. Their 'ladies' are scared shitless – no way would one testify. If they have kids and a good number of them do, the gang keeps the kids as ransom to insure mom's continued cooperation.

"You gotta understand, this business is sadistic and brutal. We might have thought slavery went away after the Civil War, but it's alive and well right here in the good old USA. We call it human trafficking – but it's slavery pure and simple - and Houston has some of the best practitioners in the world. Once they get their hands on a girl – it's pretty much over for her and if she has kids – it's over for them, too. Most don't see their 30th birthday."

Nobody spoke for a moment - the reality of Dover's world was just a little too terrible to take in all at once. Finally, Director Huff broke the silence.

"So, you don't think it's possible some of the larger, more organized cartels are moving in on the Sierpe Gang?"

"Well, I didn't." Dover responded, "I didn't, but now I'm not so sure. Two things are making me rethink it. First, your twins were found in Oklahoma. That's way outside the Sierpe's usual territory. They don't even do much cross-country - that's where they move small numbers of girls from place to place – sometimes truck stops – sometimes motels for a few days - and then move to a new place. Sierpes have pretty much been local. The second is the text message your guy was able to recover from the burn phone you found."

"What do you mean?" Holcomb again.

"The text from Viper to Wasp." He showed the group the message on the screen. Caleb couldn't make heads or tales out of the half-words, slang, misspellings and profanity, but Dover translated. "It warns Wasp not to fuck up the 2 delivery because piranhas eat snakes alive."

"And that means...." Asked Caleb, still in the dark.

Dover answered, "Piranhas are native to South America – not Mexico or Central America. "Sierpe" is Spanish for snake. I think the Sierpe Gang may be teaming up with one of the South American cartels to traffic humans. Maybe the twin kidnapping was the first joint venture. When Wasp failed to deliver, the piranhas ate him alive."

Chapter Nine

Emma, Nana and Jesse took a walk around the Tallchief yard, with Deputy Moore trailing behind, keeping watch. They talked about their ghost mystery and tried to figure out what to do next.

Emma began, "We think Billy was killed or died sometime before October, 1863, but how do we find out for sure?"

Nana said, "Can't we look it up on the Internet?"

Emma laughed, "They didn't have the Internet back then, silly." Then she reconsidered, "Nana, you're right. There's all kinds of historical stuff on the Internet. Let's see what we can find."

Emma sat down in the office and booted up the computer. She fumbled around for a bit, Nana directing her to go to different websites. Finally, a frustrated Emma got up and sat the girl down in her place. "You drive, smarty pants. Obviously, you know much more than I do."

Nana giggled, as her fingers flew over the keyboard. "We know that Billy was stationed at Perryville – and it was someplace in Indian Territory – that's Oklahoma, right? So let's start there."

The two found that Perryville was today's McAlester, Oklahoma. In 1863 it had been a major Confederate supply depot in Indian Territory, and that Union General James Blunt attacked the Confederates there on August 26, 1863. The Confederate forces were defeated and had to retreat in a hurry, leaving everything behind. After the battle was won, Blunt burned the town to the ground.

"Wow, if Billy was in the middle of that – do you think he was killed?"

"It sure sounds possible. I wonder if there are any lists of people who died in the battle." Nana did some more of her computer magic, but was unable to find a casualty list or anything definitive about their ghost's son.

At dinner that evening, the Tallchief family discussed progress of the Chapman research. No one had any good ideas, and Jenny was opposed to telling Mary Elizabeth her son had died in the Battle of Perryville unless they were absolutely sure.

Halfway though dinner, Matt blew into the kitchen in the company of some hard-driving rain. He shook off his jacket and dripped water all over the kitchen floor. "Whooee – looks like we're in for a hell of a storm tonight. Channel 10 said it was gearing up to be a big one."

Jenny jumped up and turned on the T.V. Keeping on top of the weather in Oklahoma's wild springtime was as critical as it was routine. But this time, it looked like all the focus was well to their north and east – the zone of concern cut a wide swath across most of Eastern Oklahoma, Arkansas and even up into Missouri. Luckily for them, the weather center predicted only severe thunderstorms for the Shawnee-Tecumseh area. Jenny sighed relief, but kept the T.V. turned on low – the weather could change on a dime.

That night was a light and sound show par excellence. Thunder boomed continually, rattling windows and nerves. The sky lit up like the 4th of July with cloud to cloud and cloud to ground spears of electric light and the smell of ozone. The wind howled, and the rain came down in buckets. Curly Joe shook like a palsy victim and tried to hide in every nook and cranny. When he still couldn't get away from the noise, he tried to dig a hole in the floor. That would have been okay if he'd been outside, but he was trying to dig the hole in the newly refinished hardwood floor in the master bedroom. Caleb was not pleased. Jenny finally had to give the poor animal a tranquilizer to calm him down. Clue and Jesse just took the whole thing in stride.

****

Matt had wisely decided to spend the night at his brother's, rather than try to 'feel' his way home in the downpour. He was up and out early to get the Feed Store open, sure there'd be a good number of customers waiting for him. The Feed Store also sold and rented all kinds of farming and light construction equipment, and with the storm damage from the night before, most everything would be gone by 9:00 am. The Tallchiefs had been lucky – a downed tree branch or two but that was about it. Nothing major.

Caleb left even before Matt did. There'd been a severe, multi-vehicle accident involving at least two semis and several cars on I-40 during the storm and the highway patrol had asked PottCo for help in rerouting traffic.

The big news was the F-4 tornado that devastated southwestern parts of Missouri. Like the storm that had hit Joplin a few years ago, this storm paralleled I-44, but, thank God, it had not hit any major urban areas this time. It hop scotched its way up the highway, tearing up miles of countryside. No deaths were being reported, but some 200 rural homes and farms had been seriously damaged.

Later that morning, Nana and Emma did some more research on the Battle of Perryville. They found a small museum in McAlester dedicated to the Civil War battle and decided to visit it. After all, their trip to Van Buren had provided a gold mine of information – why not McAlester?

Deputy Moore agreed, although the girls could tell he'd much rather be out in the field with the other Pott Co deputies doing real cop stuff, than babysitting them. On the other hand, he thought, directing traffic was pretty boring work – maybe babysitting adults wasn't so bad.

The trip to McAlester didn't take long. The four pulled into the tiny museum's parking lot just as it was closing for lunch.

Ms. Partridge, curator of the Battle of Perryville Museum, was thrilled to have visitors. Apparently, she didn't get many. She pooh-pooh'ed the Museum's hours of operation and cordially invited her guests – even Jesse - into the small, jam-packed room. Emma groaned inwardly, how would they ever find anything in this mess? Ms. Partridge proudly handed them the official guest book to sign. "Looks like it's been more than a month since anyone stopped by," Emma noted as she signed her name, Nana's and Jesse's, too. Deputy Moore could sign for himself.

The museum, formerly a fast food restaurant that had gone belly-up years ago, was overly filled with Civil War era memorabilia. Every shelf, every table was filled to overflowing. The walls were covered with framed photos and certificates. At first, it looked like there was no rhyme or reason to it, but in fact, its arrangement flowed logically from beginning to end. You could tell that it had been a labor of love for this elderly woman.

"My great-great-granddaddy was in the Battle of Perryville," she said proudly. "He was an artillery man with Steele's forces – in charge of one of the two howitzers on the road north of Perryville. Blunt's no-account federals snuck up on his position in the middle of the night - night fighting just wasn't done in those days, you know – totally against the accepted rules. My grandfather's troops didn't stand a chance; they held out bravely for as long as they could and then skedaddled back towards Fort Smith. Then, if that wasn't bad enough, those damn Yanks stole what they wanted and burned down the whole town, did you know that?"

There was no doubt as to where this lady's sympathies lay. Emma and Nana nodded.

Emma told Ms. Partridge what a beautiful museum she had. Ms. Partridge preened, saying first her mother and then she had devoted many years to collecting, arranging and displaying the remnants of that grand battle - not that many appreciated it these days.

When Ms. Partridge finally ran out of steam, Emma explained that she and Nana were on a quest to find out what happened to a young Confederate assistant surgeon after the Battle of Perryville. Ms. Partridge was delighted to help them. Emma wasn't so sure she would have been quite so delighted had Billy fought for the Union.

The three spent the afternoon pouring through lists, journals, letters, and photos. Unfortunately, they didn't find any mention of Billy or of what happened to the surgeons following the August 26th battle.

Sensing their disappointment, Ms. Partridge told them not to be discouraged. Finding one person out of the many who fought was not easy – but she had several other sources she would call to see if she could get help. Emma thanked her profusely. Even Jesse put up her paw to thank the lady for her kindness. Ms. Partridge solemnly shook the shepherd's paw and then laughed. "Aren't you the polite one," she said, "you must be a Southern lady." Then she scratched the fur on Jesse's head.

****

Joe Holcomb motioned to Caleb to come into his office.

"What's up?"

"Just got a call from Hamilton in Bobbi Huff's office. The cells we got from those dirtbags we arrested at McRea's didn't have a whole lot on them – just some phone numbers, including McRea's."

"Damn, I was really hoping we'd get something," said Caleb, disappointment obvious in his voice.

"Well, we did get a couple of things – I mean we got that tip from Houston and now these Denver cell records seem to pull in Kansas City, and Atlanta. McRea's description of the Escalade looks like it might'ta come out of St. Louis. And now there's a new wrinkle - the automatic they recovered from the guard was part of a load of guns and explosives hijacked from Buckley Air Force Base near Denver. Huff said the Feebs are all over it – the guns – the cells – they think maybe organized crime."

"Maybe they *are* all part of the same network, Sheriff. Can't just be a coincidence...maybe this trafficking thing is a whole lot bigger and more complicated than we thought." Lines of concern etched Caleb's face.

****

"Jenny, Caleb, I remembered something." Nana burst into the master bedroom, Jesse and Zac following close on her heels. Her face was flushed and her arms waived frenetically.

Caleb, dressing for work, turned to her, astonished at her emotional intensity. "What, sweetheart? What did you remember?"

"Well" she started, obviously proud of herself, "sometimes on Saturday me, my mom and Katie would walk to the big flea market by the old railroad park. Mom'd give us a couple of dollars to buy whatever we wanted. The flea market was really big – there were booths and booths everywhere and a whole lot of really cool stuff. Once, I bought a pink purse with feathers and sparkles all over it. Will that help?" Nana smiled widely.

"That'll help a lot," Caleb assured her.

****

Holcomb, Jenny, Caleb and Emma sat around the Tallchief kitchen table. It was late and the kids had gone to bed long ago. The Sheriff's Office hadn't made much progress on finding Katie's murderer and kidnapper, and Holcomb thought by talking it through, they might find some clue or link they hadn't explored. He was right.

Holcomb started off the conversation, "So what do we know so far?"

Emma said, "We know the twin sister's name is Katie. We know they sometimes went to school and they had a teacher by the name of Sister Mary Agnes. We know Nana is a whiz with the computer. We know they must have lived somewhere close to a railroad park that housed a big flea market. We know their mother was into drugs.

Caleb added. "We know Katie's murderer was a member of the Sierpe – that means snake in Spanish – gang, and…"

Emma interrupted, holding up her hand like a schoolgirl. "Whoa, whoa - wait a minute." She thought about the exact words Nana had used a few days before. "Nana said her mother wanted her to stay away from the dealer on the corner because he was 'mean as a snake.' What if she meant he was a 'snake' – a Sierpe."

Holcomb mentally processed the information. "That would mean that Nana and Katie lived in the Sierpe's territory. Gangs are extremely territorial – no way would they let anyone else sell drugs on their turf. Could be they lived in Houston in Sierpe territory."

"Maybe this would help." Emma went over to the stack of pictures Zac and Nana drew. She shuffled through almost all of them until she came to the one she wanted – a drawing of two hands intertwined – fingers locked. She passed the drawing around the table.

"Is this a gang sign – could it be the sign of the Sierpe Gang?"

"No, that doesn't look right," replied Caleb, "but it does remind me of something. What is it?"

"Let me look at it, Caleb," said Jenny. She held it one way and then the other.

Caleb snapped his fingers. "I've got it! It's the logo of the Boys and Girls Clubs of America. We did a couple of safety programs for them last year. That's what it is – the Boys and Girls Club logo."

"OK – maybe we're getting somewhere. Maybe Sister Mary Agnes volunteers or teaches at the Boys and Girls Clubs. I think they do some teaching of homeless and street kids, don't they?"

"They do, indeed," agreed Sheriff Holcomb.

"So," Caleb summarized, "we know or guess – some of this stuff is really thin - the twins lived in

Houston somewhere in Sierpe's territory. They lived with their mother who is a drug addict. They attended school or at least went somewhat regularly to a Boys and Girls Club in their neighborhood and there was also a railroad park and large flea market within walking distance. They haven't been listed on any missing person reports, but if Mom is an addict, she might not even know they're gone."

"The way Nana talked about her Mom, I think she'd know," said Emma.

"Either way, what do we do next?"

"I know," said Caleb.

****

Caleb, Eric McBride and Chris Dover discussed possibilities in McBride's office at the OSBI. Even though the population of the Houston metropolitan area was more than six million, and covered 10,000 plus square miles, there were only two locations within or near the Sierpe's territory matching Caleb's criteria. Dover volunteered to visit both Boys and Girls Clubs and see if he could find a Sister Mary Agnes.

"Still have the twin's photo I sent you?" Caleb asked.

"Yeah, right here. Think Sister Mary Agnes'll know I'm a lapsed Catholic?" Dover asked. Caleb wasn't sure if Dover's concern was altogether in jest.

"Of course she'll know," responded McBride tonelessly, "nuns know everything."

"Shit."

****

A somewhat presentable Chris Dover stopped at the Boys and Girls Club reception desk and asked for Sister Mary Agnes.

"I believe she's just finishing her afternoon class," said the heavily built black woman with a big smile. "I'll see if she's available. Please wait right there," she pointed to a row of molded plastic chairs arranged in a perfectly straight line against the wall.

Dover had barely made it into a sitting position, when a very petite, slender – no, skinny – 50's something lady came at him in a quick militaristic march. She was dressed in street clothes, but even without her habit, there was no shred of doubt she was a Catholic nun.

"Uh-oh, this has got to be the good sister." He stood and offered his hand. "Sister Mary Agnes?"

Somewhat mollified by Dover's polite manner, she took his hand and turned her piercing glare down a notch or two. "Yes, that's me, young man. How may I help you?"

"Is there somewhere we can talk – someplace private? It's really important."

Generally, Sister Mary Agnes would never have considered going anywhere privately with a man she didn't know, especially in this neighborhood. But something in Dover's attitude or appearance caused her to make an exception this time. She waved him through the lobby and into her office where she settled down behind her tiny desk – queen of her domain.

Dover brought out his credentials and discretely showed them to her. He explained that he worked undercover most of the time – that's why he hadn't said anything to their receptionist outside. Sister Mary Agnes raised her eyebrows, but said nothing.

"Sister, do you know this girl?" He laid the photo of Nana in front of Mary Agnes.

"Oh, my Lord," she said, picking up the picture and clasping the crucifix that hung on a long chain across her chest. "That's Carly Anderson. She has a twin sister Katie, but Katie would never look this sweet."

She handed Dover the photo. "Are they alright? I've been so worried. They just disappeared several weeks ago and, come to think of it, I haven't seen their mother, either. I thought maybe they just took off. These street families do that, you know?" She sighed.

Dover nodded. He knew very well.

"Katie and Carly are really sweet children and have been through so much in their young lives. Please tell me they're alright."

Dover told the Sister his story. Mary Agnes, tears shimmering in her eyes, made the sign of the cross.

She stood up and turned toward her small window. She crossed her arms in front of her chest and stared out onto the basketball court where children were shooting hoops.

"I'll pray for Katie – that poor child. She really loved basketball, you know? …I should probably pray for their mother, too, even though she was a horrible mother and a druggie."

The good sister was silent for a long moment, "But you couldn't really dislike Linda Anderson. She was one of those lost souls – not a mean bone in her body and she did love those girls. She would never have allowed anything this bad to happen to them – not if she was alive."

"Do you have any information you can share with me, anything that can help us track down the mother?"

"Well," said the sister, "I do have their school records and an address. But you didn't get them from me, OK?"

****

"Caleb, Eric" Dover's voice came through clearly on McBride's speaker phone. "Your girl's name is Carly Anderson. She's ten years old and will be eleven on June 2nd. Her mother's name is Linda and a father is listed on the birth certificate – a Charles Morgan Bannerman. I ran the father's name and he doesn't have a criminal record – I did find military records for that name and age."

"And now for the bad news. Linda Anderson died three weeks ago from a heroin overdose. Didn't seem to be any signs of foul play, though - she's a known drug addict. I've asked our morgue to send a sample of Anderson's DNA up there, but there doesn't seem to be any doubt this is the twins' mother. Not sure where you want to go from here. I've got an address, but I can't check it out. It'd blow my cover."

Eric McBride responded, "Dover, thanks man. You've done more than enough. Can't tell you how much we appreciate it. Send me the mother's address and the information on the father. We'll take it from here."

"Let me know what you learn. This case is becoming personal," Chris said as he disconnected.

Eric and Caleb looked at each other and grinned. Finally, a break.

****

Nana brightened when Caleb told her that her name was Carly. She nodded vigorously as if knowing her name was the most important thing in her young life. Maybe it was. But the girl fell apart when Caleb told her about her mother.

Caleb wondered if he'd ever be able to share some good news with the twin– and just how much more bad news the kid could take. "I know life isn't fair, God," he prayed silently, "but come on."

Chapter Ten

It was late afternoon when Eric McBride wheeled the black SUV into the long driveway of the Bannerman farm. He and Caleb got out, "It's pretty warm for early April," he said as he looked across the infinite expanse of fields already green with shoots of wheat. This is beautiful country – flat – but beautiful." Eric and Caleb had driven from Shawnee – up I-35 into the heart of Kansas. They were both tired and car-weary. Caleb was a little apprehensive – what kind of guy would this be?

A pretty woman in her early 30's came out on the front porch, two little boys about five or six years old tumbled out the screen door after her. Another set of twins.

She smiled, "Can I help you?"

"We're looking for a Charles Morgan Bannerman, ma'am. Does he live here?" Eric pulled out his credentials and showed them. "I'm Eric McBride with the Oklahoma State Bureau of Investigation, and this is Caleb Tallchief, Pottawatomie County Undersheriff."

"Hello… Trish Bannerman," she said, extending her hand. "This is our farm – Charlie's and mine. Is something wrong?"

"We just need to ask Mr. Bannerman a couple of questions about a case we're handling. Is he around?"

"Yes," said Trish, concern registering on her face. "He's out back, trying to kick an old tractor back into life. I'll show you."

She instructed the boys to play nicely and led the two men around back. Even before they spied the legs sticking out from under the well-worn John Deere, they could hear Charlie's voice loudly cursing the tractor and all of its respective parts.

"Charlie, language. We've got company."

An attractive fair-haired man in his early 30's leveraged himself out from under the green machine, kicking up dust and dry grass. He pulled a rag out of his back pocket, rubbing his face and hands vigorously before offering an almost debris-free hand to Eric and Caleb. "Sorry," he said, "that damn tractor isn't old enough to lay down on me yet. She just needs a little kick in the ass."

"Charlie, these men are from the FBI."

"Oh," he looked more closely at the two men, "And what have I done lately to piss off the FBI?"

Eric brought out his credentials again and showed them to Charlie. "Actually I'm with the Oklahoma State

Bureau of Investigation and this is Caleb Tallchief, with the Pottawatomie County Sheriff's Office."

"How can I help you guys? Let's sit over here in the shade." The foursome made their way over to the cement picnic table, partially shaded by a huge 30 foot tall budding silver maple. Little helicopter seedlings covered the table and the ground, and occasionally spun past their heads. Charlie brushed them aside to allow the group to sit.

Suddenly screaming broke out from inside the house, and Trish Bannerman jumped up, yelling, "Connor! Jack!" and took off for the back door.

"Mr. Bannerman, there's just no easy way to say this." He laid the morgue photo of Linda Anderson before the young man. "Do you know this woman?"

Bannerman stared at the picture for a full minute. "Oh dear Jesus – that's Linda. Linda Anderson. What happened to her?"

"Can you tell me what your relationship was with this woman?"It was clear that Bannerman was shaken. His eyes shimmered with tears and his voice trembled a little when he answered. "My God…oh man." Taking another breath, Bannerman continued, "Linda and I were high school sweethearts in Conroe, Texas. That's a little town north of Houston." He picked up the picture and stared at it.

Trish Bannerman came out on the back porch with a pitcher of chilled lemonade and four glasses filled with ice. She set the tray down and when she saw the expression on her husband's face, she looked anxiously at Caleb and Eric.

"Are you okay, honey? Do I need to go back in – or call somebody?"

Charlie snapped out of his reverie, "No, honey. I think you need to hear this. Remember when I told you I was madly in love once when I lived in Texas before I went in the service? Before I met you? This is her." He showed his wife the photo.

Caleb asked, "Would it have been possible for you to have fathered a child by her back then?"

Charlie stared at him. He thought for a moment. "Well," he said, shrugging his shoulders, "I guess it would have been possible, but if so, she never said anything about being pregnant." He went on, "Linda and I dated all our senior year in high school and then went to UT Houston for two years. I was crazy about her – wanted to get married, have a family….but Linda would have none of it. She wanted the high life - go to Hollywood or New York – be somebody. We fought about it – a lot.

"She started hanging out with some really bad-boys. Linda was convinced they had movie connections – but I didn't buy it – these guys seemed more conmen than movie moguls. I tried to reason with her – but she said I was nuts. According to Linda, they were her ticket out of Texas and into stardom. After a while she started coming home high. I'd had enough. I told her to choose – me or the rats. She chose the rats – that was a blow to my ego, I'll tell you. Anyway, that's the last I ever saw of her."

Bannerman continued, "So – just to show her I went into the service- sort of a 'foreign legion' gesture." He smiled at his wife. "I was sure she'd write me to tell me how sorry she was and that she loved me and would wait for me – but she never did. By the time my tour was over, my dad had been transferred and my folks were back in Kansas City. There didn't seem to be any reason to go back to Texas, so I came here, went back to college at Kansas State. That's where I met Trish and finished my degree. We got married – what eight years ago?"

Trish nodded.

"And I never heard a word from Linda in all that time.

"God," he said looking at the dead woman's photo again, "she was so pretty and so sweet. What the hell happened?"

Caleb told the Bannerman's the whole story – of finding the twins, Katie, and then Carly. He explained how they were traced to Houston and finally of their mother's death from a drug overdose. Bannerman's name was listed on Katie and Carly's birth certificates.

"Oh, my God, those poor kids." Trish grabbed her husband's hand.

"Do you have a picture of Carly?" Caleb handed him the photo. "My God," he said, "she looks just like Linda."

When Eric and Caleb left an hour later, Caleb was feeling good for the first time in a very long while. He liked the Bannerman family; they were solid people. Charlie wanted to meet Carly right away and bring her home immediately. Trish agreed. McBride said they'd have to do some DNA tests – to confirm Bannerman was her biological father before they could go any further. Charlie agreed to do whatever it took. He kept looking at Carly's photo.

On the way back to Shawnee, Caleb thought to himself, "Maybe – just maybe - if everything works out, Carly just might get that second chance."

****

A week later, Caleb got the confirmation he'd been waiting for. Bannerman was Carly's biological father. Now he felt confident enough to share what he'd found with the person to whom it mattered most – Carly.

He found the twin playing computer games. "Hey, Carly – I've got some news for you."

"It's not more bad news, is it, Caleb." She'd been given enough bad news for a lifetime.

"No, sweetheart. This time I think it's really good news for you. We found your dad."

Carly was taken aback. Caleb was surprised to see a shadow cross her face. "It's not that creep Hickey, is it?"

"Who or what is a 'hickey.'"

"Oh, Caleb," the preteen giggled. "You know what a hickey is."

Carly's eyes unfocused for a minute. Her entire persona transformed - she almost seemed to step outside herself. "Caleb, I remembered something."

"What, Carly? What did you remember?"

"Hickey, he was this creepy guy who really liked my mom. He was always hanging around our apartment. We – me and Katie - thought he was awful …yuck!

"Well, after school one day, me and Katie was walking home. Stinky Hickey pulled up beside us in his crappy old Chevy and told us he was on the way to the Corner Mart to get us some groceries – sometimes he did that – I guess he thought it would make our mom like him - but he didn't know what food we needed. I didn't want to go with him, but Katie said we're almost out of food and we don't have any money. So we went. Hickey had a coke for us and we drank some – he only had one – so we had to share. He never bought us one for ourselves – he was so cheap.

"Anyway, I fell asleep and so did Katie. When we woke up, it was night and we were in a van driving someplace. There were two scary-looking men in the front. One of 'em was a Sierpe – he had tats all over his face. I'd seen him around – he was one bad dude. Katie started to scream – tat-face said if we didn't shut up, he'd kill our Mom. Just like that – he said he'd kill our Mom. He would've, too. We shut up.

"There were some other girls in the van, too. They were a little older than me and Katie, but they were really scared, too. They said we had to be quiet or everybody would get hurt. One of 'em said she heard that tat-face had cut off one girl's foot – just for talking back."

"They had some drinks and sandwiches in the van and every once in a while they'd stop by the side of the road and let us out one at a time to pee. Tat-face would always go with us and watch us use the bathroom. It was awful."

"After a long time we got to this old beat-up house. It was even worse than our apartment – didn't even have lights, but it had a bathroom."

Words were just pouring from Carly's lips. It was as if a dam had burst and her memories flooded into her conscious all at once.

"Katie said we had to get out of there – get back to Mom and warn her about Hickey and the Sierpes. Everybody was asleep, so we snuck into the bathroom and crawled out the window. It was high up on the wall. Katie boosted me up, but I guess we made some noise, because tat-face came into the bathroom just when Katie was coming through the window. I could hear him screaming and his flashlight going around. Then Katie disappeared back into the house. She told me to go – yelled at me to go and leave her – I didn't want to, but she said to get the cops and come back and get her. I didn't know what else to do – I didn't want to leave my sister, but I didn't know what else to do. There was yelling and screaming and I just ran."

Carly's eyes teared and she started to cry. "I ran and ran and ran until I found that church. Sister Mary Agnes said 'you're always safe in God's house,' so I ran in there. But, Caleb, I didn't remember to get the cops. I didn't bring the cops to save my sister. Now Katie is gone and it's my fault. My Mom is dead, too. I didn't remember in time to tell her about Hickey and the Sierpes."

Carly heaved big heartbreaking sobs into Caleb's chest. Emma came running into the room to see what on earth had happened, but Caleb waived her away.

He let the child cry until she had no more tears left.

"Carly, none of this is your fault." He lifted her chin so that his eyes looked directly into hers. He said harshly, "None of this is your fault, you understand? I will get the bastards who killed Katie and your mom. If it takes the rest of my life, I will get them. Do you believe me?"

The child searched Caleb's eyes and saw nothing but determination and more than a little anger.

"Yes, Caleb, I believe you."

****

The skinny man dressed in street attire "chic" sat in Interrogation Room 6, sweating profusely. The two cops standing behind the one way mirror weren't sure whether that was because he was worried or coming down from a high. Whichever – they'd work it to their advantage. Mike Chambers, veteran Houston homicide detective and Chris Dover went over Mike's strategy. "Don't think you're going to have too much trouble with this one, Mike. He looks like a bad guy wannabe, but never had the balls to make it. He also looks like he's about to piss his pants."

"Think you're right, Dover. He's got a sheet, but nothing violent. Some B&E, some possession charges, but that's about it. Never went to prison for any of it. He comes across kind of a pussy-rat, doesn't he?"

Dover laughed. "Well, maybe you can get him to catch and kill himself then."

"I, sir, will do my best – on both counts." Chambers squared his shoulders and put on his game face.

Mike slammed into Interrogation Room #6, file folder in hand, and threw it on the table. Photos of Linda Anderson, Katie Anderson and Carly Anderson, burst from the folder and landed in Hickey's lap. "Well, Duane, looks like you're in a lot of trouble."

"Whadda ya mean? I ain't done nuthin' man," the little man whined. "You can't keep me here – I ain't done nuthin..." Hickey's eyes darted around the little room and he couldn't stay still in his chair. "You gotta let me go, man."

"No, as a matter of fact, we don't, Duane. We're going to keep you for a very long time – probably the rest of your life. Well, you may be right. Maybe it won't be so long – death sentence appeals are moving through the system quicker these days."

Hickey started sputtering. "You ain't serious, man. I didn't do nuthin…"

Chambers picked up Katie's photo and shoved it in Hickman's face. "You're being charged in the kidnapping of the Anderson twins and the murder of one of them, Duane, that's about as serious as it gets."

"Hey, man – I didn't have nothin' to do with that… that wasn't me. I didn't do that – that was…" he suddenly realized what he was saying and shut up. "I need me a lawyer."

"Well, that's fine, Duane. But you know once you get a lawyer, I can't talk to you anymore– no room for a deal then. If you didn't do this – telling me who did will go a long way in helping you out. Right now, I'd say you're looking at the death penalty for sure. No way is any jury going to give you less – not where a dead kid is concerned and not here in Texas."

Duane Hickey gurgled.

Chambers pressed his advantage, "You want to call that lawyer now – or do you want to tell me about it?"

The detective stared at the little weasel. He could see the wheels turning inside his little peckerhead.

"I gotta think for a minute," he whined. "Man, this is bad – real bad."

Chambers gave him five. When he went back into the room, it smelled so bad he almost gagged. Had the guy pissed himself? Sweat dripped from Hickey's face and he pivoted his head left and right like a weasel sure a predator was close at hand. He lowered his voice to a whisper, "Look man, I can tell you a bunch of shit – but I gotta have immunity. You got to get me away from here, OK? Otherwise, I'm a dead man."

"Tell me what you got, Duane, and I'll see what it's worth to the D.A."

"Ok, man. You just got to keep this quiet and you gotta get me away from here," he repeated, eyes blinking rapidly.

Chambers nodded, "I understand, Duane. Before we get started, I need you to sign this saying you were advised of your Miranda rights and you waive the right to talk to an attorney before we talk. Then I'm going to turn on this recorder so I get it right, OK?"

Hickey scribbled his name.

"So tell me just what happened, Duane."

The little man breathed in a bushel of air. He started slowly and then his tale picked up speed. The longer he talked, the quicker he spoke. It was almost as if he wanted to tell his story – get it over with so he could get out of the danger zone.

"Well, me and Linda was tight. She was crazy about me, you know, but those little shitty bitches – they didn't like me - they was always getting' in my way. Telling Linda this and that…sometimes she'd listen to them – but mostly not."

"Anyways, me and Linda enjoyed a little 'uh' medicinal recreational fun, you know?"

Chambers said evenly, "Drugs."

Duane swallowed hard again. "Yeah, mostly meth and a little coke from time to time. No heroin – none of that hard stuff," Hickey looked at Chambers for confirmation he understood that Hickey didn't really do anything so bad. Chambers nodded.

"Well, we – me and Linda – we was into the Sierpes pretty good – owed 'em some money…they was happy to sell on credit – but if you didn't pay on time – they charged you double and then double again. They was starting to get – downright nasty is what they was getting'."

"One day this Sierpe dude, Wasp, come to my apartment. He say if we didn't pay up in two days, he's gonna take out what we owe in other ways – bad ways, real bad ways, you know?"

Chambers nodded again, surreptitiously checking to make sure the recorder was getting everything. "I think this dude's sweating even more, if that's possible" thought Chambers. Aloud he said, "Then what happened, Duane?"

"Oh, man. He said we could get straight with them, if," Duane realized he was on shaky ground here, "uh, he said we could – all I had to do man was pick up the twins and bring them to him and everything would be okay."

"And why did Wasp want the girls?"

"I don't know, man." Hickey was lying through his teeth. "I didn't think he'd hurt 'em. It was Wasp that did them bad things, man. Not me. You got to help me, man. Get me away from here. They hear it was me talking – I'm a dead man."

It took all the restraint Chambers had to keep from reaching across the table and killing the little bastard himself.

Chapter Eleven

The phone rang loudly and Emma and Carly raced to see who would get there first. Carly won, answered and then, laughing, handed Emma the phone.

"Is this Emma Cochran?" Emma acknowledged it was indeed she, just before she recognized the sweet high voice of Ms. Partridge on the other end.

"Oh, hello, Ms. Partridge. How are you?"

"Fine, dear. Just fine. And you?

"We're all good here, too, Ms. Partridge."

Pleasantries completed, the elderly lady got to the reason she'd called. "Well, sweetheart, I may just have some information on that assistant surgeon you were looking for."

"Super, Ms. Partridge. That's wonderful news. What did you find?"

"Several of my friends in the McAlester Genealogy Club were very interested in your project. One of them,

Mr. Parker, is just a whiz at these old Census Reports. He did quite a bit of digging."

Emma was growing impatient with all the background information, but did her best to conceal her frustration. "And what did Mr. Parker find?"

"Well," she said, obviously very proud of her accomplishment. "He found your young man listed on the 1860 Crawford County Arkansas Census rolls. William S. Chapman, age 13, white, male, born in Crawford County, unmarried, not handicapped nor a convict."

Emma thought, "I sure hope this isn't all she has for us." She let the curator continue.

"He was the son of a Benjamin Blackford Chapman, age 40, white, male, born in Alabama, married with three children, owner of an estate called Nine Oaks outside of Van Buren, Arkansas, part owner of Chapman & Samuelson Shipping, real estate and personal worth of $172,000. He owned six slaves (so his estate was probably not a plantation) named, Thomas, Sissy, Mabel, Matthew, Lancelot, and Digger. His wife was Mary Elizabeth Samuelson Chapman, age 33, white, female, born in Crawford County, married. The two other children were an Anna Marie, age 10 and Evelyn Rose, age 5."

Since they already knew this stuff from the Chapman family bible, Emma hoped the census expert, Mr. Parker, had been able to find out more.

"Thank you, Ms. Partridge. Were you able to find if William S. Chapman was killed at Perryville?"

"Don't rush me, girl. He didn't find anything else on William S. Chapman, but on the 1870 Census, Mr. Parker found William S. Chapman's cousin, Lawrence Bennett Chapman. He must have survived the Battle of Perryville, because he was listed as a doctor, living in Bentonville, Arkansas, married, with two children. If any of his records still exist, they just might tell you what happened to William – as they were so close during the War."

"That's a wonderful idea, Ms. Partridge," and it was. Something none of the Tallchiefs had thought of.

"I'll keep digging," promised the old lady. "Most fun I've had in a while. A real mystery."

Later that day Carly searched the Internet for a list of persons living in Bentonville, Arkansas with the last name of Chapman along with their addresses. Then she, Emma and Jenny carefully worded a letter, asking for any information they might have regarding William S. Chapman, Van Buren Arkansas, who was a cousin and contemporary of their Civil War era ancestor Dr. Lawrence Chapman. They included return, stamped envelopes and sent the letters off with a wish and a prayer.

****

The search for the twin's killer had dead-ended with Wasp, Sierpe second-in-command, and all-around piece of shit. Without a head, he was certainly dead and couldn't provide law enforcement with any leads into the possible connection between his gang and a South American - or any other - cartel. There hadn't been any new information for a couple of days, and Caleb was getting anxious. He'd promised Carly he'd get those responsible, but that looked less and less likely with each passing day.

He called Eric McBride to see if anything new had come up.

"Funny you should call, Caleb." Eric started. Caleb sat up, "What?"

"I got the weirdest call this morning from the Missouri State Bureau of Investigation."

"And...." Eric was having way too much fun stringing Caleb along.

"OK, remember that storm we had last week – the big tornado that ripped up a lot of the area around I-44?"

"Yeah..."

"As part of the somewhat gruesome clean-up effort, a county sheriff sent in some cadaver dogs to sniff around an abandoned house that had had occasional reports of lights at night, unusual traffic – that sort of thing. Sheriff thought there might have been some squatters hanging out there or kids partying....anyway he didn't want any dead bodies from the storm strewn around there rotting. Well, the dogs didn't find anybody killed in the tornado, but they sure as hell found two dead bodies buried near one of the outbuildings – and one of 'em – a black man covered in tats - didn't have a head."

"Hot damn – got to be the rest of Wasp. Got to be, right?"

"We won't know that until the DNA comes back, but I'd say chances are good. The other body was whole, but just as dead. Both of 'em killed with a 9mm Glock. How's that for divine intervention?"

"Hey, I'll take any help I can get. Call me as soon as you get confirmation, OK?"

McBride feigned hurt feelings "Don't I always? As Kojak would say, 'Who loves ya, baby?' I should get something back in a day or two at the most."

Tallchief hung up, elated at the discovery of the bodies. Maybe they could pump some life back into this investigation, after all. "Hot damn!"

****

"Do you think he'll like me?" asked Carly, dressing for her first meeting with Charlie Bannerman and his wife, Trish.

"How could he help but love you?" said Emma as she helped her little friend wind her hair into a French braid. "You're smart, pretty, and funny. Oh, did I say tough? Oh yes, and smart and pretty, too. Besides, he's probably just as nervous about meeting you today as you are about meeting him."

"My stomach hurts," she whined. "I don't think I can go."

Emma turned the girl around and looked right in her eyes. "Look sweetheart. Jenny, Caleb, Matt and I will all be there with you. Jesse, too. If this guy turns out to be a jerk, Jesse will just bite him on the butt. How about that?"

Carly laughed. "Would she really do that?"

"Probably not – unless, of course, he was a *real* jerk."

****

Emma carefully placed her glass of Chardonnay on the table in front of her and picked up her dessert spoon. She looked across the table at her handsome date as he took a sip from his glass and looked around, "This place is great, isn't it?"

Emma had to agree – the wine was wonderful, the dinner had been superb, the service perfect. The wine list contained hundreds of choices – many rare and unusual. OPUS Steakhouse, one of the most exclusive in Oklahoma City, had sure come by its reputation honestly.

The atmosphere, too, seemed designed for lovers – or those who hoped to be. The high-backed booths and low lights invited intimacy, the soft music encouraged conversation or touching.

Everything should have been perfect – but it wasn't.

Emma toyed with her Crème Brule. "I don't think I can eat another bite," she put the spoon down.

Logan looked at her. "You know, Emma. By this time I can usually get a feel for whether a relationship will be a go or a bust. With you – I just can't get a feel at all." When he realized what he'd just said, he added – "Uh, I didn't exactly mean that, I meant…"

"I know what you meant, Logan." Emma laughed. "I really like you – you're bright and witty and we have fun together, but there just doesn't seem to be a spark, does there?"

"Well, maybe not for you…"

"Oh bologna…I can tell."

Logan shrugged his shoulders, "You're right – I should never kid a kidder. So what're we going to do about it?"

"I know this sounds cliché – but how about if we just stay friends?"

Logan was a little disappointed, but it wasn't as if his heart were broken. They soon slipped into easy conversation. Logan talked about his plans - he really wanted to go into practice either on the east or west coast – he wasn't sure which.

"So why didn't you take a job out there after you graduated?"

"Truthfully?"

"Of course, truthfully."

"I wanted to learn how Jenny does it – how she can figure out what's wrong with an animal when no one else can. It's phenomenal. I sat in on one of her evaluations the other day – and for the life of me – I can't see how she figured it out – but she was spot on. How does she do it…do you know?"

Logan honestly wanted to learn how to diagnose like Jenny, she thought.

"Logan, I don't think you – or anybody- can learn to do what Jenny does. I think she's had the talent to read animals from the time she was a little kid – she just didn't know it. When we were growing up she'd bring home this sick kitten or that hurt dog or whatever, and she seemed to know just what to do to make it well."

Logan nodded.

"Then college and raising me got in the way – her natural skill kind of got shoved under for a while, but a couple years ago, Jenny …um …"

Logan broke in…"Yeah… the convicts… the rape… She killed one of them, didn't she?"

Emma nodded.

"Annie told me all about it. That must have been terrifying for her – hell, for all of you. Jenny must be one tough cookie."

"Yeah, well after that Jenny's skill came back - stronger than ever. I don't think Jenny even knows *how* she does it – she just does."

Logan thought about that for a minute or two, a resigned look crossing his face. He'd been afraid that would be the answer.

Then he shrugged his shoulders, accepting that he might never be in a league with his boss, and asked, "So Em, what is it you want? Is it the writing thing? Maybe try New York or give California another shot?"

The question took Emma aback. She really hadn't thought about it – anyway not in the last month or so since she'd come home. Home - Emma realized she'd never been happy in California –away from friends, family... Matt.

Damn.

****

"Dover," Caleb called his new buddy in Houston. "Did you hear there's a new lead in the Sierpe case?"

"No, tell me."

Caleb brought the undercover detective up to date.

"Good news, Tallchief. Maybe we'll get something we can use... we've got nothin' here – haven't found anything to link the Sierpes to organized crime yet. But we're still trying."

When Caleb disconnected, Dover sat looking at his cell phone for a while. Something was bothering him about this whole thing. Something he heard or saw?

What was it? He just couldn't put his finger on it – but he would. He knew he would.

Later that afternoon, Chris stopped in to see Sister Mary Agnes and let her know they had found Carly's biological father and that he seemed to be a good man and would take good care of her.

"Thank you, Christopher, for letting me know. I've been just heartsick about those girls – even their mother, Linda, misguided though she was – has been in my prayers. Maybe this is Carly's chance to have a little happiness in her life."

Click… there it was – that 'something' that didn't quite jive. It had something to do with Linda Anderson's death. He couldn't wait to get back to Mark Chambers and see if they could figure it out.

Chambers met Dover at a little off-the-wall place where they wouldn't be seen by anyone in Dover's circle of gangs, druggies or pimps. Mark brought the Anderson file with him. The two went over each paper separately. When Dover got to the transcription from Hickey's interview, he slammed his fist down on the table. "Here it is…what I couldn't remember."

"Well, you are getting old, man…"

"Remember when Hickey told us he and Linda only did meth and coke – never the hard stuff – never heroin?"

Chambers nodded – instantly catching the meaning. Under the cause of death, the M.E. had listed "Heroin drug overdose." Bingo – maybe they had a murder after all.

Chambers took his concerns to the M.E. Because of the possible gang, cartel, and human trafficking aspect, the M.E. consented to give Anderson's body a closer look. Since the initial take on the case was one of accidental death or suicide, the M.E. hadn't brought all his investigative tools to bear. This time he did. In addition to confirmation that she'd died from a heroin overdose, the M.E. found some latent bruising on her forearms and throat– she had to have been in a struggle just before her death. They also found several fingerprints on the body – two belonging to Wasp and one belonging to Viper himself.

****

The letter arrived ten days after the Tallchiefs sent out their request for information on William Chapman. The handwriting was tiny and spidery – almost indecipherable. Emma and Carly sat down together to read it.

> *Dear Miss Cochran,*
> *My name is Miss Thelma Hazel Chapman, and Dr. Lawrence Chapman was my great-grandfather. I apologize for my handwriting, but my eyes are not as sharp as they once were. I will be 97 this year and my hands shake a little when I write.*

William S. Chapman was great-grandfather's cousin. Their fathers were brothers and they were originally from Alabama. Dr. Lawrence Chapman was about ten years older than his cousin, William, and was already a doctor by the time Arkansas entered the Civil War. From the letters that survive from Dr. Chapman to his dear wife Charlotte, we learned that William S. Chapman died from shrapnel wounds at the Battle of Perryville in August, 1863.

Dr. Lawrence Chapman was captured along with the hospital wounded, but was soon released when his patients were turned over to Union doctors. By that time most of the fighting in Arkansas was over and Dr. Lawrence Chapman was wounded. He returned to his home in Bentonville in late September, 1863, where he lived out his life and was much loved and respected.

I enclose a copy of the letter Dr. Lawrence Chapman wrote his wife and wherein your William S. Chapman's death is noted.

Sincerely,
Miss Thelma Hazel Chapman
Enclosure:

Mrs. Lawrence Chapman
Bentonville, Arkansas
September 5, 1863
My darling Charlotte,
I write to you from the prison hospital at Ft. Smith. Please be assured I am being well-treated, as are our wounded. I have suffered a slight leg wound, but I am still quite able to perform my medical duties. Do not be overly concerned on my behalf.

The Union forces overran our hospital at Perryville in the early morning hours of August 27th and my patients and all medical staff were captured. As the surgeon in charge of the hospital, it was my duty to accompany my injured patients to their new location until such a time as I could transfer their care to a Union doctor.

I am assured that I am considered non-combatant, and when my patients are able to be placed into the hands of Union doctors, I will be released.

I regret to tell you that our good cousin, William S. Chapman, was accidentally killed by shrapnel during the Battle. He did not suffer, but died instantly. I shall miss him deeply. However, I implore you to make no mention of this, my dear, until such time as I return and can personally speak with William's uncle. I know you will understand my desire to see and talk to William's Uncle Dwight directly.

Please do not construe exclusion of my intimate feelings and thoughts from this letter as anything other than a concern that this letter may be seen by eyes other than your own. I have been told by several of our wounded, the federals often read the mail sent from its prisoners to their loved ones in order to gather useful information.

Thus, I am taking great care to write only those things which will cause no harm or embarrassment to anyone in our family should it be read by an outsider.

Your loving husband,
Lawrence

Jenny had entered the room as Emma and Carly finished reading the letter. Jenny was really disappointed. She wanted to be able to tell Mary Elizabeth that her son had survived the War and led a wonderful, happy life. She didn't know how she was going to break this news to the mother who had waited more than a century and a half for her son's return. It would be hard for her to hear that his life, too, was cut so short and in so meaningless a way. Her one-way conversation with Mary Elizabeth later that evening would be heartbreaking.

Emma, Jenny and Carly began packing up the Chapman research papers, photographs, and memorabilia. As Jenny looked at the Chapman family portrait, she asked. "Did anyone else think the letter from Lawrence to his wife was just a little odd – a little off-kilter?"

"Well, he obviously thought the Union soldiers might read it – he wouldn't have wanted to say personal stuff to his wife… is that what you mean?"

"Yeah, well, no - not really. Why didn't he want his wife to tell Dwight Samuelson that William had died?"

"Maybe he didn't want the uncle to have a heart attack or something," Carly said.

"Yeah, maybe."

Emma had almost finished packing the letters from Chapman & Samuelson Shipping and Drayage into their folder, when she came across two odd receipts from the same source, the Chicago Medical College. The first was dated July 21, 1865, for $2,840.00 in payment of tuition, room and board for the 1865 school year in favor of a Mr. Billy Samuelson, son. The second was dated July 1, 1866, for the 1866 school year - in the same amount and again, for Mr. Billy Samuelson, son.

"Dwight didn't have a son," said Emma, looking at the receipt and turning it over in her hands.

"Why would Dwight pay such a large amount of money for an expensive medical education for a son he didn't have?"

"No," said Jenny thoughtfully. "He didn't have a son."

The inconsistencies in the Chapman & Samuelson records continued to play on Jenny's mind all that evening. She was sure she was missing something – who was this Billy Samuelson? He sure wasn't listed in the family Bible. It didn't appear that Dwight Samuelson had any offspring. Why would Dwight spend so much money on someone nobody had heard of before? After all, $2,840 was a small fortune in 1865 and there was nothing to indicate Dwight had a serious charitable streak.

The more Jenny thought about it – the more it puzzled her. Then, in a flash of insight, Jenny thought, "What if Billy Chapman didn't really die at the Battle of Perryville, as Lawrence Chapman alleged in his letters home. What if he'd survived, but for some reason, Lawrence wanted the world to think Billy was dead? Maybe that was why Lawrence didn't want his wife to say anything to Uncle Dwight. Lawrence wanted to tell the uncle what had really happened and that Billy was still alive. That made sense of the Chapman letter and the payment to the Chicago Medical College. Billy had some medical training already at the side of his cousin, Lawrence. Dwight would have paid the college tuition of his nephew – actually it was probably Billy's inheritance anyway. Jenny was excited. This made sense. But why and how could they prove it? Where else could they look?

She asked Emma. "Do we know when Dwight Samuelson died?"

"No, but surely we can find out."

Carly sat down at the computer and tried to find out what happed to Dwight Samuelson. They had his date of birth from the family Bible, but after a couple of hours of searching – nothing. Carly did find several Civil War era Billy Samuelsons in her search, one in Little Rock, Arkansas, one in Illinois, two in Virginia and even one in Indian Territory. But there was no way to tell if any of these Billy Samuelsons were related to Dwight Samuelson.

"OK – this isn't getting us anywhere," said Jenny. "How about another road trip?"

Chapter Twelve

The music inside the "Skulls" was so loud and discordant; it was like an audio blast from tortured souls in hell. Chambers shook his head. "Much more of this and my brain will turn to jelly."

Chambers, along with several plainclothes Houston detectives and uniformed patrolmen, entered the club at midnight. About an hour earlier Dover had notified Chambers that Viper and his gang were doing some serious partying and it looked like they were going to be there for awhile.

Chambers had no difficulty locating his target and crew. Through smarting eyes, he could see they held court in the back of the smoke-filled room, "More than just cigarette smoke in here," Chambers mused. "One could get high just crossing the dance floor."

Viper was surrounded by three very young women – on second look, Mike thought - not really old enough to be women – they were just girls, really. All were heavily made up and dressed identically in ultra-short sequined white dresses – one petite blonde Caucasian, a tall slender black, and a beautiful caramel-skinned Hispanic. As the homicide detective approached, all three turned their gaze to the floor. None of them spoke. Viper snapped his fingers and the girls quickly rose and disappeared into the corner.

"Hey Viper, see you've got your girls to protect you tonight." Chambers chided.

"Man, they'se not for security, you know. They'se for other stuff," his lips curled into a smile but his eyes remained dead black.

"Yeah, I know what you use those girls for," Chambers added.

"They love me, man. They like to do what I say." Viper smiled broadly and settled back into his chair.

"Well, tonight, I guess they'll have to do without you." Chambers pulled out his handcuffs. "DeLon Robinson, you're under arrest…"

"You can't arrest me, you stupid fuck. Them girls are doin' what they like – do who they want – and that be me and my crew. Just you ask 'em," the black man laughed and turned around to make sure his 'crew' was right behind him. They were.

Chambers seemed oblivious to the Sierpes' proximity. "I'm not arresting you because of your girls, you piece of shit. You're under arrest for the murder of Linda Anderson."

For a split second, Viper's eyes widened – then settled back into their normal partially hooded stare. "You full of shit, man. Who that be - never heard of that bitch." He lowered his voice, "You betta watch it, man – you walkin' in some dangerous territory here."

"You threatening me, Viper?" Several of the plainclothes detectives moved into place and blocked the other Sierpes from their leader. Mike Chambers none-too-gently cuffed the black man and led him out of the nightclub, surrounded by the detectives and uniformed patrolmen.

"Hey, wifey," Viper called back over his shoulder. "Call my shapiro, bitch."

****

The Crawford County Courthouse Clerk looked up from her paperwork at the threesome standing in front of her counter. "May I help you," she said. Somehow her tone belied her words.

Jenny made eye contact and smiled. "Yes, we're sort of on a mission to find out what happened to a Mr. Dwight Samuelson, of Van Buren, following the Civil War."

Ms. Danvers rolled her eyes and inwardly groaned. She was definitely not impressed with their 'mission.' "People come in here all the time with 'missions,'" she thought. "I've got enough to do without this nonsense."

Aloud she said, "And what records specifically do you wish to research? We have many, many documents in this Courthouse and I can't direct you unless you can give me more specifics, you know." She stared unblinkingly over the top of her half-glasses.

"Not going to get a lot of help here," Emma thought to herself.

"Well, we know that Dwight Samuelson was born in 1820, and that he lived here in Van Buren. We'd like to find his will."

"Humph...we don't even keep wills here. But I guess you can't find his will if you don't know when he died. I'm guessing you don't know that, do you?" Ms. Danvers gave Jenny a look only disappointed school teachers could muster. Jenny shook her head.

"Guess you could start with the Death Registers. That might give you a starting point. You don't have much to go on, but it's your time." Ms. Danvers hoisted her ample figure out of the chair and led Jenny, Emma and Carly to a small room adjacent to her office. She gestured to a floor to ceiling wall of thick journals, each approximately 18" x 12" filled with pages and covered in dust. Emma and Jenny looked at each other in dismay.

"Here are the Death Registers. I've got to tell you, though - they're not always complete – especially around Civil War times. It was pretty chaotic back then, you know." Ms. Danvers turned and left them. She smiled insincerely as she said over her shoulder, "Be sure to put the books back where you found them," and then disappeared.

After several false starts, the three established a search process that seemed to work well – worked well, except for the fact they found no listing for Dwight Samuelson or William Chapman. They did find the listing for Mary Elizabeth, Anna Marie and Evelyn Rose, but that was all. For hours, they searched the years from 1863 through 1900 – but nothing. Carly despondently placed the last book back on the shelf.

They exited the tiny room, defeat obvious on their faces.

"Well, you really needed much more information to find someone from back then," Ms. Danvers intoned. "You'd be surprised at the number of people who come in here with only a name and expect me to find out what happened to their great-great-great grandmother's second cousin – once removed. As if I didn't have enough work to do." She gestured towards the paperwork on her desk.

Jenny could tell Emma was gearing up to say something sarcastic, so she headed her off, "Yes, thank you for all your help, Ms. Danvers."

Carly suppressed a giggle. Emma surreptitiously pinched her arm.

"You're right. We don't really know enough to do a proper search. We just didn't realize how difficult it would be." Jenny looked so disappointed and so earnest, Ms. Danvers thawed a little.

"Well dear, few people do - few people do. Do you know anything else about this man - other than just his name?"

"We know he had at least one sister, Mary Elizabeth Samuelson – married to a Benjamin Blackford Chapman. They owned the Chapman and Samuelson Shipping and Drayage Company here in Van Buren during the Civil War years and…" Jenny's voice trailed off. A light in Ms. Danvers eyes just went on.

"Chapman – as in the Chapman Cemetery – just north of town on Logtown Road?"

"I guess that could be," said Jenny. "We know the entire Chapman family was killed during the Civil War and only Dwight Samuelson survived."

"Well," said Ms. Danvers proudly, "I belong to the Van Buren Beautiful Society and one of our main projects each year is to oversee the cemetery grounds maintenance and records." From somewhere inside Ms. Danvers, a tap of enthusiasm turned - the lady obviously loved her Society.

Emma broke in, "Yes, we saw it when we came in off I-40. It's a beautiful cemetery."

"It takes a lot of work to keep it so pretty," said Ms. Danvers. You wouldn't believe some of the shoddy landscape work done up there some years. This city and its 'take the low bid' attitude." She shook her head disgustedly.

Emma, Jenny and Carly smiled politely.

"Anyway, the cemetery land was donated by the Chapman family – I think sometime not long after the Civil War. Let me call Beverly over to the County Clerk's Office and have her check the Land Records. She belongs to the Beautiful Society, too, you know."

Not more than 15 minutes later, Ms. Danvers – telephone to her ear, waved the threesome over to her desk. She was smiling broadly as she made the 'thumbs-up' gesture.

"Yes, yes," she crooned, placing her hand over the receiver. "I was right. The land the cemetery sits on was donated to the town by a Mr. Dwight Samuelson in his will probated October 15, 1872. The land was formerly called Nine Oaks and was the home of the Benjamin Blackford Chapman family. Mr. Samuelson must have inherited the property when the rest of the Chapman family died. He donated it to the City in perpetuity as long as the City of Van Buren named the cemetery for his sister's family, maintained it in good order and cared for the graves of the Chapman family."

Emma and Jenny broke into wide grins. Carly jumped up and down, clapping her hands in excitement.

"Is Beverly looking at the will right now?" asked Jenny.

"Beverly, do you have the will in front of you?" Ms. Danvers nodded in the affirmative.

"Would you ask her who Mr. Samuelson left the rest of his estate to? This could be very important to us in our search," Jenny looked pleadingly at the Courthouse Clerk.

"Beverly, do you have an heir listed?"

"Yes, wow – that's a lot of money. Yes, I've got it. Thanks, sweetie. I'll see you Saturday."

By way of explanation, Ms. Danvers said, "We've got a meeting of the Van Buren Beautiful Society on Saturday. As a matter of fact, the Chapman Cemetery is the first item on the agenda..."

Carly stared at Ms. Danvers. "Oh yes, oh yes. Well, Beverly found out some really interesting information for you. Mr. Dwight Samuelson died on September 25, 1872, and left Nine Oaks to the City of Van Buren and the remainder of his estate to Dr. Billy Samuelson of Scullyville, Indian Territory. His estate was worth \$183,425.00 in 1872. In today's dollars that'd be about \$2.5 million."

****

"What in the world is a Scully?" asked Carly on the way home.

"Beats me," replied Emma, "guess you'll have to do some more of your internet magic."

Carly found that Scullyville was a small town just a few miles west of the Arkansas border in Oklahoma - Indian Territory in the 1860's. It wasn't named for a defleshed head, as the phonetics of the name might indicate, but for the Choctaw word "iskuli" which, loosely translated, meant 'money.' From 1832 when the

Choctaws were forced west into new homes in Indian Territory, it was the site of the government agency that distributed annual allotments to the Choctaws. And as commerce follows money, a flourishing town soon built up around the agency building. Today, Scullyville was little more than a ghost town - just a few scattered homes and an abandoned cemetery. But in its heyday, it was a thriving frontier settlement.

Carly also found that Dr. Billy Samuelson of Scullyville had played a prominent role in the town's history. He was the only doctor for many miles around. He established a medical center for the treatment of all patients – regardless of whether they could pay or not. And he was an outspoken advocate for Native American rights at a time when that stance was not popular. His date or place of birth weren't included in the on-line biography, but he married, had four children – three of whom lived to adulthood - and died in 1907 at the home of his eldest son, Dr. Liam Samuelson.

"This has got to be our Billy," said Emma, grinning broadly.

"Got to be," agreed Matt.

"Think we can track down any of Billy's descendents?" asked Jenny.

"Well, I know somebody who can," said Emma.

"Ms. Partridge!" they all shouted in unison.

****

Later that evening after Zac had been bathed and put to bed, Jenny, Emma and Carly were watching reruns of 'Dancing with the Stars.'

"How can they watch that crap," grumbled Caleb to himself. "It's bad enough the first time around, but to watch it even after you know who wins…well…" His commentary was cut short by the strident ringing of the kitchen phone. Jenny got it and, called "Hey, Em. It's for you. It's Dr. Sloan."

"Who's Dr. Sloan?" asked Carly, concern in her voice. "You're not sick, are you?"

"No," Emma assured her, fighting the overly-soft sofa cushions to get vertical. When she finally extricated herself, she added, "That doggone couch is like quicksand. If any of us disappears – the first place we'd better look is under the cushions." Then to explain to Carly, "Dr. Sloan's a college professor and a friend of mine."

Jenny handed off the phone and returned to the show.

"Hey, Dr. Sloan. It's really good to hear from you." Sloan's voice evoked a picture in Emma's mind. She could see the short, round lady – her hair obviously dyed black. She'd be dressed in some outrageous outfit – but on her it would seem right. She'd have a cigarette in one hand and the phone in the other and her body would be in motion- probably pacing as she talked. Amanda Sloan had been a Hollywood star many years ago – maybe not an "A List" star, but one who not only survived, but thrived, in the cutthroat world of acting. Emma adored her.

"Hello, dear. You're right – it's been much too long since we talked. I just don't keep up with my former students as well as I should."

They exchanged news for a few minutes and then Dr. Sloan got to the reason for the call. "Well, Emma, I want you to tell me exactly what happened when you went to visit Thomas Reynolds out in California. I understand he didn't even take the time to talk with you – nor did he read any of your scripts – which by the way are far superior to any that his band of idiots turns out."

She didn't even take a breath before she launched into her next series of comments. "When I heard that – it really made me quite angry. You know, I helped that man get started and he, more than anyone else, should know just how important personal introductions are. You can have all the talent in the world, but if you can't get in to see the movers and shakers – that talent gets you absolutely nowhere." Sloan stopped her tirade long enough to take a breath.

Emma took advantage of the momentary opportunity – they were, as she remembered – few and far between. "Uh, Dr. Sloan, how did you know Mr. Reynolds wouldn't see me? I really haven't told anybody about it and, well, to be truthful – I was sort of embarrassed to get the brush-off from him."

Silence on the other end of the line. "Oh my – now I've done it. You know, people shouldn't ever tell me things and then expect me to keep it a secret. I just haven't the ability to keep my mouth shut. I'm so sorry."

"Okay, who ratted me out?" Emma asked, but in her heart – she knew.

"Well, that very nice and I might add, very good-looking young man with the dark hair I met when we were looking for you? It's an M-name – Mike or Mitch or something like that….well, he called and told me all about what happened and that Tom wouldn't even see you and that he thought I might be able - I think the words he used were -'put the screws to *Reynolds and O'Brien* so at least they'd read your works. You know he thinks you're about the best writer there is and I had to agree that you do have a lot of talent. That sweet boy must really be in love with you."

Dr. Sloan took a long breath. Emma never met anyone who could talk as long, or as loud without breathing as she. "Must be her stage training," Emma thought randomly.

Her former advisor continued, "Anyway, your young man asked me to please, please not say anything –especially to you…. about this - and now it looks like I've messed up that part of my assignment, doesn't it? You will forgive me, won't you, dear?"

When Emma hung up some fifteen minutes later, she told Jenny. "I'm going to bed. I'm really tired and I've got some thinking to do."

Jenny and Carly just looked at each other – Emma never went to bed before midnight. What was that all about?

Even later that night, Caleb and Jenny climbed into bed. The house was quiet – everyone seemed to be asleep. Jenny snuggled up to Caleb's backside – spooning. It was her favorite cuddle position - holding Caleb close.

Pretty soon, Caleb's breathing slowed and became more regular, Jenny poked his shoulder - "so what *are* we going to do about Matt and Emma?"

Caleb groaned and rolled over to face her.

"Jen, how about just for this one night – we quit worrying about Matt and Emma, or Carly, or Jesse or ghosts or anybody else and concentrate of taking care of ourselves?"

"Oh," Jenny responded seeing the fire kindling in Caleb's eyes, "what just what kind of care did you have in mind?"

"This kind," and Caleb starting kissing her face while his hands pushed her nightgown up. Jenny laughed and pulled him toward her. "OK, big guy – just you and me..."

Much later, Jenny and Caleb lay side-by-side – breathing still elevated but passion at last satisfied. With a contented sigh, Caleb rolled over on his right side and Jenny snuggled up against his back. She threw her arm across his waist and drifted into a contented sleep.

Suddenly, Caleb flipped over, poked her shoulder and said, "So what *are* we going to do about Matt and Emma?"

Jenny groaned, sat up and smacked Caleb with her pillow until he begged for mercy. Caleb was still chuckling when Jenny fell back to sleep.

****

Jenny waylaid her sister at the breakfast table the next morning. Zac was already hard at it - perched on a regular sized chair – his chin level with the top of the table - no more baby chair for this boy. He was happily munching a bowl of Cheerios in a most Zac-like fashion. First, he'd dip his spoon into the cereal bowl, get some milk in it, and then his chubby little fingers would pick up a couple of the soggy 'O's' and put them on the spoon. If luck and gravity were on his side, the whole thing would then go into his mouth.

Emma stumbled in, yawning - a sleepless night reflected in her red, puffy eyes. She kissed her nephew on top of his head and filled her coffee mug.

Jenny let her have a few seconds before she began the interrogation.

"OK, Em – what's going on with you and Logan Penn?"

Emma laughed, intending to blow off Jenny's question with a smart-aleck response, at least that was what she had *intended* to do until she saw the steely glint in her sister's eyes. Emma learned at an early age that you never – ever - messed with Jenny when she had "that look."

She sighed. "Truthfully, Jenny, nothing. We've gone out a couple of times, that's all. He's a great guy and we've had a lot of fun together, but… we're just friends - that's all it is."

"You sure?"

Emma nodded and took a sip.

"Positive. In fact, I think one of the reasons he asked me out in the first place was to find out how you work your magic. He'd like to be that good – to be as good as you – it's the reason he came to Tecumseh. He's got his mind set on bigger and better places."

Jenny smiled. She knew Logan wouldn't be satisfied living in rural Oklahoma all his life, but she was surprised to find *she'd* been the draw that brought him to her Clinic.

"So, what'd you tell him?"

"Just that you had this special intuition – that you've always had it – ever since you were a kid. It's a talent - kind of like a concert pianist. It was just something you were born with and no amount of training could duplicate it. You've got it – or you don't. And you, Jenny Tallchief, have it in spades."

Jenny thought a minute about that. "Did he buy it?"

"Sure – it's what it really is, after all. Just a natural talent." Emma smiled over the top of her coffee cup.

The sisters sat in companionable silence for a couple of minutes. Then Jenny got to her real question. "So what're you going to do about Matt?"

Emma's eyes turned soulful. "Boy, I've really messed up that whole thing, haven't I?" When Jenny didn't disagree, she went on. "One thing Logan asked me the other evening when we were having dinner at OPUS in Oklahoma City– that's really a fabulous place, by the way – you should get Caleb take you there..."

Jenny gave Emma 'that look' again – she wasn't about to be sidetracked.

"Ok – one thing Logan asked me was what did I want – did I want to live in California or New York – and write scripts for a living? What did I want my life to be?" Emma put her mug down.

"And you know what – I knew right then I wanted to be with Matt - and now I've screwed it up so completely – he'll never have me back," and the tears began streaming down her face. "Did you know, Matt even called Amanda Sloan to try to get her help again – he loves me that much. To hell with those damned scripts..." Emma couldn't finish the sentence. She sobbed.

Carly sauntered slowly into the kitchen, rubbing the sleep from her eyes and yawning. Suddenly she came to attention, "Did you say Matt," she looked around frantically, "Is Matt here?"

A panoply of expressions played across her face - first, excitement. It was obvious she had a serious Matt-crush going on. Then dismay - Matt certainly couldn't see her in her pj's and bunny slippers. OMG-she'd never be able to face him again. The girl spun on her heel and fled toward her room and the shower.

Chapter Thirteen

Dover ate a late lunch alone at the McDonald's on 34th. He sat with his back to the wall, but where he could watch the comings and goings of the Sierpes on the street. They were an active bunch; he had to give them that.

The glass doors to the fast-food restaurant whooshed open and a jumble of street smells temporarily overpowered those of the Chicken McNuggets. Dover glanced around at the customers. There was something familiar about the young woman placing a large order at the counter. At her side was a toddler – maybe two years old. He held tightly to the girl's hand.

The girl was reading an order from a paper – it was taking some time – had to be a lot of food. "Wanted to get it right," he thought. She seemed subdued and smiled only when talking with the small boy. Even from across the room, Dover could see she had a black eye. She nervously pushed back her blonde hair and the gesture revealed colorful bruising on her neck.

Suddenly, he had it – why she looked familiar. She was one of the three women with Viper when they arrested him last Saturday night. Without her heavy make-up and here in the daylight, she looked even younger. "Couldn't be more than seventeen at most," he thought. He returned his gaze outside, yup – there was Carla – Viper's 'wifey.' She was about twenty, Hispanic and almost as vicious as the Sierpe's gang leader himself. Her eyes were glued on the white girl at the counter. As Viper's wifey, she was responsible for all new-girl training and for keeping them in line. "This must be one of the new girls," Dover thought, "and from the beating she'd obviously had - one that is proving to be a little difficult."

As the new girl stood aside waiting for her order, she held the baby tight and gazed slowly around the room. Her eyes paused for a moment on Dover, puzzled, like she knew him from somewhere – but not sure where. Then the server called her number, she turned, quickly retrieved her bags of hot food and went outside with the little boy. She didn't look back.

On and off for the next week, Dover made a point to visit the McDonalds on 34th. Each time, new-girl came in to get the 'crew' something to eat. Twice she had the toddler with her. Each time she made eye contact with Dover and in that gaze, Dover believed he saw a cry for help. In that moment, Chris Dover made a decision. He was going to help this woman and her son. It was probably going to blow his cover, but he was ready to get out of undercover work anyway. He'd had enough. He'd seen enough of the underbelly of humankind to last a lifetime. He knew he was starting to let his feelings show – starting to be more careless. And in this business, carelessness meant death.

On the next Saturday, Dover made sure he was in line behind 'new-girl.' He wouldn't have much time to talk. He drew close and whispered, "If you're in trouble, I can help. I know about the Sierpes."

The girl froze in place, glanced nervously around and then slightly nodded her head.

As the two waited for their food, Dover said, "Act like I'm hitting on you."

She nodded.

"I can take you out of here right now – out the back," he assured her.

She shook her head. "I can't – they've got my son."

Dover grimaced. Damn those pieces of shit. Keeping a girl's child hostage to assure her cooperation was SOP in human trafficking gangs.

"OK, next time we're in here and you've got your boy, here's what we'll do…"

****

Dover got the okay to extricate the young woman and her son from the Sierpes. He and his friend and fellow detective, Sally Merchant, staked out the McDonalds every day. Like clockwork, 'new-girl' came in, ordered and left with the take-out. For the first two days, she was alone.

On the third day, the young blonde with her fair-haired toddler in hand, entered the order line. Sally fell in right behind her. She waited until the two of them reached the counter, ordered, paid and when they stepped over to the side to wait, 'new-girl' quickly picked up her child. The three ran behind the counter, out through the kitchen and into the waiting black SUV.

As soon as new-girl, her son, and Sally turned toward the kitchen, Carla and two of the Sierpes slammed into the restaurant lobby. In the crowded room, Dover had no difficulty tripping the two men. By the time Carla shoved her way through the crowd, the kitchen, and reached the alley entrance, 'new-girl' and her son had disappeared. Dover walked out the front door, whistling.

The undercover cop smiled to himself as he walked down the street toward the waiting black undercover van. He thought, "I bet there'll be a hot time in the old snake den tonight." Then he broke into a grin – best he'd felt in years.

****

'New-girl's' name was Sherry Marie Zane. She'd come from a small town just west of Houston. When she was fifteen, she'd been swept off her feet by the football team's senior star player. He told her he was head-over-heels in love with her – that was, until she got pregnant. Then he wanted nothing to do with her. He told her if she exposed him as the father, he'd make sure everyone in their small town knew what a slut she was. Who'd they believe - the town's football star – or some cheap little tramp? Sherry was terrified. Her parents were strict church-going people and would never have understood. Instead of telling them, she ran away and wound up in Houston and on the streets.

After her baby was born, Sherry's life became even more desperate. She had to feed her son Jaime; she had to take care of him. That's when Carla stepped in. For almost a year, Carla bought Sherry groceries, helped her out with rent, and took care of her and the baby when they were sick. She was the girl's most trusted confidant. All the time Carla was trying to convince Sherry to come over to the Sierpes. Carla told her that being a part of the Sierpe crew was great. They provided security, a good home for her son, plenty of food and a good income. They were like family – only a family that would never judge her. It sounded so good to the lonely, desperate young woman. But, Sherry said bitterly, it was all lies – nothing but lies. Carla had said whatever she thought Sherry needed to hear. Once inside the gang, Sherry found herself in hell – a hell with no escape.

The Sierpe gang prostituted Sherry out with several johns a day – usually six days a week. She was one of their high-end girls – their best earner. No problem finding customers, they liked fair-haired, white girls best. She earned $150 a trick, but none of the money came to her – all of it went to Viper. If she protested, she was beaten and there was the constant threat they would harm her little boy. Once, Viper slapped Jaime – just to watch Sherry's reaction. He thought it was funny.

Some of the things Wasp and Viper had done to the few girls who stood up to them were beyond belief. When a girl was going to get 'punished' for some infraction, the Sierpes would make everyone watch. Usually, it was a beating, but once they cut off a girl's foot – with the poor victim awake and screaming the whole time. It made Sherry throw up. She couldn't sleep for days. Sherry didn't know what happened to the girl after that – she just disappeared and nobody talked about her.

Terror was Sherry's constant companion and the Sierpes liked it that way.

****

In her second interview, Sherry told Dover the reason she'd decided to talk to him was because she knew she had to get away – both for Jaime and herself. She'd seen what the Sierpes had done to that mother who came looking for her twin daughters – seen with her own eyes – how Wasp and Viper had held her down and injected her with a lethal dose of heroin. They laughed about it. She knew that could easily be her fate, too, and then what – they'd sell her son to somebody – maybe even somebody outside the country. That's what they did to the twins.

"You witnessed that?" Dover wanted to be clear about what he was hearing.

"Everybody did. Viper said it was a 'teaching moment,' whatever the hell that meant." Even though Dover knew how things worked inside gangs, Sherry's story got to him. He was hesitant to ask her to testify, knowing the dangers she faced and the way she'd be treated by defense attorneys. But he knew he had no choice.

"Sherry, would you be willing to go to court and testify about what you saw?"

"Dover, I understand the risks and I know Viper's attorneys will try to make me look like a druggie whore whose testimony can't be trusted. Even Sierpes told us that – just to show it was impossible to get away and even if you did, nobody'd believe you. I never ever did drugs, but they'd try to make it look like I did. I know how sleazy Viper's lawyers are. Hell, they were some of my most frequent johns."

Dover was impressed by Sherry's spunk and her savvy. "I guess with everything she's been through – she'd have to be," he thought to himself.

"I knew when I made up my mind to leave; I'd have to turn witness against the Sierpes. That'd be the only way I could make sure they're put away where they couldn't come after Jaime or me. If they get off, I'm dead and so is my son."

"So I thought and thought about how to do it. How to get some evidence. I even prayed about it, if you can believe that. God works in mysterious ways – my father always said that. And he was right; the answer came when one of my johns forgot his cell. It was a good one, too – had photo and video on it. I took it and hid it, hoping I'd be able to get some good stuff to use against the gang – so it wouldn't be just my testimony, you know? They were always talking about how they did this or that – robbed or beat up somebody – they didn't care who heard. They thought nobody could touch 'em – nobody would be stupid enough to testify. But I had to wait until I was sure I could get something that would really do it – I only had the battery power left in the cell. Once it was gone – I wouldn't have another chance."

"And did you get anything?"

"Yeah," she said smiling. "When that lady came looking for her kids, I hid up in the loft, and got the whole thing on video."

****

Sure enough, Ms. Partridge and her band of genealogists came through with flying colors. Within two weeks, the Tallchief family had a listing of Billy

Samuelson's descendants – all four generations of them. Ms. Partridge also provided addresses and phone numbers for those still living in Oklahoma.

Jenny, Emma, Carly and Matt crafted a letter and sent it to each family on the list, briefly outlining their research so far and asking for any additional information the family might be willing to share. The four of them discussed whether they should say anything about the spirit living in the rocking chair, but decided against it. After all, they didn't want the Samuelson families to think they were crackpots – they would just say they were intrigued by the initials carved on the rocker's underside. The rest was pretty straight-forward; straightforward that is, if they skipped the part where Clue found the wicker basket.

A week later Jenny, Emma, Carly and Matt stood on the front porch of the Samuelson home in McAlester, Oklahoma. Ben Samuelson, Billy's great-great-great grandson, had lost no time calling Jenny just as soon as he read their letter. He was the family historian and couldn't wait to hear more about his ancestor's early years. His unbridled excitement clearly transmitted itself over the phone line.

"You know, in all our family tales of Billy Samuelson and his wife Lucy, there have been many wonderful and wild stories. They led quite an exciting life during territorial times. He must have been one hell of a character." He laughed, obviously proud and maybe even a little envious of the man and the times in which he had lived.

"But we never knew about Billy's roots – his family before he married my great-great-great grandmother. It was all a blank. Now we'll know." The two families made arrangements to meet just as soon as they could.

A pretty, blonde teen met the Tallchiefs at the door of the Samuelson house. She introduced herself as Evelyn Rose and Jenny smiled. Mr. Samuelson – Ben – and his wife Emily warmly were waiting in the den. Family memorabilia, including some turn of the century photos and framed newspaper articles regarding Billy, decorated the walls. As a way of starting the conversation, Ben told his visitors about his recent family history – his brother's family, his mother and dad and their grandfather, Liam. According to Ben all of the Samuelson families were successful and well-liked. If there were any misfits or miscreants; he didn't say, and Jenny didn't ask.

Emma presented them with the letters from Billy to his mother and his uncle, the locket with hair inside, the papers from Chapman and Samuelson Shipping and Drayage and, most treasured of all, the Chapman Family Bible. Then they told Ben and Emily their story.

As he listened, Ben held the Bible in his hands, turning it over and over. When they finished, he said, "I can't tell you how much this means to me." His voice was choked with emotion.

"I have Billy's original journals – those he wrote about living in Eagle Town and medical college and then Scullyville – but nothing before the Civil War. This completes the picture and answers many of the questions I had after reading his journals."

Ben handed the journals to Jenny. She opened the one on top and leafed through the pages. She thought to herself how happy the spirit of Mary Elizabeth would be if she could hear – in Billy's own words – what happened to her lost son – how he lived his life – his thoughts and dreams.

So, she took a chance. "Mr. Samuelson, I know this is a lot to ask, but there's a lady in my town – she's probably been the most important person in all our research. She would love to hear the words written here. But she's place-bound and can't come to you to read them."

Jenny paused and looked into the eyes of Billy Samuelson's great-great-great grandson. "Would you allow me to take these home and read them to her? It would mean so very much."

Ben Samuelson thought about the request for a couple of minutes. "You know, I've been real protective of these journals – they're really important to me. But ..." he looked at the photo of Billy on the wall, "something tells me I should make an exception for this lady – whoever she is."

"Are you sure, Ben?" asked his wife, bewildered by her husband's decision. "You've never let those journals out of your sight before."

"Yeah, I'm sure." Samuelson turned to Jenny, "Just promise you'll take good care of them, OK?"

And so, the deal was struck. Jenny carefully took charge of the journals and promised to return them by the end of the next week.

Chapter Fourteen

Jenny rocked in the old chair and began reading aloud to the spirit of Mary Elizabeth from the first of the dozen or so journals written by her son so many years ago.

Journal

September 25, 1863

I am reborn today as a Presbyterian missionary. Father will turn over in his Episcopalian grave and lament his failure as a parent.

I begin this journal in my new life as Billy Samuelson, nephew of Dr. Thaddeus Springer. It is only fitting that I do so, as nothing of value remains of my previous life – all I love has been taken from me, murdered either by this horrible war or burnt out of existence by those who would take advantage of the country's suffering. Therefore, I am utterly determined never to return to those places of heartbreak memories, but to begin anew and forge what future there may be by personal dedication and fortitude.

I enter only this part of my history as it came to me after I had arrived in my new life and was related to me by Dr. Thaddeus Springer. I do not remember much about the journey to this remote spot, being overcome with fever and pain for most of the time, but Dr. Springer just this morning sat with me as he examined my wounds and explained how I came to be here.

I was badly wounded by shrapnel just outside the field hospital where Cousin Lawrence and I were doing our best to tend to our wounded comrades. Dr. Thaddeus Springer, en route to Eagle Town where he was to begin his missionary service under the guidance of Father Cyrus Byington, had been delayed in his passage through the city by the battle and volunteered his services to help in the hospital.

By this time, it was clear the Federal forces would overcome our position and we would have to vacate the city. Cousin Lawrence determined my wounds were too severe to allow me to retreat, and fearing for my well-being as a prisoner of war under the harsh hands of our enemy, entreated Dr. Springer to take me in as part of his retinue. Cousin Lawrence told Dr. Springer he would report me as dead and beseeched Dr. Springer to call me Billy Samuelson, my dear mother's family name. Dr. Springer, realizing that his failure to accede to this request would likely result in my death, agreed to the charade and, with the assistance of Old Thomas, took me away in the dark of night. For the next ten days, the Springer family tended to me as I lapsed in and out of consciousness. When the Federals came looking for any remaining Confederate soldiers, Dr. Springer told them I was his nephew, Billy Samuelson, who was part of his family of missionaries to the Choctaw Nation and that I had been wounded by misplaced cannon fire.

Fortunately this was a highly believable story, as there were many innocent civilians wounded or killed during the battle. Sensing a need for urgency to get away from the suspicions of the Federal officers, Dr. Springer elected to continue his trek toward the Nations as soon as I could possibly tolerate the travel. I am told we came by wagon, over somewhat treacherous land, crossing several rivers, and in unbearable heat, but at last we have arrived safely in the small conclave of buildings that constitutes the Stockbridge Mission and Eagle Town. Old Thomas died while crossing the Little River, being swept away by the strong current.

I am now arrived in the missionary center of Eagle Town, Indian Territory, Choctaw Nation with Dr. Thaddeus Springer, his wife, and two children, one boy of twelve years and one daughter of fifteen years. Dr. Springer, by invitation of the Southern Board of Foreign Missions of the Presbyterian Church, is to assist the good Father Cyrus Byington, a Presbyterian missionary of some acclaim, to the Choctaw Nation with the many medical responsibilities Father Byington has previously borne alone. I am committed to use all the knowledge and skill I have so far learned at the side of Cousin Lawrence to assist him in this effort.

September 28, 1863
I recover in a small one room log cabin with walls covered in muslin. So far my only exercise has been to kill the several scorpions and not more than a few lizards of various colors and sizes which have taken up residence with me. The walls are covered with muslin papering drawn tightly, but leaving spaces behind it between the logs, where any insect or reptile which fancies

doing so can find entry into the cabin. Although there is a tester over my bed, the invaders still manage to reach me. The scorpions are at least two or three inches in length and in the shape of a lobster. The poison is in the curved tail and when attacking drive the stringer in with great force. I have been stung thrice already, but am becoming much more skilled in executing their demise.

The war seems not to have touched this place. It is as though I have by some miracle of the supernatural been transported to a foreign land far removed from the horrific realities of war. The only time I hear cannon shot or the moaning of dying men, is from the echoes of a terrible dream from which I have awoken still sweating and writhing.

I cannot dismiss the feeling that there seems to be a dark cloud hanging over me and that my heart is cold and dead. I mourn Old Thomas, my good and faithful friend and last connection to home, mightily.

October 1, 1863

Father Cyrus Byington, the head missionary at Eagle Town, visits me daily during my convalescence. He appears to be a fine gentleman, although a little too evangelical for my likes, constantly asking whether I am a friend of Jesus and speaking of the "Great Salvation." Fortuitously, most of the time, I feign exhaustion and slip off into sleep.

It is clear; however, that this elderly, distinguished man is totally devoted to his flock. He came west with the Choctaws in 1834, settling in that year just south of the Mission's current location. That original settlement proved to be unhealthy, resulting in the death of at least one of Byington's children and his sister, causing *the Mission to be moved to its present location of Stockbridge at Eagle Town. It is known as Stockbridge in honor of Father Byington's birthplace. Over the years, Father Byington along with Rev. Alfred Wright, a diminutive somewhat sickly individual, who does not visit but works primarily in the church building and along with the help of several Choctaw interpreters, continues to refine and develop a Grammar, Dictionary, Definer and Speller of the Choctaw language. This is the grand work the two had begun in Mississippi as it was thought the Choctaw language had to be learned before English could be learned by the Choctaws. Father Byington has founded several outreach missionary churches and schools within a one hundred mile district and this elderly gentleman travels to each of them regularly; at least as regularly as his health will allow. He is a man of greatly advanced years and lives here, along with his wife, and several other missionaries and teachers.*

Much of this information was conveyed to me by Dr. Thaddeus Springer.

October 5, 1863
Father Byington visited me again today, but in the place of inquiring about my spiritual well-being, he told me a little of his sentiments regarding his devotion to his lifework. He was greatly troubled and for some reason known only to him (perhaps he thinks I will soon die and thus his innermost thoughts will remain safe with me), he spoke of the early years when as a missionary in Mississippi, he had come to love this strong, independent Indian people and abhorred the brutal treatment they received from the Government. He told me, "They are an injured people; driven from their rightful homes by the greed of the whites. I

fear, without the help of the Missions and schools, they will become an extinguished race, yet the human generosity and justice which first sent me to take on this self-denying work now conspire to dictate its end." He then went on to explain that the sponsors of Choctaw missions were all abolitionists, and wished him to speak out against slavery. Although Father Byington, too, was anti-slavery in his sentiments, many of the Choctaws owned slaves and would have ejected him from the Nations if he were to take such a stance. He was much concerned that his Mission would discontinue support.

October 6, 1863

I am finally of good enough health to allow for short excursions around Eagle Town although in my way of thinking, Eagle Town is not a real town in the true sense of the word. There is no proper town square. It is just a group of log cabins – one serving as the general store and post office, a blacksmith shop and a cotton buyer set up in a shed of some sort. The Female Seminary, Iyanabi, under the supervision of a Mr. Chamberlain and two female teachers is somewhat set apart from these structures and this compound contains the Church building.

The one official building, if a cabin built of round pine logs can be called "official" is the courthouse built in 1850 and which commemorates the organization of Eagle County, Apukshunnubbee district, Choctaw Nation. Nearby stands "execution rock." There is a large cypress tree over 100 feet tall located just west of the Mountain Fork River at the eastern end and a government ration station is nearby. From what I have learned, the town's name was derived from the throngs of eagles who nest in the swamps alongside the Mountain Fork River. I understand nearby there are cotton plantations, cotton gins and gristmills in operation, but I am not yet well enough to mount a horse and see for myself.

I have by way of Dr. Springer and his son, made the acquaintance of a half-blood Indian by the name of David Folsom. His younger sister is a student at the Iyanabi Seminary. David Folsom is exceptionally tall, more than a head and a half taller than I, and very handsome. The females, including the teachers at the Iyanabi, steal surreptitious glances at him as he passes in route to visit with his sister. He has about him an air of quiet dignity calculated to inspire respect and I understand he is a man of much standing with his people, even though he is not much older than I. He is not without humor, displaying an insight and intelligence I have come to admire and appreciate. Even after so short an acquaintance, I have come to love him as a brother.

October 7, 1863

As with all Sundays, I attended Church services twice this day. Although one church service per Sunday is enough for my soul (at least to my way of thinking); to do otherwise would be an insult to the good Father Byington and the other missionaries who have been so kind to me. Dr. Byington conducted the service in the Choctaw language, being one of the few white men who can actually speak, write and sing in that unusual but beautiful language. The sounds are quite pleasant to the ear, and the singing is melodious and true. The Indians possess an almost uncanny understanding of pitch. I refrain from singing, rather I hum along quietly under my breath, for the first time I sang out loud, several of the Indians turned and looked at me when I emitted a sour note. I am sure the congregation appreciates my new found musical restraint.

The people of the Nation always come dressed in their finest. The men wear colorful calico shirts and the women wear calico as well with a handkerchief tied across the head.

When Father Byington is riding his "circuit" to the other churches and schools, a substitute missionary will preach, but the service is in English and few of the full-blood Indians understand enough of that language to make the service meaningful. Generally, when this happens, the missionary will speak a few sentences and the interpreter, generally a half-blood, will repeat the information in the native language. Ofttimes, David Folsom will be asked to interpret, which he does with great efficacy and skill.

I have asked David Folsom to teach me his language and he has agreed to do so.

November 1, 1863

My good friend David Folsom visited today and made me a present of enormous value – a roan not unlike the one I had previously. I have named him Old Thomas, even though he is a young stallion. I was so delighted; I implored Dr. Springer to allow me a short ride with Folsom. It took much convincing on both our parts, but the good doctor finally acceded to the request. We took a track north of Eagle Town, into the woods where we espied several game animals – wild turkey, deer, and a variety of smaller animals. I was told there are also bear, but we saw none of these. I was much pleased to see I had not lost my sharp-shooting skills as I was able to take down two turkeys, hitting them fully in the head and not spoiling the meat. David Folsom took one and I the other.

December 13, 1863

On this, my 17th birthday, I am desolate - my thoughts melancholy. Although I have vowed to myself to direct my thoughts strictly to the future, I cannot help but think sadly of home, my dear Mother and my two sweet sisters. I cannot but ponder how different their lives and mine would have been had not this horrible war, comprised of equal parts madness and folly, infested the country with such hatred that all humanity has been rendered asunder. I have witnessed such outrages and brutality by both the Federals and the Confederates – each claiming divine righteousness and each having been equally aggressive, treacherous and intolerant to the other. I despair that human beings will never be of a mind to live peacefully.

I remember conversations held between my Mother and me, discussing the undeniable cruelty of slavery and finding little or no support for our views. We were forbidden to talk of it and had to carefully select our discussion sites so that none would overhear. Father was a staunch supporter of this untenable practice and was so convinced of his position and of the real or perceived injustices the black Republicans forced upon the Southern states that he would not abide a dissenting opinion from anyone and less still from his family.

What arrogance and hubris caused that otherwise good and wise man to volunteer for service with the Army of Arkansas and leave his family with none to protect or nurture them? I remember the loathsome fight I had with Father the night before his departure – he so convinced of the right of his mission and I so convinced the opposite was true. Even when the Army of Arkansas disbanded, Father failed to return home but remained with the regular Confederate troops.

I think of my dear Mother's grief when she learned Father was killed in the action at Pea Ridge and of her stoicism when his body was returned home and buried at Nine Oaks. In my eyes Father abandoned his family to participate in an arrogant, malicious folly, but Mother would hear none of it. She visited his grave side every day – even in the rain and snow. A widow, she had none to protect her, save me – a boy of barely fifteen years and Uncle Dwight who was quite elderly and crippled.

And then, I too, was sacrificed to that unholy war – to those more interested in death and enslavement than in life and liberty – our country's founding principles. Not half a year after Father's death, Mother and my sisters were left alone and unprotected once again.

I must not revisit these thoughts. They do nothing but cause me despair and loneliness. I must make every effort to only look forward.

December 15, 1863
My language training goes exceedingly well. Father Byington is very pleased with my linguistic progress and tells me I will make a fine replacement for him when he is called home to his Father in Heaven. I am unconvinced, as I do not have the religious fervor necessary for this work, but I do not say so. The fundamental reason I work so diligently at this task is far less ethereal and much more a characteristic of my ego. David Folsom takes such pleasure in my mispronunciations and improper use of the language that I have made it my mission to become as fluent as he as soon as possible and deprive him of this source of humor. I practice day and night with anyone who will listen. Several of the girls, under the watchful eye of their teacher

at Iyanabi, have made my education their project.
I believe it makes them happy to be the teachers
for a change and their giggles when I fail to speak
appropriately do not irritate me nearly as much
as David Folsom's unbridled laughter.

Father Byington is also impressed with my
knowledge and understanding of the Bible and
other good literature – but in truth this must be
credited to the excellent training given my most
educated Mother who read to us from Hamlet,
King Lear, Merchant of Venice, the Marmion and
many other classical works. As children were also
required to copy down passages from the Bible
each day, so that we would learn it well and also
learn to spell and write properly.

I continue my medical training with Dr.
Stringer. I am pleased that, here too, I can
contribute to our shared trove of medical
knowledge, having been Cousin Lawrence's
assistant for more than 10 months. During that
time I learned much, as we treated as many cases
of pneumonia, dysentery, small pox, malaria and
other maladies as we did battlefield wounds. In
the end, Cousin Lawrence allowed me to conduct
operations, determine treatments and dispense
medicine (when any medicine was to be had)
independent of his oversight as in this way we
could help more of our comrades more quickly.
Together, we would read his medical journals
as a review for him and education for me. This
experience has been of much help in our local
hospital as many of these same illnesses are also
rampant in the Nation.

December 20, 1863
This day was unseasonably warm and
beautiful. Perhaps it was God's way of telling
me that all will be healed in His time. Of this,

I do not know. I do know that dwelling on the unchangeable and dark past cannot but throw me into low spirits, so I took to my roan and rode out into the quiet of the woods, hoping to bring home some turkey or, if lucky, a deer.

I had traversed but a few miles, when Old Thomas suddenly reared up, unceremoniously dumped me on the ground, and disappeared into the trees. I lay there for a minute or two, trying to corral my senses, when I felt, rather than heard a low growling to my right and rear. I turned slowly and to my utter astonishment, spied a large - no a giant - brown bear, emerge from the bush. He stopped, stared into my eyes and began rocking back and forth on his short, powerful legs – his mouth from time to time stretching wide – perhaps to see if I would fit. My rifle, still attached to Old Thomas, was rapidly heading west and out of my reach. All I could think was that I would soon join my mother and sisters as I had no means of protection against this formidable and deadly creature.

The bear reared on its hind legs to what seemed to be a height of at least ten feet. I was certain he prepared for his charge and my finality. He emitted a deep growl. I tightly screwed shut my eyes and prayed for a quick ending, when the growl suddenly changed its pitch, and silenced. After several seconds, I cautioned to open one eye, and there, standing over the fallen great bear stood David Folsom. The bear had been brought down by three arrows, dispensed in such a rapid order and with such accuracy as to save me from the meal table. I came to my knees and vomited copiously – whether from fear or relief, I cannot say. It was amazing to me that I could have gracefully withstood the horrors of the bloody war when every day brought the threat of death, yet be so affected by that hairy beast. Perhaps it was because that no matter what cruel tortures I envisioned the Federals to be capable of, I did not think they would eat me.

David Folsom helped me to my feet and together we found Old Thomas drinking tranquilly from a stream about a mile away to the west, my rifle happily intact in its scabbard. By the time we returned to the slain bear, I had ceased shaking and was no longer in fear of injuring myself with a skinning knife. Together, we dressed the devil animal and returned with the meat and the skin to the Mission. David Folsom took great care in removing the creature's eye teeth and offered me one, but I declined, saying the glory was his alone and besides, it would give me nightmares each time I gazed upon a tooth that had nearly had me for dinner. David Folsom laughed so hard he had to sit for a few moments to regain his composure. I could still hear his chuckles as he and his horse and its bounty disappeared into the woods beyond the clearing.

May 8, 1865

On this day David Folsom brought me to meet his family. In all the months I have known my dear friend, he has spoken little of his home or his family. Perhaps this is because I, too, seldom mention my early years.

We traveled on horseback for several hours southward from Eagle Town, crossing several small streams and valleys until at once we gained the high ground. As we broke through the tree line, spread out before my eyes were many acres of freshly tilled soil. In the far distance near a wide meandering river, green grasslands stretched as far as the eye could see – pastures dotted with multitudes of black and brown cattle. I could also see a large compound of buildings –

a main house, several outbuildings, barns, and - somewhat removed from the main house – two rows of small one-room houses. I recognized them immediately – slave quarters.

As we drew closer to the main house, I noted the many Negroes tending the fields – they touched fingers to heads as we passed – in deference to their owner's son. It was a gesture I well-recognized. As a child I had received the very same gesture of respect each and every day.

The main house was large and constructed of rock and hewn log. Although much different in structure and architectural style, it somehow had the aura of my own Nine Oaks. Dogs lay about basking in the morning sunshine. Several horses tethered to the front railing slowly shifted from foot to foot, tails swatting at flies. Everything reminded me of the life I left behind.

David Folsom's parents were dear souls and as far removed from David in appearance and demeanor as was possible. Where their son was tall and powerfully built, they were small - round of countenance and physique. Where David was intransigent, they were effusive and enthusiastic. They welcomed me into their home as if I were a prodigal son. His two younger sisters never took their eyes from me and giggled constantly behind hands modestly shielding mouths. I wondered what they thought about this strange white man who was friend to their brother.

The day passed quickly. Mr. Silas Folsom, David's father, would hear nothing but to tour me around his vast farm, pointing out the various vocations - farming, ranching, leather craft, and others too numerous to mention - as we rode along. It was with such pride that he spoke of his love and connection to the land, his family and people – that he could very well have been my own father talking. Even his arguments

*supporting slavery employed the same rationale
my father used so many years ago in his attempt
to convince me of its rightfulness. David Folsom
remained silent as we wandered across the land.
For my part, I said nothing – for to vocalize my
true feelings about the wrongfulness of slavery
would have been ultimately discourteous to my
host and my friend.*

*The day had left me strangely elated, yet at the
same time melancholy and thoughtful. It occurred
to me that perhaps the reason David Folsom and
I had so quickly become such fast friends was
because we were both sons of the south - raised in
ease with others to do our bidding – children who
never considered the horrendous cost that luxury
would demand.*

*Later that afternoon David Folsom and I
made ready to leave for Eagle Town, as David had
agreed to ride partway with me. It was tradition
to present my host with a gift, and I had carefully
chosen a particularly beautiful woven basket to
give to the family. But as I prepared to say my
goodbyes, I was surprised to see myself draw
from my inner pocket the watch which had been
my father's prized possession. I handed it to Mr.
Folsom. I told him the timepiece had belonged
to my deceased father, but that Mr. Folsom had
so much reminded me of him that I felt it should
be his. The old Indian took the watch carefully,
turned it over in his weathered fingers, and smiled
his thanks.*

*The sun slowly slipped toward the horizon
as David and I crested the hill to the north of the
farm. I turned for one last long look at David's
home. Encased in the soft light, it seemed almost
magical – and as easily lost as Nine Oaks. In my
heart I knew I would never see it again.*

*Uncharacteristically, David Folsom wished
to speak of the philosophy of slavery – a subject*

we had never before discussed. I was saddened when it became clear David's thoughts and heart were completely in line with those of his father. He postulated the Negro would never be able to survive in the world without direct supervision from an owner. The owner took care of his property – assured each one had enough to eat, a house in which to live and medical care. It simply made good sense – both economically and humanely that they should be owned.

My rebuttal was the same I used with my father – that is, all people should be free to determine their own destiny, make their own way and prosper or fail by the fruits of their labors. No person should own another. To say that Negroes should be owned because they had neither the will nor intelligence to be independent was simply a rationalization. After all, I reasoned, whites said the same things about Indians and look at the success David's father had orchestrated.

David took immediate and volatile offence to my statements. It was if I had just shot my friend in the heart at point blank range. He shouted that he had come from many generations of a civilized people and to compare them with the Negro was an insult not to be forgiven. He wheeled his horse toward his ranch and galloped into the thicket.

I made the rest of the long journey to Eagle Town alone and in silence, wondering if the wounds of slavery could ever be healed.

Chapter Fifteen

Billy's journal entries for the next sixteen months reflected the daily life of the Stockbridge Mission and its inhabitants, upon his growing friendship with David Folsom and his growing respect for the Natives. Little was mentioned about the Civil War, save once when Tandy Walker and a troop of Choctaw-Chickasaws camped for the night near the Mission in early 1865. News of the War's end reached the Mission in June, 1865.

> *June 2, 1865*
> *We have received by way of a letter from the Presbyterian Mission Board word that the War has ended. The Confederacy has been defeated; the slaves freed. I am surprisingly unmoved by this announcement. I thought I would be overjoyed that those people who for so long were deprived of their freedom are now free to pursue their dreams and aspirations. And of this I am glad. Perhaps my feelings toward anything associated with this*

horrible war have been dulled – perhaps it is because we are so removed from its reach out here in the wilderness. I do not know. I only know I am happy it is finally and completely done.

Many of the Choctaw who held slaves are now bankrupt. They will no longer be able to run their cotton plantations or the mills. David Folsom is desolate as his family owned a good number of slaves. Although he and I have always disagreed on the morality of slave-ownership, he worries that his family will not survive and with this I do sympathize.

The missionaries have been directed to return home and were informed their funding is hereby discontinued. Father Byington is desolate. He has been very ill of late, and this news has only worsened his condition. This mission has been his entire life. His illness has become so severe that the good man has been unable to ride his circuit to the outlying missions for some time. David Folsom and I have accompanied the good Rev. Adams on this journey twice each month for the past three months. I do not know how to raise the hopes of the good Father, when the Presbyterian Mission seems bent on destroying his life's work.

Dr. Springer and his good wife are packing their wagon to leave amidst many tears and heartfelt wishes of thanks and Godspeed. I do believe Mrs. Springer is secretly happy to be returning to her Ohio home, leaving this wilderness and its hardships far behind.

Father Byington and his good wife, Sophia, have determined to stay and convince the Board and its sponsors to allow the Mission to continue. I do not believe he will have good fortune in this endeavor.

June 30, 1865

Father Byington has received another letter from the Mission Board, once again directing his return. The letter indicated no further appeals to allow the continuation would be entertained, as funding had already been directed toward other missions.

July 10, 1865

When the news of the War's end reached us with its message from the Mission Board, I understood this mission would soon be disbanded, regardless of Father Byington's protestations. I drew him aside and told him of my plans to continue my medical education at the Chicago Medical College so that someday I could return to this beautiful land I have come to love and serve the people here in the way I knew best. The good man enthusiastically agreed. I think he had always known I would never make a good Missionary. I implored him once again to take leave of Stockbridge and return to his home in Ohio where he might receive the medical attention he needed to return to health.

Father Byington told me he was almost at the end of his journey and he soon would be called to join his Father in Heaven. He promised to return to Ohio as soon as was possible to assure his dictionaries, the Pentateuch and New Testament translations – his life's work - were appropriately published.

August 1, 1865

Today was one of the most difficult days I have had since coming to the Stockbridge Mission some two years ago. Eagle Town has been my sanctuary – the place where I healed the wounds of War and made my peace with God, due in no small part to the goodness of Father Byington and his missionaries. No longer am I the wounded boy, devastated from physical and emotional loss. I believe I am finally ready to begin life anew. I am filled with hope and a new purpose.

I embraced my good friends and mounted Old Thomas, heading for Little Rock and the train northward to Chicago. I searched for David Folsom to tell him goodbye – to tell him I planned to return to Indian Territory once my education was complete. My good friend was not to be found. His father informed me that his son had gone "on the scout" and had not been seen for more than two weeks. Mr. Folsom did not seem overly concerned about his son's absence, as many Natives who go "on the scout" stay in the wilderness for a year or more. I was saddened not to see David Folsom prior to leaving Indian Territory – as he has been my true friend and I did not know whether I would ever set eyes on him again.

September 10, 1865

After many days of exhausting travel I am finally arrived in Chicago. I rode out of the Territory and on to Little Rock; where, sadly, I had to sell my roan, Old Thomas. He has been the most amiable of companions (excepting for the time he abandoned me to the bear) and I made sure he went to a fine and gentle family who would take the good care of him.

I boarded the train to Illinois and during the next three days watched in astonishment the countryside as it passed my window. Everywhere I saw the detritus of War - in the towns and cities through which I passed – so much destruction – and for what purpose? It is clear this country has sustained a bitter and long-lasting wound – a wound we can but hope will not prove mortal.

Chicago City is a most astounding place. People of all nationalities are everywhere. My eye can scarcely perceive a view in any direction that is not dominated by new construction, wagon and pedestrian traffic and general chaos. The streets are knee-deep in mud and filth and the smell is quite atrocious – most likely the smell is borne by the south wind coming from the many stockyards nearby. I am told that the population of Chicago is experiencing unprecedented growth, and I can well believe it. My seatmate on the train informed me the railroads now consider Chicago the hub of eastern and western transportation – there are more than thirty railroads coming and going from this one city alone.

The differences between where I resided just two weeks ago and the place in which I find myself today are unfathomable.

September 12/13, 1865

I have located a room in Mrs. Decatur's Boarding House – just to the north of the downtown district and one block from the Chicago Medical College. It is a three story home - most luxurious by Indian Territory standards, although less so than my childhood home, and my room is in the front, looking out over Lake Michigan. I do not know how this body of water can be called a lake as it is unbelievably large – the shorelines stretch to the north and south as far as the eye can see and water extends to the east as far as the horizon and beyond.

Mrs. Decatur is a most affable hostess. I believe she is most happy to have a paying customer – especially one who has prepaid for an entire year. It is my understanding she lost her husband at Gettysburg some two years ago and has had a difficult time financially since his death. All this was told to me whilst we enjoyed a cup of coffee during my first afternoon in her establishment.

The next morning, Mrs. Decatur's daughter, Amanda, escorted me to the Chicago Medical College where I officially registered for my first term.

December 25, 1865

Today I attended Christmas services with Mrs. Decatur and her two daughters, Amanda and Mary Ann. We then shared a Christmas dinner along with the other residents of the Decatur Boarding House, drank some punch and wished one another good health and fortune. It was a fine day with a heavy down pouring of snow and of good cheer. Best of all, it was a wonderful respite from the rigors of my medical curriculum.

I have not had much time for socializing since my arrival, although Mrs. Decatur seems determined to make a match of her eldest daughter and myself. Apparently, having a doctor in the family appeals greatly to this fine lady. Amanda Decatur seems to agree; however, I am not of a like mind. Amanda is a very sweet girl; however, she does not have a spirit that excites my passion and she is also very committed to a City life. I am of a mind to return to Indian Territory – a future that interests Amanda not at all. She is not of the adventurous type.

Billy's subsequent journal entries for the period of January 1866 through July of 1867 were sporadic and short. He talked about the difficulty of the new curriculum at the Chicago Medical College. Billy felt he was one of the lucky ones, having had the experiences and training with Cousin Lawrence, but even so – it was exceedingly demanding. Although the curriculum was divided into a three year program – junior, middle and senior including clinical practice and a hospital internship – Billy completed it in two years. He was anxious to return to his beloved Indian Territory and keep his promise to Father Byington.

There was a flirtation or two during this period, but none was serious.

> *July 10, 1867*
> *I am now a full-fledged doctor of medicine and I have the diploma from the Chicago Medical College to prove it. It resides in my suitcase, properly signed, dated and stamped. Someday I may even have a wall to hang it upon.*
>
> *I sit in a railway car – not heading west toward Indian Territory, but east to visit my friend and mentor, Father Byington. I fear if I do not visit the Byingtons now, I will not see them again on this earth. The good man has been long ill, and was finally forced to abandon his Stockbridge Mission. His arduous trip to Ohio further weakened my friend and he subsequently contracted smallpox from which he has since recovered. His dear wife, Sophia, has also returned from Indian Territory. She remained in Stockbridge for some time following Father Byington's departure, hoping for a new Stockbridge missionary, but none came. The mission is now deserted. I am quite saddened to hear this, as the mission was so dear to them both.*
>
> *Although I am anxious to return to Indian Territory, there is no one remaining at Eagle*

Town, so I am unsure as to what my next actions will be, but I will discuss my plans with my friends.

December 16, 1867

As I enter the town of Scullyville, Indian Territory, I feel an enormous rush of energy and happiness. How I have missed this untamed land – these fine and honest people. It is like breathing clear air again – excitement and anticipation courses through my bloodstream. Until this moment I did not realize how depressed I had become living in the 'civilized' world – a world of tall buildings, brutal cold, ego and indifference. I feel alive again.

My riding companion, Green McCurtain, was very impressed in my ability to speak his native language. We used that tongue as we rode. Just east of town, Green points to a large structure, sturdily built with rock on the bottom and huge logs above. He tells me the logs came from the Cavanal Mountains some fifteen miles from here. He said although it was originally the Choctaw Agency station, it had also been the Butterfield Overland Mail station and when Tandy Walker was elected first chief after the Skullyville Constitution meeting in 1857, he made it the governor's mansion and moved in. He still lives there – but now it's just known as the Choctaw Agency-Walker Station. The Choctaw Nation's capitol is to the southwest at Chahta Tamaha. Although my friend does not say it, I detect there is no love lost between the McCurtains and the Walkers.

As we ambled down the bustling main street, I saw many stores, a barber shop, a hotel and several restaurants. The pungent odor I caught on the southwest wind told me there had to be a stockyard not too far distant – I learned that smell all too well living these past years in Chicago. There were grain mills and a cotton gin. Lord help us, I could see the steeples of at least three churches. There was even a Spring Water bottling station. When I asked, Green said the springs nearby had such good water that it was bottled and sold to neighboring towns in the Territories and Arkansas. The Natives crowding the streets appeared to be from several tribes, including some Cherokee, I thought. There were as many whites as Indians and a scattering of Negroes as well. Some of the natives thought there were too many whites, Green informed me. That attitude does not bode particularly well for my new medical practice, I thought to myself dismally.

We talked at length about my stay at Eagle Town and Father Byington. Green promised to introduce me to his father, Cornelius McCurtain, in the next few days. He said his father was a man of great influence in the Choctaw Nation and could do much to assure my welcome and acceptance.

I left Old Thomas (not the same roan I left Stockbridge upon – but I have since determined to call all my horses Old Thomas in honor of my friend and companion) at the Livery and took a room at the Scullyville Hotel. It is a clean and functional establishment of some ten rooms and I am given a front on the second floor by the most beautiful woman I have ever seen. She is the daughter of the owner, Liam Martin, and her name is Lucy Landon Martin. All previous thoughts of failure disappear. It is an auspicious beginning.

January 4, 1868
Through the good works of Cornelius McCurtain and his associates, I have secured

rental of temporary offices above the Scullyville Barber Shop. It is a fine suite, having a small but adequate outer reception area, two examining rooms (one of which I will make into a surgery) and an ample space at the rear for my living quarters (although I am somewhat reluctant to leave the Scullyville Hotel – more importantly to leave Lucy Landon Martin). I have ordered medical supplies from Fort Smith and they should arrive within the next week or two.

Green McCurtain and I shared dinner last evening. He is about my age, a fine man with a moon-shape countenance, dark-haired with a bushy mustache. He is easy to laugh and possessed of a quick intelligence. He is a good companion and full of the history of his people. I find myself endlessly fascinated. His family arrived in the first coming of the Choctaw in 1832 and he shared many stories of the early years in Scullyville, as told to him by his father. At that time there was much hardship, the difficult journey from Mississippi, a smallpox epidemic, the great flood of 1834, Fort Coffee and the whiskey runners, but through it all, the Choctaw people remained strong and independent.

This is not to say there has not also been much controversy, in-fighting and disagreement. A current one rages over the governance and structure of the Choctaw Lands. There is much speculation that now that the War has ended and the Confederates defeated, there will be an even greater push to 'territorialize' the Nations. Some railroads have already been granted access across tribal lands and many of the people fear this is but the first step in their loss of independence.

I cannot disagree.

January 14, 1868

I saw three patients today in my new offices. I cannot help but think this is due to the efforts of my new friends, the McCurtains. None of the cases was life-threatening, the cures easily identified and the remedies quickly dispensed. I have high hopes my practice will soon begin to flourish.

In the late afternoon, I walked about the town, noting the construction of two new general stores, a commodities warehouse and what appears to be a volunteer fire station. One can almost feel the energy in the air. One of the men heading up the fire station's construction told me there were plans to build a freedman's school just to the west of town. He was unsure whether this would be a positive step or not. Apparently, there are many differing opinions regarding this subject. There is still much resentment against the Negroes and their newly freed status.

As on most evenings I supped at the Scullyville Hotel. The meals there are quite good, but I must admit it is more the company than the food that draws me. Mr. Martin's daughter, Lucy, generally serves the meals and I look forward each day to our mutual discourse. She is very sharp of wit and has a sense of humor that keeps me constantly on the watch. She is also in my mind quite beautiful – raven dark-hair and skin the color of cream. Of late, Liam Martin has joined me for the meal. He shares his stories of Ireland and his early years in Boston, where, he tells me, he learned the hotel trade from some of the finest establishments in that fair city. Miss Martin later clarified most of these establishments were bordellos.

On many evenings Mr. Martin entertains us with his music, playing tunes on his old upright piano and singing in his magnificent baritone voice. He is also most astute in the politics of the town and the Territory. We laugh much and each evening has become the highlight of my day.

February 14, 1868

I asked Miss Lucy Landon Martin to the Valentine's Day celebration and dance and much to my surprise and delight, she accepted. We enjoyed a fine evening. She is a most accomplished dancer, light on her feet and graceful. Unfortunately, I am not; however, she was kind enough to refrain from bringing this to my attention – even when I repeatedly assaulted her dancing shoes with my boots. This was one area in which my mother's repeated lessons found no fertile soil for growth and improvement. Mr. Liam Martin also attended the dance and he put on quite a show with his many Irish dancing steps and laughter.

Although alcohol is forbidden in the Territories, Mr. Liam Martin and some of the other shop owners managed to find a way to become quite inebriated. Mr. Martin, in particular, seemed to overly enjoy the evening as Miss Martin and I had to escort him home, one on each side holding him erect in order to avoid his collision with several obstacles along the way. The lyrics of the songs he sang on the way back to the hotel would have made the fine ladies in Chicago blush; however, Miss Martin seemed to take it all in stride. All things considered, it was an evening I shall hold dear in my memory.

By mid-1868 Billy's journals entries were no longer long epistles of daily life. With few exceptions he wrote in summary, covering weeks or months in one single entry. There were; however, some exceptions.

June 2, 1868

Today must be the most happy day of my life. For today, Lucy Landon Martin and I were married in the Scullyville Baptist Church. She is all I could ever hope for in a wife and partner. She is as beautiful as she is intelligent, witty and independent. She is a strong-willed woman and can handle herself as well as any man with a rifle or a bow. She easily keeps her father, Liam, and me in line, but with such a sense of humor and sweetness that neither of us can complain. I am the most lucky of men.

The roses around the church bloomed radiantly and Lucy carried a bouquet made from the most exquisite buds. For the first time in many months, I thought of my mother and the lovely rose bushes she so tenderly nursed. I feel a touch of sadness that my young sisters will never experience the joy that is mine today.

The entire town has turned out to help us celebrate. Even the Walkers and the McCurtains seem to have put aside their ill feelings for a time. Liam is in fine form. I was concerned he might drink himself into such a state before the wedding that he would be unable to walk Lucy down the aisle. But happily he did not, whether from a feeling of propriety or because Lucy put the fear of God into him – I do not know – nor will I ask. The poor man has not stopped crying yet – Lucy is his only child.

September 2, 1868

Early this morning Green McCurtain came by the hotel and collected Lucy and me. We rode southwest out of town to a great field called Charby Prairie, there to witness one of the great Choctaw ball games. Hundreds, maybe even as many as a thousand Choctaw appeared at various points surrounding a large open expanse of grass. This was the field of play. There were two crudely built goals at either end.

Throughout the crowd of spectators there was much laughter, excitement, and betting – especially among the women. According to Green, this was a contest of great honor between teams of the former districts. He said some of the people bet everything they had on their team.

Lucy turned a bright red when the players came out onto the field as they were naked, save for a breech-clout with a tail. It will give me much pleasure in the future to duplicate their costume for her private viewing in our bedroom. Each team had ten players – every player carried two sticks. They marched onto the field behind a medicine man, and then several of them broke away and began banging their sticks against the goals, shouting and making odd sounds. Green told us this was to scare away bad luck.

The game began at about nine o'clock in the morning with a rush and much confusion and scrambling on the field. The ball was either carried or thrown by using the sticks and the object was to get the ball in the goal. There did not seem to be any other rules. Once the game was underway, there was so much shouting, cajoling and name-calling, we could not hear one another speak.

The game never stopped, but continued throughout the day. Players were shuffled in and out as one after another fell from heat and exhaustion. Green shouted the game would not end until one team had one hundred goals. There was much rejoicing and many lamentations when the final goal was scored just before sunset. I wondered how many had just lost their life's savings.

There were many wounded with cuts, broken arms, legs and noses. I do not believe anyone died. I have never in my life seen anything like that Choctaw ball game.

January 1869

I have just received word that my friend, Father Byington died on December 31, 1868 at his daughter's home in Ohio. He was 75. God grant him the peace he deserves.

Chapter Sixteen

Bobbi Huff sat in her office chair, staring out at the Devon Tower and thinking about the information that had just come in from Chris Dover. She'd received the results of the DNA and fingerprint tests on the two bodies found in Missouri – one of them was Wasp, and the other was Julio Mendez – a naturalized citizen who worked for Lordes Realty in St. Louis.

As the director sat thinking, Mark Hamilton knocked on her door frame and added a couple of facts and some speculation of his own.

"The cell the Houston P.D. pulled off Viper had a lot of numbers, text messages and the like on it. Most of it was local garbage, but there was one that seemed out of place. They sent me the data, and I think I've found something interesting."

"Sit down. What is it?"

"Well, there's this cryptic message – maybe not so cryptic as it obviously refers to Wasp – it says 'a man who can't keep his head during a delivery doesn't need one,' but what's interesting is that the text came from a burn phone bought just outside St. Louis."

"We also got a copy of the Anderson woman's murder on video. Just before they shoot her up, Wasp turns to Viper and says something like, 'too bad we can't send this bitch to Serbia, too,' and Viper replies something like, 'Nah, too old and too used up. He wants 'em young – real young.' That sounds to me like the Sierpes are 'shopping' for very young girls to send to Serbia."

"Makes sense," speculated Huff. "St. Louis keeps popping up, doesn't it?"

"Yeah," Hamilton ticked off the information on his fingers, "so we've got connections to Shawnee with the kidnapped girls, Denver from the women in the van and the stolen automatic pistol, Atlanta from the Denver driver's cell, Viper in Houston and now St. Louis - where the message to Viper and the cell from the Denver guy were bought."

Huff thought a minute, "We're looking at something pretty big, I think – maybe an international crime syndicate or something like that. What do you think?"

"I think you're on to something." Then she made up her mind.

"Let's ask the task force to get together first thing tomorrow. Call Stuart Compton at the FBI and make sure he brings somebody knowledgeable about the international crime syndicates. I think it's time we went over everything that's happened in the last week."

The next morning all the familiar faces and one extra – Bill Freemont from the FBI's International Organized Crime Division, sat around the table in Bobbi Huff's office. Dover and Chambers joined in from Houston via Skype. They went over all the information they had – including the arrest of Viper and Sherry Zane's story and video. They reviewed the DNA results from the two bodies found in Missouri.

Freemont listened to all the discussion, but didn't add much. However, as soon as he left the building and was assured of some privacy, he called his boss Paul Ridler, in Washington, D.C.

"Hey, Paul. I think I got something good – *really good*. Didn't we just get some intel that Lordes Realty in St. Louis is really a front for the Marta Cartel in Colombia?"

He listened for a few seconds, "well, looks like they might have added a new line of product to their guns and drug smuggling operations - human trafficking. …Yeah, no kidding. You know that kid who was murdered in Shawnee, Oklahoma – you know – just outside of Oklahoma City…yeah the twin. Well, looks like an employee of Lordes was involved in that… I'm surprised too, but maybe it was just economics. They've been taking a licking from the Mexicans for a couple of years now. Yeah, its tenuous I know - but maybe now we can at least get a judge to let us ramp up the surveillance on Ortiz."

****

Viper reclined as much as possible in the interrogation room's hard plastic chair. He couldn't do a full 'fuck-you' posture because his handcuffs were secured to the table in front of him – but he did his best to display an aura of insolence and indifference. Next to him sat his 'shapiro' or attorney, Melvin Clarence, a perfect example of a well-heeled lawyer in his $5,000 navy blue suit, custom-made shoes and leather briefcase. Clarence opened the top of the briefcase and settled back to wait for the detectives. He unobtrusively advised Viper to keep quiet until Clarence had determined just how much trouble his client was in. Viper ignored him.

Chris Dover and Mike Chambers entered the room and sat down. Chris had shaved his beard, got a haircut, and discarded his street clothes. Sister Mary Agnes would be proud. Now relieved from his undercover assignment, Chris felt good at being able to come eye to eye with this sack of shit.

"How about if we take the cuffs off my client," Clement began.

"How about if you shove it up your ass, you worthless piece of crap," Dover answered.

Chambers cut in, "Well, DeLon, looks like you're in some serious trouble."

'"Name's Viper, you stupid fuck. You got nothin' on me, man. Nothin'" The black man turned his insolent gaze from the two detectives and contemplated the ceiling tiles.

"Well, DeLon," Mike continued. "That's not exactly true. You see, we've got your fingerprint on our deceased victim, Linda Anderson."

"That can be easily explained," said Clarence arrogantly, "they could have brushed against each other anywhere – they live in the same neighborhood, after all, and drug addicts seldom wash. If that's all you have, I'll have my client out of here in an hour." He started to close the lid to his briefcase.

"We also have some very interesting phone numbers and text messages retrieved from your cell phone linking you to some interstate human trafficking and the death of a ten-year-old child."

That got Clarence's attention. "What evidence?" He looked at Viper, but got no response. He sat back in his chair, trying to convey an attitude of mild interest, but not concern. However, he did retrieve his Mont Blanc pen from his inside jacket pocket and pull a notepad out of his briefcase. "What evidence?" Clarence repeated.

Chambers ignored him, keeping his eyes glued to the gang leader. "We've also got eye witness testimony saying you and your headless lieutenant, Wasp, murdered Linda Anderson by injecting her with a fatal dose of heroin when she came to find her twin daughters at your gang's crib. You remember them, don't you? The daughters you kidnapped, sold and murdered."

Clarence was madly scribbling away. Apparently there were several items of information his client had neglected to share.

"You talking 'bout Sherry? That your witness – ha! That bitch? She nothin'." Apparently Viper had already heard of Sherry's sudden and unanticipated departure from the fold. "She's nothin' but a two-bit, drugged-out ho. Can't trust nuthin' that cunt say."

"Oh, and I almost forgot." Chambers snapped his fingers as if he'd just remembered something important. "We have video, DeLon. A good, clear, time-stamped video showing you and Wasp committing that murder. As I said – some serious trouble, my man. Serious trouble. Death penalty trouble."

****

Attorney Clarence caught up with Dover and Chambers as they walked down the hallway toward the detectives' bullpen.

"Gentlemen," he began, walking quickly to keep pace. "Perhaps we can talk some kind of deal for my client."

"Right….the only deal your client deserves is the chair," retorted Dover.

Gone was the attorney's former arrogance. His voice was nothing but conciliatory. "I know. I know he's been involved in some questionable activities over the years...but he's willing to give you some extremely valuable information in exchange for consideration of his situation." Clarence was sweating – he was practically groveling. No telling what ultimatum Viper had given him. "It would be in your best interests to hear him out."

Dover started to say something – but Chambers cut him off. "It'd have to be something real good, Clarence," he said. "Something the D.A. couldn't possibly pass up."

"It is, believe me it is. He can tell you who ordered the twins."

Chambers responded, "Clarence, I don't think that's gonna be enough to make a difference to our D.A. He's a real hard-ass."

It was obvious Clarence didn't want to offer anything else, but he also didn't want to piss off Viper. "I guess –better the enemy you know..." he thought.

Aloud, the attorney said, "And ... Viper knows enough about the other gangs' activities to put a significant dent in Houston's organized crime operations."

Chambers and Dover looked at each other and grinned. Now that was something that might be worth bargaining for.

****

The D.A. agreed to take the death penalty off the table in exchange for everything Viper knew about the sale of the twins and Houston gang activities. Viper knew a lot. He gave up the names, locations and drops for drug distribution sites.

He described the man to whom he sold the twins and he named the accounting firm in St. Louis he dealt with for payments to and from the Sierpes. In short, he gave them everything they needed to seriously cripple Houston's gang activities.

****

The next few journals were filled with the comings and goings of Billy's family, his friendships with the McCurtain family and his growing medical practice. His first son, Liam Landon Samuelson, was born on August 8, 1869, followed by the birth of his only daughter, Evelyn Rose Samuelson, on February 22, 1871. The Samuelsons built a two story frame house on the corner of 6th and Walker. Billy moved his medical offices from above the Scullyville Barber Shop into a wing of the house built especially for his practice.

August 31, 1872

There are "Green McCurtain for Sheriff" posters splattered across Scullyville and now Lucy has put one in our front yard, too. Will I never be free from these infernal politics?

Lucy and Evelyn Rose have gone off to a suffrage meeting in Fort Smith (more blasted politics) and luckily Liam was able to come and help out with his namesake. He's much better with the baby than I. Maybe it's because Liam never really grew up. I am feeling out of sorts. I miss Lucy and the little one very much.

September 3, 1872

This evening Henderson Walker, Tandy Walker's son, came up to the house. Lucy had still not returned from her journey and Liam and I were out on the front porch taking in the cool evening air. Little Liam was still awake, playing chase with one of our dogs across the porch and onto the front lawn.

Henderson was quite angry and out of sorts as he strode up to the house. He asked that I accompany him to the station east of Scullyville, as there was an exceedingly drunk Indian making a ruckus and shouting my name. Not knowing who this person could be or whether he was injured in any way other than being drunk, I gathered my bag, saddled Old Thomas and followed. We rode quickly through town and directly to the station.

Sprawled across the front porch was a large, filthy, obviously drunk Indian. I could smell him the moment I climbed from Old Thomas. Liquor was forbidden to the people of the Nations as they had no tolerance for it. Old Andy Jackson had even built a fort just north of Scullyville to get rid of the illicit whiskey trade, but the fort had burned during the Civil War. Nothing seems to help stem the flood of this vile liquid – whiskey still pours into the Nations. And the people continue to suffer from its evil influence.

Henderson helped me turn over his unwelcome thoroughly inebriated guest. I stared at him for a long moment and then suddenly recognized my old friend, David Folsom. Sweet Jesus, it was David Folsom. I could not imagine what tragedy had led him to this state.

Henderson helped me take David Folsom to my house, where Liam and I stripped off his unsavory attire and bedded him in the downstairs den. I did not wish to put him in the guest room upstairs for fear he would become disoriented and fall down the stairs.

For the next two days, Liam and I plied my friend with every antidote for drunkenness we could conjure. Lucy and little Evelyn Rose returned the second day and, without even so much a question as to why I had brought such a derelict into her home, she took over the nursing responsibilities so that I could care for my patients.

When David Folsom regained his sobriety, he thanked me for his care. When I inquired as to his family, he told me they had lost all they had following the War. His father had committed suicide and his mother and sisters had moved west. He had not heard from them in several years. The Stockbridge Mission at Eagle Town had fallen into disrepair. My heart ached for my old friend who had lost so much. I determined I would do all I could to help him regain his life and his dignity.

I told David Folsom he always had a place in my home and at my table and he laid his head on the pillow. I told him he must never drink whiskey again, and he promised he would not do so. I only pray that he is able to keep that promise.

October 4, 1872

Green McCurtain stopped by today and begged me to accompany him to the New Hope Seminary. There was to be a dedication ceremony at the opening of a new building – a project his father, Cornelius, had devoted much of his time and energies into seeing accomplished. Green could not disappoint his father – the whole McCurtain family was pressed into attendance. There would be hell to pay should he miss the event, but he could not bear the boredom of the afternoon alone.

I could not help but laugh. This strong, independent man, who aspired to be the law for the entire area was quaking at the thought of disappointing his father. I checked my schedule and assented to go. It was much too great an opportunity to have a chance to place Green in my debt. We asked David Folsom to accompany our little party, but he declined. Apparently, tea, cookies and speeches were not on his afternoon's agenda.

We returned home early that afternoon, Green sheepishly waved his goodbye. When I entered the kitchen, Lucy told me that David Folsom had packed his few belongings and left without a word sometime after Green and I departed for the dedication.

November 15, 1872

Cornelius McCurtain, patriarch of the family, died on October 23rd this year.

Green was elected sheriff – although in my mind there was never any doubt he would be. I see less and less of Green since the election. Apparently, sheriffing is an occupation that keeps one very busy. I have heard nothing from David Folsom. I pray he is well and sober.

E. H. McEachern

December 12, 1872

    I received word this day that I am the sole beneficiary in the will of my uncle, who passed away earlier this autumn. He was my last tie with the home of my youth. I have not thought about my early home for many years now, it is odd to think of it now. It is as if that whole segment happened to another person – in another life and in many ways, that is true.

    The inheritance is substantial. Lucy and I have often wished we could build a real hospital. If she agrees, this will be our opportunity to do so.

December 31, 1872

    Green McCurtain rode up to the house early this morning. I was most happy to see my friend, but he had about him an air of sorrow. He asked that I accompany him and his deputies (there were two stout Choctaw men with him) to the old Fort Coffee ruins. As we rode north he told me he'd received word that there had been a fight of some note between whiskey traffickers and some of the people. I felt there was something he did not add, but as he thought it wise to keep the matter to himself, I did not press him for information.

    We arrived at the ruins. The fire that destroyed it during the War had been fierce. No wood remained – only the stonework foundations showed the outlines of the original structure. In a cleared area near the center of the debris field, we came upon five dead men and a scattering of whiskey barrels and several glass bottles. Two of the bodies were white men dressed in rough backwoods attire. The other three were Indians - one was David Folsom. Since none were left alive, there were no witnesses as to what precipitated the massacre – we could only speculate it was

over whiskey. I looked sadly at the body of my
first real friend here in the Nations and thought of
the waste of such a fine human being. I wondered
how many other Southern sons – sons who lost
everything in the War – had suffered his fate.

January 1873

Lucy is again with child. Our family continues
to grow and remains healthy. For this, both of us
are most grateful. We have hired a Negro woman,
Mandy Pickens, as a housekeeper, nanny, and
cook. Mandy is a plain-looking woman of middle
years, very hard-working and has a most pleasant
attitude. She is a freed woman, having lived her
early years on the Harkins family plantation near
Eagle Town in the south. Mandy is ever-grateful
for her position in our household. Those who were
freed following the War have not been welcome
in many of the towns in the Nations – including,
I am sad to say, Scullyville. Mandy's youngest
son attends the Freedman's School just outside of
town, and the wages she earns will be more than
adequate to pay his tuition. Well-paying positions
for Negroes have been in extremely short supply
since the War. I have promised to hire her son
during the summer months as a general handyman
around the house.

****

Joe Holcomb pulled off his hat as he entered the
Office. Mary Ellen raised her eyebrows and pointed to
the little conference room.

"Got a big shot FBI man waiting for you, Sheriff. Wouldn't tell me what he wanted." She was obviously miffed at being left out of the loop.

Sheriff Holcomb got a cup of coffee and headed into the conference room.

The big man seated at the table looked familiar, but Holcomb couldn't quite place him.

"Sheriff Holcomb, Special Agent Bill Freemont, FBI Organized Crime."

"Right, you were at that task force meeting in Oklahoma City a couple of days ago..."

"Yeah, well something's come up and I'm hoping you can help me with it."

"Sure Agent Freemont, what can I do?"

"Well," Freemont was obviously looking for just the right way to put this across.

Holcomb went on guard. It always made him suspicious when folks took too long trying to figure out what to say. In his experience, the truth never took that long.

"... We got a tip that one of the men you have in custody might be able to identify a suspect we've got in a case we're working on..." It was clear the Organized Crime Division of the FBI didn't want to share any more information than was absolutely necessary.

"And what case would that be?"

"Well, I'm not really at liberty to tell you..."

Something stunk big time....Holcomb's nose twitched.

"Look Freemont, if you can't tell me what's going on….well, I don't see how we can help." He pushed his chair back.

Agent Freemont backed off. "OK, Sheriff. But you've got to keep this confidential."

Holcomb didn't say anything.

"I need to run some photos by your witness, uh - Clement McRea – to see if he recognizes the man who rented his property."

"You've got a lead in our kidnapping and murder?"

"Well, no….well, yes….We think the man might be associated with a Colombian Cartel operating out of a base in St. Louis…"

"And I didn't need to know this because…." Holcomb was pissed. He figured – quite rightly – that Freemont had gotten his tip at the OBNDC task force meeting and was using the information the other agencies had worked to uncover to leapfrog his own investigation forward. He hadn't shared his information with the rest of the law enforcement personnel on the task force because the FBI wanted sole credit. Who cared if Pott County ever solved its case? Holcomb leaned back in his chair and crossed his arms across his chest.

"Look, Sheriff." Freemont was using his most conciliatory tone, "This whole thing is much bigger than just the murder of one child…we're talking gun and drug smuggling and billions of dollars. We've got a chance to bring down the whole damn Marta Cartel – if we can just get enough evidence to convince a judge to issue surveillance warrants. Mr. McRea's identification just might be that extra piece we need."

Holcomb didn't respond for a minute or two. He really didn't want to punch out an FBI agent – but he was struggling not to do so. He put both his elbows on the table and intertwined his fingers.

"I guess that's where we differ, Mr. Special Agent Bill Freemont – to me - there ain't nothing more important than the murder of a child."

Three hours later, Holcomb was on the phone with Bobbi Huff.

"Hey, Bobbi…you ain't gonna believe who was just here and what he wanted…"

****

Late the following Sunday afternoon, Carly jumped out of the Bannerman's big white Tahoe and ran to the kitchen door. All the family accompanied her into the kitchen, where the twin threw down her suitcase and kissed the Tallchief family – each in turn.

Charlie turned to Caleb, "So are we a go for the 15th?"

"Far as I know, everything has been done that needs to be done with all the thousands of bureaucracies," said Caleb, shaking his hand. "I'm hoping Carly won't have to testify, but the Houston D.A. wouldn't give me any guarantees."

The three boys were playing 'wild child' through the living room and kitchen. "Boys, boys – come on. We've got a long ride home."

The Bannermans said warm goodbyes to Jenny, Emma, Caleb and, of course, Zac.

Carly kissed them all goodbye and waved as their truck pulled away from the door, did a 180- and headed west.

The Tallchiefs waited in muted anticipation of the twin's reaction to her first weekend stay at what was to be her new home – with her new family.

"Oh, my gosh - I'm going to have my own room and I can decorate it any way I want – isn't that cool? Trish said she'd help me if I want. She said I could call her mom if I want to, but I don't know. And I get to go to school every day on a bus – I don't even have to walk by any scary corner dealers. They don't even have corners there!" She laughed at her own joke.

"And, guess what, they have lots of animals and best of all - horses. Charlie – uh Dad – said he'd teach me to ride one. Isn't that the coolest thing?" She picked up her suitcase and almost floated upstairs, Jesse following close behind.

The adults breathed a collective sigh of relief.

Chapter Seventeen

The two FBI agents on surveillance duty at Ortiz's offices watched as MacIntosh exited the building and drove away in his black Escalade. Freemont had been right, McRea's positive identification of MacIntosh as the man who rented his grandfather's house had done the trick. The two men followed – although at a discreet speed and distance. They'd placed a small tracking device on the car –and kept close using their sophisticated equipment.

"Ain't technology grand?" commented the agent as they watched Ortiz's right-hand man pulled up near the docks on the west bank of the mile-wide river – right in front of the offices of Mississippi Barge Shipping. MacIntosh got a briefcase out of his trunk and went inside.

The two agents settled in to wait; their SUV perched on the shoulder of a raised parking lot just above the office area. From there, they could see the entire complex, including the barge dock, parking lots, and barns where the loading equipment was stored. Steady barge traffic moved slowly up and down the wide expanse of muddy water. The driver watched the building through high-powered binoculars, while the other video-taped. Suddenly, there was a subdued tap-tap on the passenger side window. Both men jumped and looked over to see a giant of a black man, dressed in a dark hoodie, pressing his ATF badge against the window.

"You Feebs trying to fuck up our operation?" he said softly as the window was powered down.

"What're you talking about – what operation? What Feebs? We're just tourists taking in the lovely sights of the Mississippi River."

"Well, that's not what your license plate says – how about before we blow both operations - we go someplace and talk." The black guy flashed a toothy white grin.

The Alcohol, Tobacco and Firearms (ATF) had been watching the Mississippi Barge Shipping operation for a solid month. They'd been gathering evidence that the company was a major player in running stolen guns down to New Orleans via their barges and then selling them abroad – mostly to South American customers. They had collected enough evidence to charge Mississippi Barge, but they wanted the organization behind it. Rumor was it was the Marta Cartel out of Colombia.

They just hadn't been able to make the connection. The FBI was glad to help.

****

Emma pulled the door of the Feed & Seed towards her to the accompaniment of a tinkle from the small bell just above the door.

"Be right with you," Matt's voice wafted in from the storeroom.

Suddenly, Emma heard Matt's voice yell, "Get down from there – get down!" Then followed two loud, but distinct crashes – like really big things falling. Emma leaned as far over the counter as she could to see what happened, but then a huge – must have been as big as a small dog – black and white long-hair cat shot out of the back room, up on the counter, down into the store, across the floor and disappeared behind a large stack of seed bags.

A few second later, Matt appeared, covered in what looked like a fine film of chalky white powder and some clumps of grey, gritty stuff that clung to his hair, eyebrows, and shirtfront.

"That's not cat litter, is it?" Emma asked.

Matt turned beet red. "Yeah, I – uh – never mind – it'd take just too long to explain." Matt was notorious for getting himself into the funniest predicaments. They weren't really accidents and were generally not something resulting from carelessness. Just weird stuff happened when Matt was around. Caleb never tired of telling and retelling Matt stories.

Matt tried to brush some of the litter from his hair and face – regain some dignity – some composure. "What's up, Em?" Emma put her hand in front of her mouth to conceal her smile. Matt was just so damn adorable.

She soon sobered, though. What she was about to do – about to say – would forge the rest of her life. It was important she get it right - she couldn't afford to be a smart-ass or fumble it. She took a deep breath and began.

"Ok, Matt. I just want you to listen – don't say anything until I'm finished."

Matt opened his mouth.

"I mean it, damnit. This is really hard for me – so just shut up and listen."

Matt snapped his jaws shut and made the zipper gesture across his lips. He stared at the woman he loved.

"I know I've been a horse's ass for the past few months," she began.

Emma looked up at him – hoping for a facial expression, a gesture – a word of encouragement, but Matt said nothing – his facial expression remained neutral.

"Maybe I shouldn't have asked him to shut up," Emma thought belatedly. But she had to go ahead anyway - encouragement or not. She had to say what she came to say -what was in her heart.

"And I've had a lot of time to do some serious thinking about what I really wanted from life..." she said slowly and deliberately.

She hesitated again. Finally, she gathered the courage to say the next words, "but, Matt, what I want from life is only one thing – I just want you. I want to live with you, love with you, have kids with you, and grow old with you. You're so much more important to me than writing or any other stupid career."

Matt still didn't say a word. Emma's heart hit rock bottom, her inner voice said, "It's over, stupid – you've done it again – you've lost him."

She turned away, heading to the front door – eager to get away so she could let loose the tears that were building up behind her eyes. "OK-that's what I wanted to say. You don't have to say anything right now, in fact, I really don't think you should – you probably need time to think....I just had to tell you how I felt...."

She stopped because Matt was coming around the counter like a tight end going for the end zone or a defensive linebacker heading for the quarterback. He wrapped her up in his arms and kissed her fiercely and kept on kissing her until neither of them could breathe.

When he finally released her, Emma stepped back and found her face, her hair and the front of her jacket covered in cat litter. Emma brushed at the grit on her face, "Does this mean you forgive me?"

In response, Matt laughed and kissed her again.

****

The next two years of Billy's journals centered on the building of the Samuelson's Clinic – the Choctaw Nation Free Clinic. Lucy and Billy paid for the construction of the hospital out of Billy's inheritance monies and hired two additional doctors to staff it. They established a foundation to assure The Clinic's continued operation – even after he and Lucy were no longer there to oversee its activities. The Clinic provided free medical care to anyone in need of it – without regard to race, or tribal affiliation. The Samuelsons felt it was their legacy to the land they both loved so well. There was one notable entry in late summer 1874 which concerned Billy's good friend, Green McCurtain.

> *August 15, 1874*
> *On the afternoon of August 12th one of Green's deputies came to the Clinic's building site saying Green had asked me to come quickly and to bring my medical bag. As was generally the case when dealing with this particular deputy, he gave me no further information. We took off at a fast pace to Old Spiro town, and there I found Green and one of his brothers standing over a lifeless male form. The lifeless form was Robert, Green's younger brother. His shirt front was covered in*

blood and he had been shot once through the chest. The expressions on the brothers' faces left no doubt I was too late to render any assistance – Robert was already dead. Jackson and Green said nothing to me, but mounted their horses and quickly rode off in the direction of Tandy Walker's home. The deputy and I returned Robert's body to his father's home near Sugar Loaf.

I later learned that Robert had been shot by Henderson Walker, Tandy's son. Apparently Robert and Walker's daughter were courting and Henderson had forbidden Robert to come anywhere near his sister. When Robert refused, Henderson shot him. Robert mounted his horse and rode away, but the severity of his wounds was too much. He travelled as far as Old Spiro before he succumbed. Henderson Walker has fled – or as the people say – 'gone on the scout.'

1876 – 1906

There were not many entries in Billy's journals from 1876 to 1906 – mostly just notes or a scribbled sentence or two - sometimes nothing for a year or more. There appeared to be little time for anything else. Lucy became pregnant again, but lost the child.

Daily life revolved around the raising of their three children and running the Clinic. A few entries made Jenny laugh out loud. Apparently family dynamics in 1876 were not so different from today.

June 12, 1876
I was called upon to play the 'great arbitrator' once again between Lucy and her father, but in this effort I sorely failed. Little Evelyn Rose has

shown to have an almost magical gift for music, and Liam has been teaching her to play on the old hotel lobby piano. The instrument is decrepit and sorely out of tune, but our little angel can coax from it the most heavenly of sounds.

Today, when Lucy went to fetch Evelyn Rose from her lesson, she found the child entertaining several of Liam's unsavory confederates – and I am informed by the most irate mother in all of Scullyville that all of them were drunk. Lucy commented there was quite a party going on and the song Evelyn Rose was playing was one totally unsuited for a child.

Lucy does not know how Liam manages to have such ready access to liquor when it is banned from the Nations, but somehow he does. What followed was, by all accounts, an epic verbal battle – most of it Gaelic – and the outcome was that Lucy will never let her baby near the hotel or her father ever again. Nothing I could say would assuage her from her decision. Lucy is resolved.

Five-year old Evelyn Rose is inconsolable as she dearly loves both her scalawag grandfather and the piano. I am not sure how I will resolve this dispute.

June 13, 1876
As I emerged from the house this morning, I found the old piano from Liam's hotel on the front porch. I could but laugh and shake my head. At the sound of my laughter, Lucy emerged from behind me and burst into tears.

Shortly thereafter, Liam sold the hotel and moved in with Lucy and Billy. The Samuelsons built an entire new wing on their house, complete with a sitting room and bedroom, just for him. Although Liam loved his family very much, he appreciated having some space to himself and away from the chaos of the Samuelson's daily life.

One interesting note in 1876 concerned the blood-feud between the McCurtain and Walker families. Henderson Walker returned to Scullyville from his foray into the wilderness and Jackson and Green McCurtain were there to meet him. One of them shot their brother's killer to death – some said it was in revenge and others said he'd been killed while evading arrest. Others said it was justice - ancient Choctaw law dictated when an individual took a life – whether by design or by accident – that person's life was forfeit. Regardless, the blood feud between the McCurtains and the Walkers was over.

Billy remained close to the center of the Choctaw Nation's politics throughout the rest of his life. In 1880 Jackson McCurtain was elected to Principal Chief. He moved the Nation's capitol from Chata Tamaha where it had been since the War to Tuskahoma in 1882. He sanctioned the building of a beautiful Council House and worked with the Frisco Railway Company to secure a right of way – the proceeds from which would profit the Nation. Jackson's brother, Edmund McCurtain replaced his brother as Principal Chief in 1884. During his time at the helm of the Nation, he dedicated some of the funds to the continued operation of the Free Clinic. A position for a third doctor and several rooms were added to the existing structure.

In 1887, young Liam went off to the Chicago Medical College in Chicago. The Samuelsons had always known Liam would follow in his father's footsteps. In 1888, Liam returned for the summer accompanied by another second year student – John 'Jack' Minor Brown – a Virginia gentleman of a genteel Southern heritage. He had never been to the 'Wild West," and was anxious to see if all the stories he'd heard were true. He and Liam helped out all summer at the Clinic – between hunting and fishing expeditions into the countryside. Jack fell in love with the Nations – rather, Jack fell in love with Evelyn Rose. And, much too soon in her parents' eyes – she with him. The two agreed to wait until Jack and Liam had graduated from medical school before they made any permanent plans, but Billy recognized the inevitability each time he looked at the light in his daughter's bright blue eyes when she looked at Jack. It was the same light his eyes reflected every time he looked at Lucy – even to that day.

Soon after Evelyn Rose's marriage in 1891, David Folsom Samuelson, Billy's youngest child, moved to Oklahoma City to work for the Kansas City railroad. He'd never been interested in medicine or in staying put; the nomadic life was for him.

1893 was a year of blessings and tragedy, Liam Samuelson married Mary Elise Green, a Choctaw half-blood, distantly related to the McCurtains and his son's namesake, Liam Martin died of pneumonia.

1895 was a year of heartbreak.

October 15, 1895

    Today must be the most desolate of my life since I learned of the deaths of my mother and sisters, for today we buried my beautiful Evelyn Rose. She was the light of my life, my smile, my heart, my song. I don't know how her mother and I will be able to go on without her. She died during the birth of her second child, a small stillborn perfect baby girl. Nothing Jack or I could do could keep the two from slipping away. God called his angels home and left us mortals in despair.

In 1900 Lucy began writing for the Van Buren Press. She was especially interested in women's suffrage issues. Her editorials were well-reasoned and brilliantly written. She was often called upon to give speeches throughout Arkansas, Missouri and Kansas on the subject, and traveled on speaking circuits. Sometimes she was gone for several weeks at a time, and Billy hated being apart, although he would never tell her so. Just as medicine was his passion, winning the right of women to vote was Lucy's. As much as she had supported his profession; he supported hers.

But save for one journey to Washington D.C. in 1902, Billy stayed close to home and his Clinic. On that occasion, Billy accompanied Green McCurtain, now Principal Chief, to meet with members of the Dawes Commission regarding the forced enrollments and land allotments mandated under the Curtis Act. Billy spoke eloquently on behalf of his adopted land, but in the end, it was to no avail. The die had been cast and nothing he or any of the Choctaw leadership said would change it. The era of tribal land ownership was at an end.

July 15, 1906

As Lucy and I sit on our porch on this most beautiful of summer evenings, I feel the urge to write once more in my journal. It has been several months – actually as I look at the dates – several years since I last entered my thoughts and dreams in this epistle.

Statehood for our land is inevitable, although in my present state of health I may not be here to see it. Perhaps that is just as well. The Choctaw Nation I loved is all but gone. I was here when it was The Nation of the People – unique and strong. Now it appears it will become only one of many states in the U.S. nation – the people robbed of their distinctive history and character.

I pray we never have another War such as the one which brought me to this land. But in the decisions made today I see the same seeds of destruction that drove this country to rend itself apart in hatred, malice, and blood. Just as we stripped the slaves of any voice in their own well-being and governance; now goes the treatment of the peoples in the Indian Territories. History has shown us again and again that when a people's voice is quelled in the interest of greed – the result is always disaster. I had hoped we as a people learned this lesson in the war between the Union and Confederacy, but I fear this is not so.

In the building of the state that is to come, it will be up to our children and their children to create a world which is good and true. To build a society that is fair and in which all voices are heard - to allow no man or woman to be enslaved.

Perhaps I am just an old man rambling. I find my thoughts these days turn more and more often to my early years at Nine Oaks - my childhood home - and the beautiful white roses in my mother's garden. I think of Mother often now, her beautiful smile, her quick intelligence and wit – how much I have missed her wise counsel over these many years.

I have never been a religious man – at least not in the ways our protestant brothers would recognize. But I have tried to be a good man by the way I lived each day– not by the words I spoke. I feel sure when I reach those Pearly Gates and St. Peter, he will allow me entry – although, my friend Green would say, probably in a probationary status.

I hope to see my good father. Perhaps there we can reconcile the harsh words spoken so many years ago. Perhaps we can become the friends we were never able to be here on this earthly plane. I know my dear mother and my sisters will be waiting there, too.

I am content and happy.

As Jenny slowly closed the last journal, a small folded paper slipped from its pages and settled to the floor. It was a child's drawing of a large antebellum home - stained, folded and refolded so many times as to be worn through in places. At the bottom was the inscription:

To Billy Nine Oaks House
From Evelyn Rose 1863

Jenny stared at the old drawing for some time, refolded it, and carefully placed it back in the pages of the journal.

She rocked for a bit, letting Billy's words course through her mind and body. Then she spoke to her friend,

"Your son, Mary Elizabeth, was a wonderful, thoughtful man. What an exciting life he led, and how many people were better for knowing him. Your family lives on through his descendents. You should be very happy and proud."

Jenny's comments were met with silence. It was an unusual silence; almost as if Mary Elizabeth was not there at all. Before, as she read of Billy's post-war adventures, Jenny could sense his mother's joy and fascination. But now that they had reached the end of the last journal - there was nothing. Jenny was mystified. Had Mary Elizabeth Chapman, now knowing her son's life story, moved on?

After two days of stillness, Jenny tried to provoke a reaction by moving the rocker into her bedroom. But unlike times past, the chair never returned to the window in the sitting room. Finally Jenny moved the rocker back to its spot and succumbed to Matt's advice. She invited Paul White Horse over; perhaps he could make sense of it.

The two sat together in the sitting room – Jenny in the rocker and Paul White Horse on the settee. At one point, White Horse got up and circled the room – not speaking, but humming some nameless tune to himself.

Each time Jenny would begin to say something, White Horse would hold up his hand – palm first –

demanding her silence. Jenny was furious. Paul White Horse always made her feel like a child - uncomfortable and vulnerable. After a few minutes he said,

"Your spirit is still here, Jenny, watching."

Jenny didn't understand. "But we told her all about her son. She still can't be waiting for him to come home, can she? He died more than one hundred years ago. What more can she want from us?"

Chapter Eighteen

Ortiz turned as MacIntosh came into the room. The director for the Marta Cartel's Midwest operations was hurriedly shoving what few records he kept on site into a large leather briefcase.

He sighed deeply. "What are you doing here, MacIntosh, didn't you get my message?"

Thirty minutes earlier MacIntosh had received a coded text telling him to disappear. The feds were on their way to arrest Ortiz and seize all his records.

MacIntosh nodded. He'd received the message, but he wanted to make sure Ortiz had evaded arrest – he owed his old friend that.

The two shook hands; then embraced. Ortiz was the first to speak. "Well, my friend, I believe the time has come for us to go our separate ways. Apparently the feds have all they need to send me away for a very long time. They should be here shortly to arrest me and

I plan to be long gone." Ortiz looked around the room to be sure he'd gathered up everything important.

"I don't believe I'd last very long in a federal prison, eh? You can be sure our friends in Colombia would see to that." He slammed down the top of the case – a little too harshly, thought MacIntosh.

"If that damned redneck sheriff had kept his nose up the ass-end of his horse where it belonged, none of this would have happened." He lovingly ran his hand over the back of his custom desk chair.

"Will you do one last job for me, old friend?" Ortiz' voice shook with anger as he spoke. "Get rid of Tallchief and his family – and that kid, too. The one that started all this."

One last favor for his old friend and mentor. MacIntosh nodded.

Ortiz continued, "Ah, well, it's been a good run. At least we have enough money to disappear in style." Ortiz sadly gazed around his room. "Perhaps we'll be able to work together again when we don't have so many fucking cops knocking at the door."

They shook hands once again. Then Ortiz hurried out, well ahead of his federal pursuers.

****

"Shit! Shit! Shit! How'd we miss him?" Bobbi Huff stood at the door to Ortiz's lavishly appointed office. FBI Special Agent Bill Freemont, officially in charge of the arrest, signaled his team to scour the building. Maybe they'd get lucky and find Ortiz hiding someplace, but none of them really thought so. All around were signs of a hasty departure – file drawers open, papers thrown on the floor. Ortiz's comely secretary told them her boss had taken off two hours earlier in one hell of a hurry and didn't tell her where he was going.

Bobbi Huff and Eric McBride had wrangled a spot on the arrest team, because of all the work their task force had done in uncovering the connection between the Cartel and the human trafficking operation. "Hell," thought Bobbi, "should have been our arrest, but I guess we'd have been totally left out if it hadn't been for Joe Holcomb." At least her agency and the OSBI would get some of the credit now.

"Well," said McBride, "don't worry, Bobbi. This guy may have slipped through our fingers right now, but we've still got enough to shut down the cartel. Drugs, guns, human trafficking – the whole enchilada. They're history in this part of the world. It'll take them years to rebuild – if they ever can."

Bobbi replied, "Yeah, I know. I know. But I really wanted Ortiz. He ordered the kidnapping of those twins. His orders got Katie Anderson killed. No telling how many other kids' lives he's ruined. He's a soulless animal who doesn't deserve to breathe the same air we do."

"We'll get him. He can't get out of St. Louis – we've got a watch on all the airports, all the roads out of the city. He can't stay hidden forever."

But McBride's confidence was sorely misplaced for Ortiz was no longer in St. Louis – but high above it. As the private jet owned by one of his satisfied customers winged its way northward toward a secluded Canadian landing field, the former head of the Marta Cartel's Midwest operations thoughtfully sipped a glass of Chardonnay – perfectly chilled.

****

The phone on Dover's desk blared. He picked it up and heard the familiar smoke-cured voice of his former partner. "Hey, man, how's life on easy street?"

"Great, I'm actually getting used to shaving every morning. How're the rats and fleas?" "Same ol', same ol'… thought I'd brighten your day …. The Sierpes were hit hard early this morning by at least one – maybe two – local gangs. Apparently in retaliation for some major drug busts that went down yesterday. The gangs think the Sierpes gave 'em up. Word is – the Sierpes are done and gone – we're counting six dead and the rest scattered to the winds…just thought you'd like to know before it hits the news."

****

Ortiz sat on his private patio, sipping the mojito his gorgeous 'date' Lucinda had just delivered, along with a lingering and very wet kiss. He congratulated himself on the ease of his escape from St. Louis to Canada and then on to this small, beautiful and isolated Caribbean island. He chuckled. Soon he and Lucinda would eat a gourmet dinner, prepared by his personal chef, followed by a night of love-making. Life was good, he thought. No, life was very, very good.

Ortiz hated to leave this place, but he had to get on with his plan. Tomorrow he'd board a private jet for Montreal and the plastic surgeon who would alter his looks. Not too much though - after all Ortiz was a handsome man and he wanted to stay that way. The ladies preferred it – maybe a little more rugged look – but he'd see what the surgeon had to say. Then lay low while he recovered at that secluded lodge he bought last year. Summers were beautiful in Montreal. Maybe he'd bring in another lady or two to see to his recovery. Ortiz smiled at the thought. Then he could begin to get back on his feet – start small, grow big. Ulmani in Serbia was the perfect contact. There was more money to be made – lots more money.

The afternoon was picture-postcard perfect, the skies an incredible blue, and the tropical breezes cooled his body perfectly. Ortiz was becoming very sleepy. "That's odd," he thought to himself. "I had a nap this afternoon." He took another sip of mojito.

"Maybe I just need some feminine company to perk me up," he chuckled at his own joke. "Lucinda, come here for a minute, will you?"

But Lucinda did not come. A haze suddenly appeared in front of his eyes and seemed to grow thicker and thicker with each passing second. "That doesn't make any sense," the fugitive thought pulling off his sunglasses, "we've had bright sunshine until now."

Ortiz thought he'd better get inside in case a storm was brewing. But his legs wouldn't cooperate and he was having difficulty keeping his eyes open.

"What the hell," he thought as he drifted into a heavy, drug-induced sleep.

****

MacIntosh waited until Jenny's SUV drove past his parked rental.

When she was out of site, he started the dark pickup and circled the block around the Tallchief's house. It sure looked like nobody was home. A small white curly haired dog romped in the yard and came up to the street as the hit man slowly passed by – curiously checking him out. "I'll have to take care of that," he thought, "don't want a damn dog alerting the neighborhood I'm here." There didn't seem to be any other dogs – thank God.

Taking the family out by long distance – MacIntosh was an excellent sniper – appeared to be out of the question. There was no high perch from which he could shoot. Up close and personal seemed to be the only way for this one, and maybe that was best, anyway. He'd make sure the Tallchiefs paid dearly for destroying his life and that of his friend.

MacIntosh made several slow passes around the block. The Tallchief property was quite large – almost an acre. There didn't appear to be any good places to conceal himself- at least not anywhere he could hide undetected for a good period of time. There was one side of the house that backed up onto a small ditch – maybe a shallow creek – from there he could make his way across the far side and maybe – if he did it just right – sneak into the house through the back door. As a matter of fact, that was probably the only way he'd be able to fulfill his promise to Ortiz.

****

The first day of Carly's new life dawned bright, cloudless, and for the first time in several months – worry-free. The update from Huff couldn't have been better - the Sierpes and the Marta Cartel were done for – Ortiz was on the run and Viper was locked up. Linda and Katie Anderson had received what little measure of justice this world could offer. Carly – well, the future looked bright for her.

Today would be her big day, the end of a nightmare. Caleb wanted to make sure everything was perfect. He'd been up early, mowing the lawn, trimming the bushes, cleaning the grill. Zac ran in circles around the yard, alternately chasing and being chased by Curly Joe.

Upstairs, Emma and Carly carefully packed her few belongings into her brand-new swivel suitcase – bright pink, of course.

"OK," said Emma. "When Matt and I get married this fall, you'll be one of my bridesmaids, right?"

"Wow, Emma. I've never been a bridesmaid before. Will I get to wear high heels?"

"Why not? You've got to learn to walk in those ankle busters some day, right?" They continued making small talk, both of them torn between happiness - now that Carly had a loving family - and sadness because she was leaving. They laughed and then they cried.

Jenny mixed a big salad in the kitchen, shucked some corn and surreptitiously checked on the small brown puppy secreted away in the pantry. Jenny, with a lot of advice from Jesse, had carefully selected the brown and black mix from their local rescue shelter. She was sure this puppy would grow up to be Carly's good and faithful a friend – just as Jesse was hers. Charlie and Trish Bannerman agreed.

Noon arrived and the Bannerman's large Tahoe pulled into the Tallchief driveway, throwing dusty gravel all around. The two younger Bannerman kids piled out and ran to play with Zac and Curly Joe. Charlie and Trish came up to the house and rang the bell. Carly, dressed in a new pair of shorts and shirt answered. "Please come in," she said formally.

Jenny met them in the front hallway and the three adults hugged and talked about the trip from Kansas, the weather. No sooner had they sat down at the kitchen table than the phone started to ring. Jenny gave the others the food, plates, silverware, napkins and drinks to take outside, while she ran to answer it. Caleb was already busy at the grill sizzling hamburgers, steaks, and hot dogs. It would be a perfect picnic.

Jenny picked up the phone. "Hello."

The deep voice on the other end of the line said, "Hello, I'm looking for Emma Cochran. Can you tell me if this is her residence?"

"Yes, this is Emma's sister. How can I help you?"

"Is Ms. Cochran there by any chance? This is Tom Reynolds of *Reynolds and O'Brien Scripts* in Hollywood, California. I'm interested in talking to your sister about the screenplays she recently submitted to our office and perhaps about some rather lucrative employment opportunities."

"Oh my God," thought Jenny. She said into the telephone, "Just a minute, Mr. Reynolds. I'll get her for you."

Emma ran into the kitchen and picked up the phone while Jenny hovered nearby. Emma listened for quite a while and then said, "No, Mr. Reynolds, I appreciate your interest – I really do and I'd love to further explore this opportunity. But if I must come to California and work there – I'm really not interested. Right here is where my heart and home are ...."

Matt entered the kitchen with two bags full of groceries. He looked at Emma's earnest expression and raised his eyebrows in a question. Jenny whispered and gestured, but Matt just looked bewildered.

"Where's the ice?" Jenny asked Matt.

"Damn, damn, damn. I knew I was forgetting something" he said, never taking his eyes off Emma. "I'll go back and get some."

Emma motioned Matt over to the telephone. "Mr. Reynolds, how about if I let you talk to my business manager, Matt Tallchief? He'll be the one to handle any possible contracts or agreements anyway. OK – here he is."

Matt mouthed "what the hell?" as Emma handed him the phone.

Emma put her hand over the speaker and whispered, "This is one of the guys Dr. Sloan tried to get me an appointment with – out in California - but his office staff wouldn't give me the time of day when I went to see him in person. I guess Dr. Sloan called him and gave him hell and he found my scripts and actually read them. He's interested – very interested. He loves the script I wrote about Jenny and Jesse and he wants to create a TV series with a vet just like Jenny. My script would be the pilot and then I'd write the episodes. He loves my writing. Can you believe it?" Emma began jumping up and down with excitement.

"So what about this going-to-California thing?" asked Jenny.

"I said no way I was leaving Oklahoma again. This is where I belong. If he can't deal with that, then maybe I can sell my scripts to somebody who'll be willing to work with me here. I've learned my lesson – my home is where Matt, you and Caleb are. And that's right here."

The two could hear Matt talking jovially with Mr. Reynolds. He finally hung up and came into the kitchen, picked up Emma, and twirled her around. "Wow – from a store clerk to the manager of a Hollywood scriptwriting star – in just the matter of minutes. Can life get any better?"

"What did he say? Come on – come on," Emma was practically strangling Matt.

"We're going to talk again on Monday. He just didn't want you selling the rights to your scripts before he had a chance to get them for himself. I told him we'd wait until we saw what he was offering." He broke into a big grin, "See, I always told you you'd make it."

Emma socked him with her fist and they danced around the kitchen.

"You guys go tell everybody the good news," Jenny said. "I'll get the ice."

She and Jesse got in the Tallchief SUV and headed to town.

****

303

MacIntosh stole quietly through the unlocked back door and into the deserted kitchen. "Easy," he thought to himself. "You'd think a cop would be more careful about security, wouldn't you?" He'd decided his best course of action would be to sneak inside and hide until dark. Once the family was asleep, he'd take out Tallchief, his wife and the kids, and, unfortunately for them, anyone else in the house. Such was his absolute faith in himself, he had no doubt he could murder them all and get away cleanly.

The tall man quietly ascended the kitchen stairs to the second floor and into the main hallway. To his left and right, he could see bedrooms. One was obviously a nursery; another had a pink suitcase open on the bed. "Guess you won't need that after all," he mused.

The master bedroom was at the far end of the hallway and beyond it was an area open to the front stairwell. On closer inspection, MacIntosh determined it was small sitting room that was accessed through the master and he checked it out. There was a large window overlooking the picnic party. In front of the window was an old rocking chair. He quietly scooted the chair over to the far wall so he could get a good look outside without being seen.

Kids were everywhere. Everyone seemed to be having a fine old time. "Well, I guess that's good," he thought. "They should have fun on the last day they're alive."

He pulled the photos of the Tallchief family from his belly pack, easily identifying Caleb, Matt, and Emma. There was a toddler running around, too. "Must be the Tallchief's kid, and there's the Anderson twin." There seemed to be another family, too, man, woman and two kids. He wasn't sure who they were, but hopefully they wouldn't spend the night. If they did, well...

An SUV turned into the driveway. "Oh, there's the wife," the intruder thought.

Jenny got out of the truck, laughing, her arms full of ice and diapers. Jesse jumped down after her. Suddenly the shepherd went on alert, her hackles standing at attention, her nose in the air, swiveling her head slowly left and right. Her growl turned into a strident bark as she took off for the Tallchief's front door. Zac, startled, started wailing at the sudden noise while the others stopped what they were doing or saying, astonishment turning to alarm as they watched the big dog charge across the front yard.

****

"Oh, fuck," thought MacIntosh, "where'd that dog come from?" He thought the Tallchiefs had only one dog – the one he'd seen when he'd checked the place out yesterday – the little white one who was happily snoozing now in a tranquilized state of euphoria. He'd not seen this big dog before, damn it to hell - where'd it come from?"

He shook his head, "Doesn't matter, I've got to get out of here right now."

MacIntosh quickly turned and tripped heavily over the old rocking chair. "What the hell…" he thought, "I moved that thing across the room just a minute ago."

He hurriedly scrambled to his feet – he could hear that damn dog scratching on the front door. "Hurry," he screamed at himself, "get out."

Then – something impossible happened.

Right before his eyes, the form of a woman materialized out of nothing. She clearly stood in front of the rocking chair, yet he could see right through her to the window beyond. She was dressed in a hoop skirt, white blouse, tattered slippers and her light-colored hair was parted down the middle and captured into some sort of a net. Blood caked across the front of her blouse and cascaded down her skirt. The air in the room crackled with her fury. MacIntosh could clearly see her enraged expression, and it horrified him to the bone.

MacIntosh was not a religious man, but in that instant he was terrified for his very soul. His eyes fixed on the eyes of the apparition - and in those menacing black pools of darkness, MacIntosh saw his death. The woman spoke his name, and MacIntosh screamed, hurriedly stumbling backwards to get away from the phantom – the phantom who knew his name. The back of the hit man's thighs slammed against the sitting room railing, and MacIntosh lost his balance. He hung in midair for just an instant, arms flailing in an effort to regain his footing. Gravity and justice won out, as MacIntosh pitched over backward into the open stairwell and oblivion.

Matt and Caleb reached the front door in the same instant. Caleb threw the door open, just as the body of a man hurled down from above, bounced its head against the wide newel post and lay unmoving at his feet.Caleb felt the neck for a pulse. There was none. The rest of the Tallchief clan and their guests rushed up onto the porch as Caleb pulled out his cell phone to call the Sheriff's Office.

****

"Man didn't have any ID on him, Caleb. But there were photos of you, Jenny, Emma, Matt and Carly. He also had a gun on him that's been tied to the deaths of Mendez and Adams. We think this must be the mysterious MacIntosh, enforcer for Ortiz."

"I thought we were finished with that bastard. Do you think there'll be any more attempts?"

"No, as far as we can tell, Ortiz has fled the country. The Marta Cartel is looking for him just as hard as we are. I don't think he'd risk coming out of hiding for another try at you– it was probably just Ortiz' last hurrah at revenge."

Caleb agreed. Some of these scumbags just couldn't stand to lose, but right now Ortiz would be more interested in protecting his life than coming after the Tallchiefs.

****

The black hood was pulled roughly from Ortiz' head. The prisoner shook his head and blinked in the harsh light of the underground room. At least it looked like an underground room, the thick stone and mortar walls were covered with a sickly black mold and an aroma of damp permeated the space. It was cold, too, a cold that struck all the way into the bones. Ortiz involuntarily shivered.

"Welcome to Colombia, my friend," said the tall, stocky mixed-blood Hispanic standing in front of him. "Glad you could join our party. I am Ernesto." The dirty bearded man ran his hand slowly down the front of Ortiz' brightly colored shirt. His voice had an odd, muffled quality, "my business partners here and I have been anxiously awaiting your arrival." Several of the rough-looking members of a local gang, shot black, tooth-gapped smiles at him.

Ortiz knew he was a dead man. All during the trip, he silently prayed his end would be quick. But as he gazed around the room assessing the collection of his executioners, he knew it was not to be.

A well-dressed man in a grey business suit stepped around Ernesto into view. He leaned over, speaking quietly to the handcuffed man. "Sr. Ortiz, it is so good to finally meet the man whose greed and stupidity have effectively destroyed the most lucrative branch of the Marta Cartel. My patron, Sr. Gabriel sends his regards." Gabriel – that bloated bastard on the Cartel board. This was bad – very bad. Ortiz willed himself to maintain a neutral expression.

"When word arrived that you had been found, Sr. Gabriel was very pleased – very pleased. You know, the other cartel members wanted to cut your head from your body or perhaps remove your limbs one by one before death. You cost them a great deal of money, senor, but Sr. Gabriel thought these methods of punishment too crude for a man so refined as you." Ortiz wasn't sure he should be more relieved or terrified.

"Sr. Gabriel thought long and hard about a punishment that would appropriately fit your crimes against the Cartel," the man paused, "and against God."

The gentleman slowly looked about the room. "So he asked our good friend here, Ernesto, to assemble some of his very best friends from prison. Friends, who, during their stay in those most disagreeable of places, learned to take pleasure in certain intimate activities which, how do I say it, are just not generally acceptable."

It took a moment for the horrible reality of Ortiz' sentence to set in. When it did, his eyes grew large and his voice shook. "Please, senor. You cannot do this.

Please, senor, do not allow this!" Ortiz' voice became more agitated – he was almost screaming. He began to writhe against his restraints. His chair banged up and down with his efforts to get free. Not this- not this…

Two rough-looking men came out of the shadows and moved closer to their victim. They smiled widely at Ortiz. For them, intimidation was almost as much fun as the forbidden pleasures that awaited.

Ortiz begged, "I know I must die for my crimes against the cartel, but not this. Do not allow this. It is not right in the eyes of God."

The man in the grey suit regarded Ortiz dispassionately. "Neither," he said, "is the rape of children."

Sr. Gabriel's emissary gathered up his coat and glanced at Ortiz frantically trying to free himself. He gestured for Ernesto to follow him outside the cell and into the hallway, noting the rest of the men in the room behind him had emerged from the shadows and begun to crowd around Ortiz, patting his hair, touching his face. Ernesto pulled the door closed.

The man in the grey suit said clearly – he wanted no misunderstanding about what was to be done with this piece of shit – this defiler of the innocent.

"When your men have finished with him," he said slowly, "kill him and make sure his body is never found."

Ernesto nodded, turned around, and opened the door to the cell. Beyond the door Ortiz could be heard screaming. The executioner looked at the man in the grey suit and smirked. "He squeals like a little girl," he remarked sarcastically, and pulled the door closed behind him.

The man in the grey suit shrugged into his coat and walked briskly down the corridor. "Poetic justice," he thought to himself as he emerged into the clear, starry Colombian night. "Poetic justice."

Epilogue

Jenny sat in the rocker holding her precious son, the slow back and forth rhythm mesmerizing the child into sleep. Back and forth, back and forth, the chair gently creaked its quiet song. Jenny stared out into the deepening twilight. Slowly she became aware of a change in the air around her – a stirring – a softness that only enhanced her sense of peace. She knew Mary Elizabeth had joined them.

"You're the one, aren't you, Mary Elizabeth? You saved us all." Jenny rocked a little more. "I don't know how, but you caused that monster to fall over the banister, didn't you? How can I ever thank you….how can I tell you how cherished are the lives you saved?" Jenny pulled Zac even closer. "But….then I guess you know that, don't you? After all, you've been looking for your son for more than a century and a half."

Zachary stirred in Jenny's arms and stuck his thumb in his mouth. Then he sighed. Jenny continued, "I don't know if you were with us when we went to see your son's descendents, but we left them your family bible.

They were so happy to have it. Did you know there's still an Evelyn Rose in your family?"

"They were so proud of what Billy accomplished in his life. He took your name to honor you and, like you, he fought injustice – no matter the cost. Now his family knows about you, too."

"I know you're happy, too, to know that Billy's life wasn't wasted in a war he hated – to know he grew into a fine man – loved and respected by everyone who knew him. He made a real difference in his world."

Jenny rocked for a little longer, and then she said, "I don't think you have to wait for Billy to come home any longer, Mary Elizabeth. In fact, he's probably been waiting for you all this time."

Suddenly the room exploded with the vibrant scent of roses – strong and sweet and full of happiness. It settled like a blanket tenderly over Jenny and her sleeping son. The two sat together in the chair, immersed in the aura for quite some time – until eventually the scent slowly faded away. Jenny knew Mary Elizabeth was finally at peace.

The tattered drawing found inside
Billy Samuelson's journal.

Author's Note –

Until the images of a local teen's tortured and dismembered body exploded across the headlines of newspapers and media in the late summer of 2012, the idea of slavery – the buying and selling of human beings – was considered by most Oklahomans to be an aberration of the past. After all, in the mind of the average American, the eradication of that inhumane activity took place 150 years ago in the bloodiest and most divisive war ever fought by this nation.

But it's back – or perhaps it never really went away. Maybe it just went underground and is only now beginning to rear its ugly head within the public psyche. Human trafficking is a particularly insidious crime, preying on the young, the helpless and the disenfranchised. Court documents indicate the young woman was murdered in such a brutal way as a warning to others. Confidential informants have painted a picture of a criminal organization that is ruthless and soulless.

An April 26, 2012 article in the Daily Oklahoman quoted the U.S. Immigration and Customs Enforcement Agency as saying human trafficking is one of the fastest growing crimes in the country and that an estimated 300,000 young girls in the U.S. are enslaved each year. They fully expect that number to rise.

According to experts, Oklahoma is fertile ground for this criminal element. Statistically, the state ranks near the top in its percentages of women incarcerated, domestic abuse, teen pregnancy, children in poverty and youth homelessness. Oklahoma also sits at the crossroads of major north-south and east-west interstates – I-35 and I-40 – affording traffickers ready access to the entire lower forty-eight states.

In late 2012 the Oklahoma Legislature passed laws giving broader authority to the Oklahoma Bureau of Narcotics and Dangerous Drugs Control to investigate human trafficking cases, as it was deemed those groups who deal in drugs often deal in human trafficking and illegal arms sales as well.

Although the Tallchief stories are fictional, it is important to note they are set in an environment that is very real.

About The Author –

Evelyn McEachern, (pronounced *Mac-KAREN*), holds a doctorate in Higher Education Administration from Oklahoma State University. Serving as a teacher, administrator and as Assistant Vice-President for Curriculum and Policy in regional public universities, she retired from academic life after more than thirty years of serving students.

Being energetic and focused, Dr. McEachern has found retirement to be a springboard for various ventures and activities including; charity fund raising, traveling and miniature doll house construction.

The *Jenny Tallchief* series is the result of more than two years of thoughtful research and planning. **Human Gold** is the second novel in this series. Fans of *Jenny Tallchief* will also want to read, **Missing Emma**, available through their favorite bookseller in either print or e-book.

Dr. McEachern and her husband live in Edmond, Oklahoma where she continues to spoil their Lhasa apso, *Maggie*.